Romance
CHARLES
Allyson
Charles, Allyson.
Putting Out Old
Flames.
WITHDRAWN
SEP 1 3 2018

Friends to Lovers

He missed Jane as a friend. If they were going to live in the same town, he wanted that back. A new, mature friendship between two adults.

Chance squared his shoulders. So that was that. If he wanted to forge a solid relationship one thing was clear.

From now on, hands off Dispatch Jane.

He glanced at her out of the corner of his eye, watched her breasts rise and fall beneath her thin sweater.

And lips off of her, too, he told himself sternly. And tongue. No touching her with his tongue.

She leaned her head against the back of the seat, exposing the long, silky column of her neck. His body tightened.

Christ. This friendship was doomed.

D0772022

Putting Out Old Flames

Allyson Charles

LYRICAL SHINE
Kensington Publishing Corp.
www.kensingtonbooks.com

To the extent that the image or images on the cover of this book depict a person or persons, such person or persons are merely models, and are not intended to portray any character or characters featured in the book.

LYRICAL SHINE BOOKS are published by

Kensington Publishing Corp.
119 West 40th Street
New York, NY 10018

Copyright © 2016 by Allyson Charles

All rights reserved. No part of this book may be reproduced in any form or by any means without the prior written consent of the Publisher, excepting brief quotes used in reviews.

All Kensington titles, imprints, and distributed lines are available at special quantity discounts for bulk purchases for sales promotion, premiums, fund-raising, educational, or institutional use.

Special book excerpts or customized printings can also be created to fit specific needs. For details, write or phone the office of the Kensington Sales Manager: Kensington Publishing Corp., 119 West 40th Street, New York, NY 10018. Attn. Sales Department. Phone: 1-800-221-2647.

Lyrical Shine and Lyrical Shine logo Reg. US Pat. & TM Off.

First Electronic Edition: August 2016
eISBN-13: 978-1-60183-603-8
eISBN-10: 1-60183-603-1

First Print Edition: August 2016
ISBN-13: 978-1-60183-604-5
ISBN-10: 1-60183-604-X

Printed in the United States of America

Chapter One

On a good day it could take a backhoe to pry Jane out from beneath her soft cotton duvet. The goose down bedspread in a faded blue paisley had been an indulgence, but one that was worth every penny. When she snuggled into bed at night, the duvet kept her cozy through the long Michigan winters, but was light enough to breathe through the warm summers. Sleeping under her duvet was like being cocooned in a cloud. It usually took her three rounds of hitting her snooze button in the morning before she could drag herself out from its inviting comfort.

And that was on a good day. Not a day when her head pounded like the drum section of a marching band and her limbs ached with fatigue.

Jane kicked the twisted sheets from her feet, and cocked her head. There it was again. The knocking was definitely coming from her front door, not her head. She groaned. Couldn't a girl get a sick day to herself? She wasn't asking for much. The last time she'd taken time off work due to illness, a different president had been sitting in the Oval Office.

Looking into one disgruntled green eye, she sighed. Cyclops didn't approve of visitors almost as much as he didn't approve of her sleeping the day away. The orange tabby circled three times on his pillow before turning his back on her and coiling himself like a garden hose.

Message received. Her ornery pet couldn't have said *Get your lazy butt out of bed* more clearly than if he'd written the message on a whiteboard.

Crawling through a sea of used tissues to the edge of the mattress, she swung her legs over. Whoever was at the door was persistent, she'd give him that. Stumbling, she took two steps to her closet, pulled a cotton robe on over her boxer shorts and T-shirt, and headed for the front door to her apartment.

Before opening the door, she gave one more solid blow of her nose, happy to discover she'd mostly dried up while she'd napped. Her face felt altogether too crusty for her liking, but considering her head was so congested it just might explode, Jane didn't care. Even if that hunky *Thor* actor stood behind her door, he was just going to have to deal with how she looked.

Concerned blue eyes and wind-blown tufts of white hair greeted her across the threshold. "Jane, are you all right? When you didn't answer the door right away, I thought maybe you'd forgotten about our meeting."

Her head fell back on her shoulders. "Judge Nichols. I did forget. I'm sorry." She stepped to the side and swept an arm toward the living room. "Come on in."

The older man paused, his eyes narrowing as he studied her face.

"It's okay. Dr. Murphy said I'm not contagious." She coughed into her sleeve. "He said it's just a twenty-four-hour bug and my time's almost up."

With another sidelong glance at her head, the judge of Crook County, Michigan, entered her small apartment and took a seat on her couch. Catching her eye, he rubbed a hand through the hair at his left temple and frowned. "If you're not feeling well, we can reschedule the meeting. The charity ball for the Pineville Fire Department isn't for another month, so we still have lots of time to plan." Leaning back on the sofa, he shifted his softly rounded belly and pulled a cell phone out of the front pocket of his trousers.

Jane laughed. "I'm glad you asked me for help with this fundraiser. Only a man would think a month was plenty of time to plan a charity ball and fireman auction. We have a lot to do."

Judge Nichols pulled the phone away from his ear. "Well, I'm glad you feel that way because the third member of our meeting isn't answering his phone. I can't cancel anyway. He should be here shortly." Brushing his hand through his hair again, he said, "But if you really don't feel well, I can wait for him outside and tell him we're rescheduling."

"Today's fine." Jane walked to the attached open kitchen and washed her hands. "I do feel a whole lot better than I did a couple of hours ago." The clock on the wall above her oven read 5:30 p.m.

She'd slept for almost eight hours straight. Pouring water into her teapot, she set it on the stove to heat and shuffled back to the living room, flopping on the other end of the couch. "And we really don't have any time to waste. I want this fundraiser to be a success."

As a local dispatcher for emergency calls, Jane knew most of the firefighters well. Knew their families. Every couple of years the town held a fundraiser for the Michigan Firefighters Widows' and Orphans' Fund. After a large refinery fire had killed two firemen in upstate Michigan last year, reminding Jane of just what their local firefighters faced, she'd jumped at the chance to help out and be one of the cochairs of the fundraising committee.

"So tell me about our third cochair," Jane asked. "I have yet to meet the new assistant fire chief. He just started last week, right? I can't believe he was already roped into helping with this fundraiser."

A devious smile turned up the edges of the judge's lips. "I believe it was a part of his initiation. He was given a couple of choices of what he, as the new guy, could do. I believe this was the least objectionable."

"The boys in Firehouse 10 gave him a choice?" She shook her head. "They must be going soft."

A firm knock on the door interrupted them.

"That must be the lucky man now." Jane pushed to her feet. "What's the new guy's name?"

"Assistant Chief McGovern." The wrinkles in the judge's forehead deepened. "First name Thomas, I believe."

"Huh." That was funny. She used to know someone with that name. But that T. McGovern would never have been caught dead wearing the blue-collar uniform of a firefighter. She moved to open the door.

"Wait, Jane!"

She turned, hand on the knob. The judge had risen to his feet. Even though the older man only stood at about Jane's own five foot six, he had presence. A sense of authority and calm that made few question his decisions. But right now, he just seemed agitated.

"I think you should know, uh . . ." He brushed violently at his hair.

She raised an eyebrow. Very odd. "Hold that thought."

Shaking her head, she pulled the door open.

And everything stopped. Her heart. The faint pounding in her head. Her breath. Time itself seemed to suck in a deep breath and hold it.

The chiseled jaw in front of her dropped. “Jane? Jane Willoughby? Is that really you?”

She didn’t know how long she would have stood there, staring at her high school love. The boy who’d ripped her heart in two, stuck a bite in his mouth, chewed it up, spit it out, and then ground the half-masticated bit under his heel. Not that she was still bitter about it or anything.

She knew her eyes were as wide as her open mouth, but couldn’t pull herself together enough to close them. The shrieking whistle of the teapot snapped her out of her shock.

Turning from the boy she’d once placed all her hopes and dreams on, she stumbled to the kitchen, removed the teapot from the stove. From the corner of her eye she watched the judge and Chance shake hands.

“You two know each other?” Judge Nichols asked.

Chance’s gaze burned between her shoulder blades. “We were friends in high school in Lansing.”

Friends. Jane snorted. “Anyone else want some tea?” The men shook their heads, and she prepared her own mug before returning to the living room. She took her first good look at the man still wearing his department-issued blue slacks and snug matching navy T-shirt. The back of her throat dried up and she took a scalding sip of tea.

He’d filled out since she’d last seen him. The wiry muscles he’d earned from varsity football had thickened. He was more solid, his wide chest and broad shoulders looking like he’d have no problem slinging an unconscious body into a fireman’s carry. Except for small lines radiating from the edges, his chestnut eyes hadn’t changed in nine years, still filled with a mischievous twinkle. He examined her apartment with curiosity before turning his scrutiny on Jane.

Her heart clenched. The way his gaze swept up and down her body, the curiosity was aimed all at her. She took stock of her appearance. Faded robe. Month-old pedicure, the purple polish chipped off half of her toenails. And a nose probably as red as the sunburn she’d gotten skinny-dipping with Chance their senior year. Just perfect.

She took another sip of tea. “You’re the new assistant fire chief of

Pineville." She hadn't said it as a question, but he nodded his head anyway. "A pretty big departure from your life plan, Chance."

The judge drew his brows down. "Chance?"

"Thomas Chance McGovern," Jane said. "He goes by his middle name. Or, at least, he used to."

"I still do." Chance rubbed the back of his neck, ran his hand up the back of his head, ruffling his short hair, the color almost an exact match to his eyes.

Judge Nichols pursed his pink lips and looked at the two of them. Jane could see the wheels turning in his head as he came to all sorts of conclusions. Unfortunately, he was probably coming to all the correct conclusions, something that did Jane's ego no good.

Sinking onto the sofa, she crossed her legs, trying to look as unaffected as possible. "Well, should we get down to business?"

Chance sat on the edge of an armchair across from her, a low glass and metal coffee table filling the gulf between them. The judge remained standing. He rocked up onto the balls of his feet. "Well, the first thing I wanted to talk to you two about was taking point on the fundraiser committee. There's no need to have three cochairs, and now that I know you two are already friends, I feel much more confident leaving the decisions in your capable hands."

Jane opened her mouth to object.

"I will, of course be a volunteer on the committee," he continued. "But as the only acting judge for Crook County, my schedule makes it difficult to take a leading role." Smiling, he looked between Chance and herself. "I can't wait to see what you guys are going to do. For the charity ball."

Jane narrowed her eyes. That seemed a tad manipulative. They were all busy, but how did you call out a sweet old man who just happened to have the power to throw you in jail for contempt of whatever-the-hell-he-wanted?

Nevertheless, she had to try. No way was she going to be cochair with Chance McGovern at her side. If he was involved, she needed a buffer.

"Judge Nichols, we've already organized part of the ball, and we've been working well together. I think it would be in the best interests of the widows' and orphans' fund if the two of us continued to run the committee."

Chance's gaze rested on her, a heavy presence, one she refused to acknowledge.

"I appreciate your vote of confidence in this old man, but to be honest, I think I took on too much when I agreed to be cochair. These bones need a little rest from running around all day." The judge rubbed his hands together. "No, the two of you will do great."

Her pulse kicked up to match the restless drumming of her fingers on the couch's cushion. "I probably don't need any help at all. I'm sure the new assistant fire chief is very busy, and I can handle the fundraiser by myself."

"Don't be silly," the judge said. "Who better to help with a fireman's fundraiser than Mr. McGovern? Besides, you were the one saying how a month isn't very much time and there is a lot still to do."

Damn. She had said that. Her mind ran through a list of excuses, but none would be good enough to convince the judge. She glared at Chance. Why wasn't he jumping in with his own reasons? He had to want to get out of this more than she did. But no, he sat there as silent as . . . something really quiet, not helping out at all.

His eyes never leaving hers, Chance slowly raised one eyebrow and cocked his head to the side. She bit back a growl. How dare he give her that look, the one that practically screamed *What are you going to do now?* Had he forgotten that she'd been there at its inception, when a scrawny fifteen-year-old boy had practiced it in front of a mirror, using his fingers to hold one eyebrow down as he raised the other, Jane sitting on his bed, laughing at the goofy faces he made? And now he used it on her? Hell no.

She shot to her feet. The pressure in her head from her cold messed with her balance, and she wobbled. Chance rose and put a steadying hand on her shoulder, but she shrugged him off. His touch messed with her head more than her cold did.

Jane dug her fingers into her hips. "Mr. McGovern—"

"Can't wait to help with the fundraiser. It's a worthy cause and a great way to get involved in the community." Chance held a large hand out to the judge. "Don't worry. I've got it from here."

The men shook hands. "Perfect," Judge Nichols said. He walked to the door. "I'll leave you to it. Get a lot of rest tonight, Jane. Pineville needs you healthy." And with a smile and a nod, he was gone.

Leaving her alone. With Chance McGovern.

She inhaled deeply, the sounds of snot tunneling up her nose loud in the silence. She looked around for a tissue. Remembering the tissues were in her bedroom, she wiped her nose on the sleeve of her robe. Not something she would normally do in front of company, but she didn't want Chance to have any misunderstanding of how he ranked in her life.

"Let's sit down," he said. "We have a lot to catch up on."

With a huff, she flopped down on the sofa, crossed one leg over the other. Her robe gaped open, revealing her bare thigh before she grabbed the edge and tugged it closed. "I don't want to catch up. Let's just get some planning done so you can get out of here."

His eyes flicked to her legs before settling back on her face. He leaned forward in the armchair and rested his elbows on his knees, lacing his long fingers together.

She stared at those hands, and swallowed past the lump in her throat. As a teenager, his hands and feet had been too large for the skinny kid they'd adorned. When they'd met freshman year in tennis practice, he'd reminded her of a Great Dane puppy, all paws and clumsiness and potential. By the time he'd left for college, he'd grown into his shoe size, no longer gawky and awkward.

But the man he'd filled out to be left her mouth dry. The fabric of his trousers strained across his hard thighs, and his exposed forearms were corded with muscle.

She picked up her mug from the coffee table, gulped down some tea.

"I'm sorry, Jane. You don't know how often I've thought—"

"What part of not catching up didn't you understand?" She bobbed her foot up and down. "Can we please just pretend we don't know each other and get this done?"

Chance clenched his jaw, breathing in deeply through his nose. After a moment's pause, he agreed. "Fine. Just fundraising business. I can do that. Where do you want—"

"I can't believe you'd show up here without giving me any warning." She uncrossed her legs and leaned forward. "You didn't have any suspicions when you were told to go to Jane Willoughby's apartment that it could be me?"

"The chief gave me the address of 'Dispatch Jane.' That's what everyone calls you. I had no idea you were a dispatcher in backwoods Michigan." His nostrils flared. "And even if I had been told your last name, how was I to warn you? I don't have your phone number."

Jane bit down on her tongue. That made sense. She knew of her nickname, knew most of the guys at the fire station called her that. And of course Chance, the evil defiler of virgins, as he'd come to be known in her head, wouldn't have her current phone number. He laid out a very sensible defense.

All that sensibility just ticked her off even more.

"Like I said, I don't want to talk about us. Let's just get to work." She reached for a yellow notepad and pen at the corner of the table.

"Fine."

"Good."

They glared at each other. Jane started out the staring contest digging deep, hoping for a heretofore unknown superpower of setting people on fire with her mind. How deliciously ironic would that be? The fireman who burned her nine years ago getting a taste of his own medicine.

The edges of his gorgeous brown eyes tilted up the smallest bit. Humor chased out the annoyance that had sparkled in their depths. She remembered how he could always find comedy in any situation, damn him. It had made him irresistible to her stupid teenage self, the way he'd laughed through their first awkward fumblings, helping her shed her self-consciousness as they learned about making love.

It had been so good between them.

And suddenly she was the one on fire. One look from Chance and she still melted into one big pile of goo. God, she was an idiot.

The body that betrayed her came back to save her. She sneezed, breaking the eye contact, breaking their connection.

Chance rose to his feet. "Look, a day or two won't matter. Why don't we meet up again after you feel better? Give me your phone number."

She hesitated.

"We're going to be working together for a month," he said. "We need each other's phone numbers." He settled his hands on his lean hips. "I promise not to prank call you in the middle of the night."

Jane ground her teeth. When did Chance become the reasonable one? She used to be the voice of sanity, trying to rein in his silly pranks and adventures.

She rubbed a knuckle into her eye socket. She was being an idiot. It had been almost a decade. Of course he'd grown up. She didn't know this Chance McGovern at all.

She gave him her number.

He punched it in, waited to hear her phone's muffled ring come from the bedroom, and slid his phone into his pocket. "Okay, now you have my number . . ."

An unearthly howl stopped Chance's words. A streak of orange rocketed through the living room, into the kitchen, and out the open window above the sink. A bowl in the sink rattled, and a paper towel Jane had left on the counter drifted slowly to the floor.

"What the hell was that?" he asked, eyes round.

"Cyclops. My cat." She took a sip of her cool tea. "He doesn't like the sound of my phone ringing. Or strangers in the apartment. Or people in general, really." She smiled at Chance, the first genuine one to cross her face since opening the door on her teenage mistake. "You're lucky all he did was run away. Usually he's more . . . aggressive in showing his displeasure."

"What does he do?"

Her smile widened. "We have a month of meetings ahead of us. I'm sure you'll find out."

Chance narrowed his eyes. "Call me when you feel better. We can meet, uh"—he shifted on his feet—"maybe downtown somewhere."

The grin on her face didn't quit, even after she'd shut the door on the man. It probably didn't say much about her as a person, but it was deeply satisfying that her little one-eyed cat could instill fear in a six-foot-something fireman. All in all, if she had to meet up with the man who'd broken her heart years ago, this reunion had gone down as a win for her. Even with her red nose and sloppy robe.

Still, for their next meeting, she'd make sure to wear something tight and sexy. Not too slutty. She didn't want to look like she was trying to make an impression. Wandering into her bathroom, she gathered her hair at the nape of her neck to see if a loose chignon would be the way to go.

A moan escaped her mouth at her reflection.

"No, no, no, no, no," she wailed. Raising a shaky hand, she brushed her fingers through her hair. And she knew what Judge Nichols had been trying to tell her with his weird hand gestures. Because there, near the crown of her head, was a used tissue. Stuck to her hair.

She pulled the crumpled white square, tugging a couple of strands of hair off with it. She didn't even want to look at what had cemented the tissue to her head.

Shoulders slumped, she tossed it in the trash can. Perfect. Just perfect. Chance hadn't seen her in nine years, and the first time he did, she had a used tissue stuck to her head.

Her win had been imagined. Chance had stood before her, all muscly and oozing testosterone, and she'd been . . . She looked in the mirror again and sighed.

Nope. It was definitely fifteen-love, advantage all to Chance.

Chapter Two

The scents of lavender and rosemary enveloped Jane when she opened the door to her mother's store. A small space tucked between a deli and a real estate agent's office, the Apothic Garden sold an eclectic mix of soaps, herbal remedies, and garden supplies.

Her mother lifted her salt-and-pepper head from the *Pineville Gazette*. "Hi, honey. How's it going?"

Jane set her messenger bag on the counter beside an old-fashioned cash register. "I'm fine."

"Your color looks better." Her mother eyeballed her critically. "I see my rose hip tea worked."

Jane just barely contained her sigh. She loved her mother. She really did. But she'd never use one of her mother's herbal remedies when over-the-counter cold and flu medicine was available at the local drug store.

Edith Willoughby was a product of the sixties, and a firm believer that positive thinking and good energy could cure most ills. When her husband had been diagnosed with cancer, along with chemotherapy he had tried every ancient Chinese herb, healing yoga practice, and Native American prayer ceremony that Edith could find.

Jane's father had lived five more years than his doctors had expected. While Jane believed it was the advances in modern-day medicine that had made the difference, she'd still driven him to many of the alternative treatments. Just in case.

Edith dug into the pocket of her flowing tunic and pulled out a pair of eyeglasses. Perching them on the end of her nose, she examined her daughter. "Your color may look better, but something's still off." She reached out, grabbed Jane's earlobe, and tugged her head to the side.

"Mom!" Jane yanked her head away.

"Your chakras are funky. What's wrong?"

Jane poked at a bundle of dried lavender hanging from an exposed wood beam. "Nothing's wrong."

Pinching her lips tight, her mom stared at her over the top of her glasses.

"Well, nothing's *wrong* wrong." Jane blew out a breath. "Just had a bit of a bad surprise."

"Well?" Edith asked. "Unfortunately, I'm not a mind reader. You're going to have to tell me."

"Chance showed up at my apartment. He's the new assistant fire chief." Just saying the words made her stomach twist and her heart pick up its pace. A man she hadn't seen in nearly a decade shouldn't have such an effect on her.

"Chance?" Her mother widened her amber eyes. Her eyes were the only trait she'd passed on to Jane. "Your Chance, from high school?"

"One and the same. Although it's debatable whether he was ever my Chance." Good God, was she sulking now? Bring back an old high school boyfriend, and she started acting like a teenager.

"Is he still as good-looking as he used to be?" Edith asked.

Jane sighed. "Better."

"Mmm."

Jane rolled her shoulders. "Mom, that's gross." She didn't want to think about her mother lusting after the same man she did.

"It would have been gross if I'd done it when he was a teenager, but not now that he's an adult." Edith peered at her over the rim of her glasses. "I may be older than you, but I'm not dead. I can still appreciate a good-looking man."

"You haven't even seen him."

"So bring him around so I can see him instead of just imagine him. It would be nice to talk to that boy again. He was always so sweet helping your dad with the composting." Her mother's voice took on the wistful tone it always did when she spoke of her deceased husband. Jane had grown up embarrassed by her parents' overt displays of affection. Now she was just envious. She didn't think she'd ever find a love like theirs.

"We're not friends, Mom. I'm not going to bring him around after school. But Chance is my cochair for the fundraiser so you'll get the opportunity to drool over him. You're still on board to be a member of the committee, right? We're going to need all the help we can get."

"Of course. I love our boys in blue." Edith's cheeks turned pink.

Jane tilted her head to the side. Her mother rarely became embarrassed. "I think that's supposed to refer to the police."

"Firefighters wear blue uniforms, too."

Jane waved a hand in front of her face. "Regardless, can we get back to the problem? I'm supposed to work with Chance on the charity ball. I can't work with him for a month!"

"Honey." Her mother covered Jane's hand with her own. "It happened a long time ago. You need to get over it."

"I'm over it." At her mother's raised eyebrow, she said, "I am. That doesn't mean I want to work with the man." Have to spend time looking at his broad shoulders, smell his spicy aftershave. Nope, she didn't want that at all.

"I'm sure you'll rise to the challenge." Edith turned to the aromatherapy bar on the wall behind the counter. "But to help you out, I'll make up just the thing for the funk you're in." Stretching, she pulled a bottle from the top shelf, one from a middle shelf. "I think a mix of lavender, chamomile, and eucalyptus will fix you right up."

"Mom, I don't think aromatherapy is going to help." Still, she plucked an empty amber stopper bottle down from a shelf and placed it next to her mother. Her mother's tinctures didn't solve any problems, but Jane had to admit her mom brewed great-smelling oils.

"Remember, just a couple of drops on your pillowcase at night."

"Yes, Mom." Jane tucked the bottle into her bag.

"And if you want to perk up for your date tonight, you can put a drop or two behind your ears." Edith wiped down the reclaimed wood counter where she mixed her oils. She had a sixth sense about what aromas worked well together. When the two of them had first moved to the small town in central Michigan, her mother's hippie clothes and attitude had turned a few heads. But each trip Jane made home from college, she saw more and more people in her mother's shop. The aromatherapy bar was the most popular draw.

"I forgot about Leon tonight." Jane sniffed, still heard a slight congestion. "Maybe I'll call and tell him I still feel under the weather."

"Your only social life is your Sunday and Thursday night dates with Leon." Her mother shook her head like that was the biggest disappointment a parent could have in her child. "You don't want to go backwards."

To the dark days when Jane spent her evenings reading mystery novels, childless and alone. That thought was clearly implied.

Jane blew out a breath. "Fine." With a kiss to her mother's cheek, she breezed out the door, the bell above it tinkling a goodbye.

Game night at the American Legion was usually fun. It probably was a good idea that she go out. Take her mind off things she shouldn't have her mind on. Like dropping a quarter on Chance's butt and seeing how high it'd bounce off the hard muscles. That part of his body had really filled out. She'd spent the better part of yesterday afternoon lying in bed thinking about that, much to her shame.

And Leon was perfectly nice. Dependable. A good friend.

Strolling to her car, her steps grew shorter and shorter.

And not nearly interesting enough to keep her mind off Chance.

Jane groaned. It was going to be a long night.

Chance pulled his SUV into a parking space at the American Legion and cut the engine. He should be at home. There were still boxes to unpack, and a free night was better spent playing games with his son rather than with adult men. But his new chief had thought it would be a good way for Chance to meet the members of the community he now served.

Chance didn't want to start off his new job ticking off his boss. Creating a stable life for Josh was his primary concern.

Still, he had a plan for the night. Get in, shake some hands, get out.

Wind slapped his face as he stepped from the car. The night air held a bite, a warning that although winter was over, this was still Michigan, and it didn't tolerate sissies. Shrugging into a windbreaker, Chance strode to the entrance.

A dimly lit bar lay off to the right. Its walls were adorned with sports pennants, and a few old-timers scattered the barstools. Straight ahead, double doors opened onto a large meeting room. The fluorescent lights made Chance blink. Fold-out tables filled the area, their surfaces covered with cards, board games, and poker chips. The room was full. People sat at the tables, smiling and laughing, attesting to the fact that they at least enjoyed playing games with other adults. Others stood, congregated in groups, chatting and drinking.

Chance muffled a grunt, and headed for the fun and games. Searching for his chief, he spotted the man easily. A head taller than anyone else in the room, the leader of the Pineville Fire Department reminded Chance of the Brawny paper towel model. A flash of red standing in front of Chief Finnegan made Chance pause. All he could see of her was her back, but he recognized Jane instantly.

There was nothing overtly sexy about the red blouse, jeans, and low pumps she wore, but Chance's body reacted just the same. Her hips had filled out since high school. Where she'd once been slim as a boy, she now had the rounded curves that begged for a man's touch. Her thin robe hadn't done much to hide the ripe swell of her breasts the day before, and that flash of smooth leg had made a frequent appearance in his head for the past twenty-four hours.

She tilted her head back to laugh at something the chief said, the ends of her hair brushing the collar of her blouse. The hair was different, too. His Jane had worn her hair down to her waist, pulled back in a thick braid.

The new Jane kept her hair short, wisps just curling at her collar. Chance didn't usually like short hair on women, but Jane's whiskey-colored locks looked soft and feminine, and framed her delicate face beautifully. It was just long enough for a man to dig his fingers into and grab hold.

Shoving his hands in the front pockets of his jeans, he shifted. Jane was no longer his to think about that way. In fact, Jane was downright pissed off at him. Not that he could blame her. When he'd left that card on her front porch years ago and taken off without her, it had been a dick move. But they'd both been stupid kids. She couldn't hold that against him forever. Could she?

In three long strides he was behind her.

The chief smiled at him over Jane's head. "McGovern. Glad you could make it." He extended a hand as Jane whipped around, her eyes flaring.

Chance gripped Finnegan's palm. "Glad to be here." He leaned a little closer to Jane, enjoying the heat from her body. She smelled earthy, different. Was that . . . eucalyptus? Weird. But somehow it worked on her. Anything would.

She took a quick step back, putting space between the two of them. "I didn't know you'd be here."

"Oh, that's right," Finnegan said. "You two have met for the fundraiser."

Chance must be a sadistic bastard. Why else would he enjoy the flush that crept up Jane's neck and the tense set to her shoulders? "We met a long time before that. Jane and I are old buddies from high school."

"Yeah, buddies." Jane spit the words out like they were bullets from a gun.

Chance smiled. He'd forgotten how much fun he used to have riling her up. She'd always been too serious. He'd needle her until she'd finally shake her head in exasperation, unable to stop the smile from spreading across her face.

It would take a lot longer to wheedle a smile from her now.

Finnegan raised his eyebrows. "Where'd you go to high school?"

"Lansing."

"So you're a local boy, or near enough. I thought you were an import to Michigan, like me. Though not from so far away." If Chance listened hard enough, he could just hear the trace of the man's Irish accent that attested to just how far away he'd come from. The chief clapped his hand on Chance's shoulder. "Still, I knew I liked you too much for you to be from California."

"The West Coast isn't full of crazies like you've heard. And the guys on Cal Fire are some of the best." Turning to Jane, he said, "I just moved here from Northern California. I was a firefighter there for five years."

"And one of the best, from what your old chief told me. You moved up the ranks quickly. He was sorry to lose you." Finnegan took a sip from the beer in his hand. "But his loss was our gain. We're lucky to have you."

A furrow appeared between Jane's eyebrows. "You became a firefighter after college? That wasn't part of your plan."

His plan. His set-in-stone life plan that he'd spent hours talking to Jane about in the backseat of his father's Jeep. College, med school, then becoming the youngest neurosurgeon in US history. The plan he'd outlined in obnoxious detail, trying to impress the sweet girl in his arms, but always knowing he was keeping a couple parts of it from her.

Like where he intended to go to college. And that he didn't plan on having her by his side for his meteoric rise. His teenage heart had loved Jane, but even then he'd known that at eighteen he was too young to plan a life with someone.

"Plans change," he said. Did they ever. After getting his college girlfriend pregnant junior year, he'd done the right thing. A small wedding. A new plan. No more dreams of medical school, with crushing debt. He'd had a family to take care of. And once he'd held his squirming, blotchy baby boy in his hands for the first time, he hadn't regretted the changes for a second.

A man sidled up next to Jane. His short hair was pale blond and thin enough to reveal glimpses of his pink scalp. He slung an arm around Jane's shoulders, and she smiled up at him.

Chance looked at that arm and decided the man looked pudgy instead of solid, and his chin was decidedly weak.

Weak chin whined to Jane. "I've got everything set up for us. You're delaying the game."

"One minute." Jane tucked a shiny lock of hair behind her ear. "Leon, have you met our new assistant fire chief? This is Chance McGovern. Chance, this is Leon Gabriel. My date."

"Nice to meet you." Leon took Chance's hand. Christ, his handshake was as weak as his chin. The man looked at the chief and nodded. "Finnegan." He pulled Jane closer into his chest. "Come on. I want to get at least two games of Dominion in. No time to waste chitchatting."

With a smile of apology to the chief, Jane turned and walked to one of the tables where two other people sat waiting. Her snug jeans caressed her hips with every step.

Finnegan took another pull from his bottle. "Leon is Judge Nichols's bailiff. He really likes game night." His lips twisted wryly, and he shook his head. "So. You and Dispatch Jane. There's a history there." The chief's voice made it known it wasn't a question.

Chance hooked his thumbs in his belt loops. "Ancient history. We were friends, then I went to college. We lost touch."

"Uh-huh." Finnegan finished his beer. "Jane's a professional, so I'm not worried about your 'ancient history' affecting work. But a lot of people like her in this town. If she keeps glaring at you like you're scum on the bottom of her shoe, it might be a little harder for you to make nice with the folks."

"I'll make out fine." Chance tried to keep the edge out of his voice. It wasn't his new boss's business what Jane's and his history was. And surely Finnegan's concerns were overblown. Everyone he'd met so far had been nothing but nice to him and his son. That wasn't likely to change if they found out he and Jane had had a bad breakup a decade ago.

"I'm sure you will," Finnegan said. "But community relations are important. Especially with our fundraiser coming up. We don't want to give anyone an excuse to give their money elsewhere."

Chance blew out a breath. "It's not a big deal. Jane and I are fine." He thought back to that card he'd left on her porch, the one that must have cemented in Jane's mind his status as asshole for life. Hopefully she wouldn't let that information get around town. He'd been just a kid, but it still wasn't his proudest moment.

"Make sure you are." The chief turned and nodded at a woman walking past. "You and Jane have to work together to get this fundraiser going. If you two have any issues that will get in the way of your working relationship, sort them out now. A bouquet of flowers and an apology go a long way in soothing a woman's ruffled feathers."

"I'll take care of it."

"Good." Finnegan clapped him on the shoulder. "What say we go find a game to join?"

Chance followed his boss to a table with a Texas Hold 'Em spread. Unbidden, his gaze drifted to Jane's table. She was laughing at something the woman next to her said, her breasts jiggling delightfully beneath the silk blouse.

She caught him looking at her and scowled.

It was going to take a lot more than flowers.

Chapter Three

Jane reread the last paragraph on the page. The novel she'd found to be a page-turner last week just couldn't hold her attention. The description of the hero cop now struck her as too similar to her former flame, and every time he was in a scene, she pictured Chance.

Giving up, she placed a bookmark between the pages and tossed the book onto her desk. She spun in her executive chair and looked at the posters on her cubicle's walls. A golden sand beach drew her in, an aquamarine ocean serenely lapping at its shores. That should be her next vacation. Somewhere warm and quiet. Just her, a hammock, and a piña colada.

Jane made a mental tally of her finances. Maybe a weekend camping by Lake Roanoke instead. Michigan had plenty of natural beauty that she loved to explore. But at the moment it also had one fireman too many.

The cord to her headset tangled around her neck. Cursing, she spun back the other direction, unraveling the mess.

"Everything okay over there?" Sharon asked.

Jane couldn't see the woman, but knew she sat in the next cubicle playing solitaire on her computer. Contrary to its name, Crook County was low on crime. Aside from the occasional car accident, heart attack, or cat stuck in a tree, the basement of Pineville's courthouse, headquarters to county dispatch, didn't receive too many calls.

There was a lot of downtime to fill, and each of the county's five dispatchers had different ways to spend it. Most shifts were worked by two dispatchers, and this Monday Jane and Sharon were holding down the fort.

"Everything's fine," Jane answered.

The snap from a popping piece of chewing gum cracked through the air. Sharon was partial to Big Red, and the scent of cinnamon followed the woman wherever she went. "You choke yourself on the headset cord again?"

Jane's shoulders slumped. "Yeah."

Another bubble popped. "You and Leon go out last night?"

"Uh-huh."

"Does that boy still shake your hand at the end of the date?" Sharon asked.

Jane took off her headset and stood up. Resting her chin on the top of the cubicle, she looked down into her coworker's small square of space. Sharon's dark hair was teased and sprayed into a hairstyle that should have stayed in the eighties. Aside from that fashion faux pas, her friend always dressed to the nines. Although Jane thought the trendy outfits were wasted on someone who worked in a hole in the ground, she had to admit her friend looked great. Sharon's rose-colored slim skirt and silk blouse complemented her smooth dark skin and showcased her trim figure.

Jane looked down at her own jeans and sweatshirt. Working a job where she was just a voice on the other end of the phone, she *might* have let herself get a bit more casual than she should.

"We don't shake hands after our dates. Don't exaggerate."

Sharon's brown eyes flicked up from her computer screen. "You don't kiss, either. That's the weirdest kind of dating I've ever heard of. It's like you're Amish or something."

Jane tugged on the hem of her University of Michigan sweatshirt. "I'm not a prude. Leon and I are just . . . we're just friendly dating. It's not serious."

"Friendly dating?" Sharon snorted. "If that's a new thing, I don't want anything to do with it. You go out with your friends. When you date, there should be heat."

Jane thought back to the goodbye hug Leon had given her the night before on her porch. Definitely no heat. Not even a stray tingle. Still, she did usually have fun with him.

She chewed on her bottom lip. Well, she had fun playing the board games, at least.

"In all these months, has that boy ever made a move on you?"

Jane shook her head.

"Is he gay?"

"Of course not." Jane didn't think so, at least. And just because he didn't maul her at her front door shouldn't be a reason to gossip about his sexuality.

"Hmm." Sharon cocked her head. "Maybe if you didn't dress so frumpy, you'd get more action." She blew a bubble the size of an apple. "We should go shopping together this weekend. I can hook you up with clothes so sexy the boy won't be able to keep his hands off of you."

Jane shuddered. "No, thanks." A handsy Leon didn't appeal. And who was Sharon to dole out fashion advice? She loved her friend, but she'd be damned if she'd take style tips from someone whose bangs created a wall high enough to cast a shadow.

The phone rang. "Call on line one," Sharon said. "Do you want to take it, or me?"

"I'll get it." Better a conversation with an injured person than continue talking about her pathetic dating habits. She grabbed her headset, slipped it on, and pulled her chair up to her computer.

"Hello. 9-1-1. What's your emergency?"

Silence greeted her.

"Hello? Can you answer? What's your emergency, please?" Jane hated the silent calls. Was it a simple misdial or was someone choking to death, unable to speak?

"Hello," a soft voice answered. "Is som'body there?"

Crap. Even worse. A child. "Sweetie, you've dialed nine-one-one. Do you need some help?"

"My aunt," the little boy said.

"What about your aunt?" Jane kept her voice gentle. "Is she hurt?"

A sniffle. "She fell. I shake her, but she don't wake up."

Jane tapped some keys and waited for an address to pop up on the screen. Bingo. She recognized the street name. It was in a solidly middle-class neighborhood, one that had a fierce Christmas decoration competition each year.

"Is your aunt inside the house? Are you with her right now?" Jane's fingers flew over the keyboard, sending the information to Pineville's emergency response services. An ambulance, fire engine with a medic, and a police cruiser would be rolling out any second. It was only a question of who would arrive first.

"We're in the kitchen. She's making me a PBJ."

"Sounds yummy." Jane typed some more, adding information as she received it. "What's your name, sweetie?"

"Josh." A long sniffle ripped through the line.

"My name's Jane." Her heart tore at the tremor in the boy's voice, but she shoved past it. In her line of work, she'd learned to take the emotion out of it. It didn't help the person at the other end of the line if Jane cried with them. "Is there anybody else in the house with you?"

"No."

"Okay, Josh. Can you tell me if your aunt is bleeding? Did she hit her head?"

"Aunt Katie's not bleeding. But when I was four I cut my finger real bad. The doctor glued me back up."

"How old are you now?"

"Five."

Jane smiled. That year made a difference in his mind. "You're a big boy now, Josh. Can you do me a favor? Can you put your hand in front of your aunt's mouth and tell me if you feel her breathing?"

The sound of the phone clacking on a hard surface reached Jane. She held her breath, waiting to see if the child could follow her instructions and relay any useful information back to her. The seconds dragged on. Maybe she should have kept the boy on the line instead.

Heavy breathing finally came back on the line. "She blew on my hand. It tickled."

Jane typed in that information. According to her computer, Deputy Jerome Davis was only two minutes away from the house and closing. "Josh? Don't hang up the phone, okay? I have to talk to someone else, but stay on the line."

She pressed a button and was transferred to the police radio frequency. "Jerome, this is Jane in dispatch. We have a five-year-old boy reporting that his aunt fell and is unresponsive in the kitchen. Victim's still breathing according to the boy. I'll keep him on the line until you arrive. It looks like you'll be the first responder."

The phone line crackled before clearing up. "Copy. My ETA is less than a minute. Ask the kid if he can open the front door. Over."

"Understood." Jane switched back to the emergency line. "Josh, are you still there?"

"Yes, but I have to go potty."

"Before you do that, can you go make sure the front door is unlocked?" Jane asked. "Officer Davis will be there soon to help you and your aunt and I want you to let him inside, okay?"

"Then can I go potty?"

"Go open the front door for Officer Davis. After you show him where your aunt is, then you can go potty. Deal?" This kid was a trooper, and Jane could only pray that his aunt would be all right.

"Deal."

The phone clattered to the counter again. Jane monitored the lines and knew the instant Jerome arrived, followed shortly by fire engine 21 and an ambulance. Her small part in the emergency response was over, but her worry over the young boy and his aunt remained. He'd sounded like such a sweetheart over the phone, and showed more calm under pressure than many adults in that situation. For the rest of her shift she wondered where Josh was and how his aunt was doing.

Working in a place where life and death could be on the line helped keep her life in perspective. Her angst over working with her ex-boyfriend was petty in comparison. She could handle a little discomfort.

Resolved, Jane picked up her novel and refused to let thoughts of a certain firefighter keep her out of the story. After work, she'd call Chance and set up a meeting to get started organizing the fundraiser.

Chance held a wriggling Josh on his lap and glanced at the clock again. Only five minutes since he'd last checked. This wasn't San Francisco General. Pineville's small emergency room was only half full of patients. As far as he could tell, they consisted of one possible broken ankle, a man complaining of chest pains, and Chance's unconscious sister. The doctors didn't have their hands full, and Chance had to stifle his impatience at not knowing what was wrong with Katie.

His son did a back bend and almost fell off Chance's lap. He grabbed the waistband of Josh's jeans, hauled him back upright. "I know you're bored, but we have to sit here a little while longer. Until we find out how Aunt Katie's doing."

"I'm booored." After Josh's initial fright over his aunt's collapse, the boy had rallied. Sitting in one spot wasn't easy for an energetic five-year-old. When the two had first arrived in the waiting room of the ER, Chance had let his son race around, hoping his energy would soon wane. Dirty looks from the other anxious people in the waiting area had soon put a stop to that.

"I know, kiddo. Just a little while longer." A woman in a white coat entered the waiting room, getting Chance's hopes up, until she moved to a young couple in the corner. Not Katie's doctor then.

Josh gave a full-body shimmy. "Gaaah."

Sighing, Chance pulled his smartphone out of his pocket. He went to the app store and downloaded something that looked kid-friendly before placing the device into his son's hands. He tried to limit his son's time spent in front of computers and tablets. He really did. But right now, he gave up. In order to keep his own sanity, he let his son become engrossed by the mindless game.

The warm weight of his son tucked up against Chance's chest combined with the stress of the day caught up with him. His eyes were just beginning to slide shut when a doctor who didn't look old enough to be out of med school entered.

"Mr. McGovern?"

Chance stood, settling Josh back on the chair, and shook the doctor's hand. "Yes, that's me. How's my sister?"

"She's doing well." The young man ran a hand through his hair. "Why don't we have a seat?"

Chance nodded, sat next to his son. The doctor pulled a chair around so he could face Chance.

"I'm Doctor Sampson. We've stabilized Katie's blood pressure, but we're going to keep her here tonight so we can keep pushing fluids."

Chance nodded. When the call had come through to the firehouse with his home address, he'd practically knocked Doug, the engine's driver, to the ground in an effort to get behind the wheel. Chief Finnegan had had some choice words to say about that. But he'd stayed out of Chance's way when they'd reached his house, letting Chance help load his sister into the ambulance. He'd spoken to her, seen the dizziness swamp her when she'd try to sit up. It had been a textbook case of hypotension.

"How long since she was diagnosed with Type One diabetes?" Doctor Sampson asked.

Josh's shoe was dangling at the tip of his toes. Chance shoved it back on, retightened the laces. "About six months now. She'd been feeling tired for months before she went to the doctor and got the diagnosis."

Doctor Sampson nodded. "We see this a lot with those new to the disease. It's an adjustment. We'll have a dietician talk to Katie before she leaves here."

"It's information she already knows. I've told her she needs to be stricter with her diet." The knot in his stomach that had started to unravel when the doctor said his sister was okay cramped again. This time in irritation. When would Katie start to take her condition seriously? His little sister acted like a Type One diagnosis shouldn't affect her life in the slightest.

"Well, it never hurts to hear it again. We're moving her up to a room right now," the doctor continued. "You can go visit with her when she's settled."

Chance shook his hand. "Thank you." He gathered his things and pocketed his phone amid his son's noisy protests. "We're going to see Aunt Katie now. You're not going to be playing a game while we do it."

Josh jutted his jaw out, but he wisely remained silent. He allowed Chance to take his small hand and lead him to the bank of elevators in the lobby. The hospital right outside Pineville wasn't large. Emergency services and administration were on the first floor, and the patient rooms on the second.

"Press the up arrow," he told his son.

Pique forgotten, Josh poked the button repeatedly, then hit the down button for good measure. Josh loved it when the buttons lit up.

Chance ruffled his son's hair. Kids were so cool. They got over their anger so quickly, never held a grudge longer than their next smile. Unlike a certain adult he knew.

The elevator dinged and opened its doors. The car was thankfully going up, not down to the parking garage, and Chance herded Josh inside. "Press the button for two."

Josh got it on his first try. Chance felt a bit embarrassed that such a small accomplishment made him proud. God help him if Josh turned out to be a football star.

With the help of the information desk on the second floor, they found Katie's room. She was propped up on three pillows and looking as happy as a cat getting a bath. Her brown hair lay tangled around her shoulders, and her eyes, almost the same color as Chance's, were flinty with anger. Seven years separated the McGovern siblings, but their features were similar enough they could be mistaken for fraternal twins.

Katie's thinned lips relaxed into a smile. "Josh! How are you, buddy?" She held out an arm and Josh scrambled up on the narrow bed to sit beside her.

"I'm bored. Hos'pedals are no fun. They didn't have my 'toons on the TV even." Josh gave the pout that had garnered him sympathy and sweets from many an adult before Chance had gotten wise to the manipulation.

"I'm bored, too," Katie told him. "I'm trying to get out of here tonight so I—"

"Not going to happen." Chance pulled a tan recliner up to the bed. It squealed as he dragged it against the polished wood floor. "The doctor wants you to stay here tonight for observation and that's what you're going to do."

Her jaw jutted out in a manner very similar to what his son had pulled minutes earlier. Must be a McGovern family trait. "I feel fine now. It was just low blood sugar."

"When was the last time you checked your glucose levels?" Chance's voice was harder than a woman lying in a hospital bed deserved, but damn it, he knew she wasn't taking proper care of herself.

She ignored him. "Pretty exciting day, huh?" Katie asked her nephew. "I hear I owe you one for calling for help."

Josh rubbed a fist beneath his nose. "I hoped Dad would answer the phone, but he came later."

Chance picked his son up from the bed and sat him across his lap. "I know you don't want to face your medical condition, but you can't keep pretending that your life hasn't changed."

"My life hasn't changed." Katie crossed her arms across her chest, careful not to bump the IV poking out of her right hand. "I have to make a couple of modifications, but no major changes."

"Right. Which is why we're having this conversation with you in the hospital." Chance shook his head. "You're supposed to be watching out for Josh. He's not supposed to be taking care of you."

The skin bunched around Katie's eyes, and she gave Chance a pained stare. "He doesn't. . . . This was just a mistake today. It won't happen again."

Josh did another one of his backbends. It was like the kid didn't have a spine. Chance tightened his grip. "You can bet your behind it won't." Glancing at Josh, Chance wished he didn't have to censor himself. Katie probably wouldn't pay attention to the PG version of this lecture. "I'm not going to be taking a passive role in your health anymore. I'm going to be on you like white on rice."

"That was you being passive?"

"Yep." He stared her down. It was a look he'd had a lot of practice with. He'd given it to her when she used to try to tag along with him and his friends as kids, when she'd wanted to join the big kids jumping off a twenty-foot boulder into a lake, when he'd caught her bringing back their parents' car at age fourteen. He'd never told their parents about that particular escapade, but he'd hoped the patented big-brother glare had gotten his point across.

Katie fiddled with the thin blanket covering her legs.

"You sleeping here, Aunt Katie?"

She sighed. "Just for tonight, kiddo. I'll be back home tomorrow."

"You get 'toons on your TV?" Josh had found the flat-screen television bolted onto the wall across from the bed.

She picked up the remote control. "Let's find out."

They spent an hour watching cartoons together. Chance knew he needed to hammer his point across harder, but the dark smudges beneath his sister's eyes sucked the will right out of him. When those eyes grew heavy, Chance picked his son up, kissed his sister on her cheek, and headed for the elevators.

"We didn't see the end," his son whined.

"The rabbit comes out on top." The elevator dinged before the doors slid open. Chance stepped inside. "Aunt Katie needed to sleep. We can watch a bit more TV when we get home." Shifting Josh around to balance on one hip, Chance pulled out his phone and began scrolling through his contacts. He hadn't formed a tight relationship with his coworkers yet, but he hoped that one of the guys would be able to switch shifts with him until his sister was well enough to take care of Josh.

The collision was all his fault. Without looking up from his phone, he stepped out of the elevator. A startled cry was the only warning he got before he bumped into a slight form and a flood of water drenched his left leg.

"Oh my God. I'm so sorry, I didn't see you." The familiar voice sent a current of electricity through Chance. "This bouquet is so big . . ."

Jane shifted what had to be the biggest vase of flowers Chance had ever seen. Shock rounded her face when she spied him.

"It was my fault." Chance shot her the aw-shucks grin that had never failed to make her heart melt when he'd been late for a date in high school. "I wasn't looking where I was going. I don't know how I missed seeing that forest you're holding."

Arms straining, she hefted the glass vase until it rested on her hip. "What are you doing here?" Her tone was frosty. She'd obviously become immune to his smiles. A crease furrowed the skin between her eyebrows. "I mean, I hope nothing's wrong." Shifting on her feet, she darted a curious glance at his son. "Since this is the hospital and all."

The skin above the V-neck of her plain white tee turned a lovely shade of pink, a sure sign that Jane was flustered. Chance rocked onto his toes. She hadn't lost all of her tells. Jane looked from his son, to him, to his son again, and Chance decided to put her out of her misery.

"We're visiting my sister, who took a fall today. She's going to be fine," he added when her eyes widened in alarm. "And this is my son."

"You have a son?" A flurry of emotions washed across her face, too quickly for Chance to interpret. Her grip on the vase slipped, and she readjusted her load.

Chance frowned. Even with half of the water now covering his pants, the three-foot stems and accompanying glass vase and water still must weigh a lot. He nodded his head toward the front desk, and she followed him over, resting the vase on the counter and rolling her shoulders.

Smiling at the older woman who volunteered at the information booth, Chance asked, "Would it be possible to get a cart for these flowers? And we'll probably need a mop to clean up the water that spilled before someone hurts themselves."

The tight curls on the volunteer's steel-gray head bobbed. "I'll call maintenance right away."

"I can carry the flowers." Jane pressed her lips into a thin line.

"I'm sure you can, Jane. But why carry something heavy when you don't have to?"

His son popped his head up from his shoulder. "Jane? You're Jane?"

Chance's stomach dropped. Crap. Had Josh overheard more of Chance's fights with his mom than he'd thought? When things had started to go bad, Annette had started accusing Chance of still holding a flame for his first love. A woman Chance had mentioned a grand total of two times to his wife.

Jane stuck out a hand. "Yep, that's me. And you are?"

His son looked excited to be offered a handshake. The weight on Chance's chest lifted when he saw his little guy acting like a little man.

"I'm Josh."

Chance didn't expect that information to have an effect on Jane. He was wrong.

"Josh." Her lips, a pretty shade of peach, stretched into a wide grin. "Sweetie, I'm so glad to meet you. I was wondering how you were doing all day."

The pieces of the puzzle fell into place. "You answered my son's 9-1-1 call."

"I did." She held out her fist and waited for Josh's small one to bump it. "And your son did an awesome job. He was cool, calm, and collected. A real pro."

A handshake and a fist bump? His son bounced up and down with excitement. "I tol' her Aunt Katie was still breathing, and opened the door for the ociffer."

"Officer," Chance explained to Jane.

"Yeah, I talked with Officer Davis later," Jane said. "He told me you did really well. He just might nominate you for the junior officer program."

"He will?" Josh's eyes got bigger than his open mouth.

"Yep. Your dad should be real proud of you." She bit her lip. "And your mother—"

"Not here." Chance hugged Josh closer.

"Mommy's gone."

"I see."

Chance could tell by her eyes that she didn't see. By the way she was looking at his son, like she just wanted to gather him up and smother him with kisses, he knew she assumed Annette was dead. There were times in the past when Chance might have hoped that, and he wasn't proud of those times, but last he'd heard she was still alive and kicking up shit.

His shoulders sagged. Every worry he had crawled onto his back and decided to go for a ride. He was exhausted, and he didn't want to get into the details of his marital status with his first girlfriend. He just wanted to take his son home, curl up on the sofa together, and watch cartoons.

"Well, we've got to get going," he said. "Are you visiting someone?"

"No." She turned the vase on the counter. "Once a week I deliver flowers here for the Flower Rangers."

Chance raised an eyebrow.

"It's a group of volunteers who take donated bouquets, you know, the leftovers from weddings, funerals, parties, then rearrange them and give them out to people in the hospital," Jane said. "This bad boy"—she patted the large vase—"is the result of us running out of time, so we just threw all the remaining flowers into one huge arrangement. We heard there was an eight-year-old girl here who just had her appendix out, so I'm heading to her room."

Of course she was. His Jane had always been bighearted. In high school, she'd been a candy striper for two years. Chance scratched his chest. Damn, he'd loved that little uniform.

Two men, one wearing a janitor's uniform and the other wearing a volunteer badge, walked up. The janitor pushed a rolling cart and mop, and the volunteer an empty cart. He stopped in front of Jane. "You need a ride for those flowers?"

"Thanks, Jerry." She reached for the vase, but Chance beat her to it, settling the heavy cylinder in the corner of the hand cart so it wouldn't topple over. She gave him a tight smile. "Thanks. Well, I'll see you later?"

"We still need to meet for the fundraiser," he reminded her.

"There's going to be a meeting tomorrow at noon at the Pantry with some of the volunteers." She shifted in her sneakers. "I, uh, was going to tell you about it when you were at my apartment Saturday."

Sure she was. She was going to tell the stranger she'd been expecting to work with, but she'd probably debated long and hard about telling Chance.

"I'll try to stop by."

She nodded, flashed a big smile at his son, the lucky kid, and walked toward the elevators, a wheel on the cart squeaking with each turn. The sweatshirt tied around her waist blocked his view of her sweet ass, but Chance's memory filled in the blanks.

His pulse kicked up a notch.

With a view like that, he'd try very hard to make the meeting. He'd missed that view for the past nine years. Life had thrown them back together. He didn't have to miss it anymore.

Chapter Four

Chance paused, his fork halfway to his mouth. A bite of meat loaf slid to the edge before he dropped the utensil back on the plate. Jane stood in the open doorway to the Pantry, a popular downtown coffee shop, scanning the crowded restaurant. The temperature had shot up to a balmy eighty degrees, and she was taking advantage of the pre-summer weather in loose linen pants and a tank top.

A clingy tank top that highlighted her every curve.

Chance smiled. His move back to Michigan was looking better and better. He couldn't wait for bikini weather.

Catching sight of their group wedged in the corner, she headed over. "Hi, Mom. Everyone." Jane dropped a quick kiss on her mother's upturned cheek before settling in at the only available seat. The one next to Chance.

His smile widened.

Jane scooted her chair in. "How's your sister?"

"Doing better. She's back home, but I wanted her to get her rest, so that's why I brought—"

A mop of brown hair leaned over the table on Chance's other side. "Hi, Jane!"

"Hey, Josh." She reached out and gave his son the fist bump he was waiting for. "You here to help out with the fundraiser, too?"

"Uhh . . . no?" Josh darted a quick glance at Chance before bringing his gaze back down to his paper placemat, gripping a blue crayon in his hand. "I'm drawing."

Leaning over, Chance whispered in Jane's ear. "He's not a big fan of the words 'help out.'" He inhaled. The eucalyptus was gone, replaced by the feminine scent of lavender. "Whenever he hears that, it's usually followed by us cleaning his room, the kitchen, my car. Josh isn't a fan of cleaning."

The edges of her eyes crinkled. She opened her mouth, but Judge Nichols interrupted before she could speak.

"Great. We're all here now." Nichols took a sip of coffee. "Jane and our new assistant fire chief, Chance McGovern, are the cochairs of this committee, and I know Jane has a lot of ideas to help us meet our fundraising goal. Jane?"

"Yes. Well." She cleared her throat and looked around the assembled tables. "You all know how important it is to contribute to the widows' and orphans' fund. I don't need to waste time trying to convince anyone of that." A chorus of agreement proved her point. "So, we'd agreed to a black-tie ball and auction. It's scheduled four Fridays from now. Martha, how are you coming on the invitation design?"

A plump, middle-aged woman with large, sparkling eyes spoke up. "I've narrowed it down to two possibilities. I thought I'd email the two options to all of you this afternoon for a vote, and then send it to the printers tomorrow. They said it wouldn't take but a day, and then Jean and I will start mailing them out."

Jean, a twenty-something Chance recognized as the sister of one of his fellow firefighters, started describing the invites, giving Jane time to whisper her lunch order to the waitress.

"Sounds great," Jane broke in after the waitress hurried off. "We can't wait to see them later. Mom, you're in charge of decorations. What do you think you'll need?"

"Well, that will depend in large part on the space you get for us. If it's the Regency, their ballroom is fairly plain. I've talked with Party Rentals and we're set for tables for the auction items, ten large potted plants, and they have a stage we can use. Since the ball is going to be formal, I thought we could do black, white, and silver colors, maybe have the ceiling covered in helium balloons."

Jane wrote something down on a small spiral notepad before clearing the way for the plate the waitress deposited. She dipped the end of her sandwich into au jus, took a large bite. "Good," she said, the word muffled. She swallowed. "I know the rest of you are looking for silent auction items, and Judge Nichols is in charge of coordinating that, so if you have any questions about what is appropriate, direct them his way."

"Anything that brings in money is appropriate," the older man said.

"I'm discussing the menu right now with a caterer." Jane flicked her pen against her list. "So I think that's it for the actual event." She took another bite of food and reached for an untouched glass of water across from her. Her bare shoulder brushed against the sleeve of Chance's polo shirt, and the neckline of her tank gaped. Chance forgot the mouthwatering meat loaf in front of him. What was on her bra? Ducks? Flowers? It was dotted with something yellow, but before he could solve that mystery, she sat back up.

Chance sighed. "What about ticket sales?" he asked. He was a cochair. He should say something to contribute, not just ogle his fellow cochair.

Jane wiped her mouth. "Jeremy, do you have the website up and running yet?"

"It's up." Jeremy, a young accountant Chance had met at game night, picked up his phone and tapped at the screen. "I'm sending you a link right now. It still needs to be beta-tested to make sure the ticket sale links all work with the credit card processor. Also, I talked to several store owners downtown and most have agreed to help. I'm going to give each store where tickets are available for sale a poster to stick in the window." He sucked on his straw, making a slurping noise when he drank the last of his soda. "If everyone can send me photos of the auction items as you get them, I'll upload them to the site." He looked at Jane and waggled his eyebrows. "That includes—"

"I know," Jane said. "I'm on it."

"On what?" Chance asked.

Cheeks pink, Jane didn't raise her gaze from the notepad. "Just items for the auction I said I'd organize," she said in a low voice Chance had to strain to hear.

He wanted to ask what exactly that was, but she moved the meeting forward.

"Okay, good." Jane wrote down a couple more notes. "I guess that just leaves me to lock down the Regency Hotel."

"Us."

She snapped her head around. "What?"

"That leaves us." Without taking his eyes off Jane, he reached down and grabbed his son by the back of his shirt, pulled him out from under the table. "I'm your cochair. I should help with something."

"Oh, I'm sure we could find something else—"

"Great!" Edith clapped her hands, the sleeves on her tunic billowing. "You two should get on that. Today. We need to have a confirmed ballroom."

Jane glared at her mother. "I'm sure Chance is busy right now. He and his son—"

More excited clapping. "I'd love to watch Josh while you two get to work. If you're okay with that, Chance."

Josh crawled onto his lap. "Can I get pie, Dad?"

"No." He smiled at Edith. "If you're going to watch him, you don't want him to eat any sugar. He can get wild."

"I'm sure he'll be no problem." Edith clasped her hands together, the large silver rings she wore on several fingers glittering under the lights. "So, we good here? I watch Josh while you two go check out the hotel?"

"Sounds like a plan," Chance said. Jane's miserable expression brought his enthusiasm down a notch. "But if Jane's too busy . . ."

"Her shift just ended. She's free the rest of the day." Edith raised an eyebrow. "Isn't that right?"

Jane's shoulders sagged. "Yep. Free as a bird." Her words said one thing, but her tone pounded home that she was acting under duress.

He gritted his teeth. How long was she going to give him attitude? When she'd swung open her front door and Chance had seen the first woman he'd ever cared about, joy had ballooned up in him. Yes, it hadn't ended well. And yes, that was entirely his fault. But beyond their teenage romance, they'd been friends. Good friends. And if they were going to be living in the same town, he wanted her scowl to disappear.

An image of Chance pressing his mouth against those hard lips until they softened beneath his, darted through his head. She probably wouldn't appreciate that. Remembering just how riled up his Jane could get, he figured she'd try to punch him in the nuts if he tried.

He'd have to think of some other way. Some way to remind her of their friendship. That he'd been the only one who could make her smile when she'd learned of her dad's cancer diagnosis. That he was basically the same guy.

Some way that didn't put his family jewels in the line of fire.

* * *

Chance clambered out of Jane's small Mazda and stretched, his cotton shirt rising to reveal a bronze strip of abs. The skin above his hips indented in two lines of pure muscle. Jane's jaw dropped. Snapping it shut, she turned toward the hotel. She needed to minimize her time ogling Chance. Being cochair with him wouldn't make that easy, but she had willpower. She could be strong.

He caught up with her halfway across the parking lot, his long legs eating up the pavement. Something fluttered deep in her stomach. Damn, he'd filled out into one fine man. The past two days she'd made several trips past the fire station, just to pick up odds and ends she kept forgetting, but hadn't caught a glimpse of him.

Not that she'd been looking. And if Firehouse 10 had stopped its practice of making the newbies wash the firetrucks in the station's driveway, covered only by water, soap, and a pair of skivvies, then good for Chance.

She swallowed. Wasn't there a little park across from the station? Sitting on a bench catching up on her reading was something anyone in Pineville might do. Not suspicious at all. Did he still wear briefs or had he graduated to boxers?

"So this is where you want to hold the charity ball?" Reaching in front of her, Chance grabbed the door and held it open. They stepped into the lobby, the burgundy and gold carpeting muffling their footsteps. "It's nice."

She paused on her way to the front desk. "You don't like it?"

"I just said it's nice."

She snorted. "Your words said nice. Your tone, not so much." She walked up to the counter and nodded when the receptionist, phone receiver tucked up between her face and shoulder, held up one finger. "What's wrong with this hotel?"

"Nothing's wrong with it." He shrugged at her continued stare. "There's just not much personality. It's . . . generic."

Jane scowled. "This place is very nice. And there aren't any other hotels in the area that have a space the size we need."

He placed a hand on her shoulder, and heat seared her bare skin. "Like I said, it's fine. And I'm sure when your mom gets done decorating the ballroom, it will be great. If anyone can make a boring space look fun and interesting, it's Edith."

The receptionist hung up the phone. "Good afternoon. Can I help you?"

Jane stepped closer to the counter. Chance's hand slid off her shoulder, and she resisted the urge to step back into his warmth. "Yes. Hi. I'm Jane Willoughby and I'm going to be holding a fundraiser in a month. I'm interested in renting out your ballroom. I was hoping I could get another look at the space and maybe talk to the manager about a contract afterwards."

"Of course." She picked up the phone again and pressed a button. "Let me just find someone to show you the ballroom."

Jane nodded, turning to look out at the lobby as she waited. Her lips pursed. It was true. This hotel didn't have any character. It looked like any other three-star hotel trying hard to work its way up to four. A large chandelier dominated the room, similar to the ones in the ballroom, if her memory served her correctly. The glass prisms didn't have the same shine as crystal. The artwork adorning the walls were inoffensive abstracts, their subdued colors asking for nothing more than an offhand perusal.

"Miss Willoughby?" The receptionist hung up the phone. "Our manager, Mr. Yu, will meet you up in the ballroom. Do you know how to get there?"

"Yes, thanks." Walking over to the bank of elevators, Jane pushed the up button. Chance rocked on his heels beside her, his thumbs looped in the front pockets of his faded jeans. He started whistling, and Jane ground her teeth.

How could he be so relaxed about this? Didn't it churn his guts to be around her? Just seeing his slightly crooked smile, hearing his deep baritone, made her heart feel like a pincushion. The fact that he was totally unaffected by her presence made her ache.

She hadn't meant anything to him at all.

The doors slid open and they walked inside. The elevator was roomy, the far wall covered in floor-to-ceiling mirrors, but when the doors shut, the air felt close, the area tight. Chance's broad frame dominated the space.

She punched the button for the second floor. A grinding squeal erupted when the car began its climb. That didn't sound good. "I hope they grease the wheels before the fundraiser."

Chance frowned and looked at the ceiling, as if he could see through it to the gears above. "It doesn't need grease. It—"

The elevator lurched to a stop. The lights flickered, and Jane reached out a hand to brace herself. Chance gripped her elbow, steadied her.

She looked over at him, her eyes stretched wide. "Holy crap. Are we stuck?"

Guiding her a step back from the control panel, Chance smiled. "Don't worry. We'll be fine." He pressed the door open button. Nothing. The button to go back to the lobby. The elevator groaned but didn't move.

Jane sucked in a deep breath. She hadn't thought she had a problem with enclosed spaces, but she'd never been trapped in an elevator before. How long did it take to run out of air? The box appeared to be about six feet by four feet wide, eight feet high. So the square footage was . . . oh, who was she kidding? She sucked at math.

Chance punched another button.

"Why did you pull me back?" she asked, her voice sharper than she'd intended. But better to sound bitchy than scared. "I could have pushed random buttons."

He raised that damned eyebrow. "Relax. We'll be out of here soon. You're not claustrophobic, are you?" Running his finger down the certificate taped to the wall, he frowned. "Christ," he muttered. "It figures."

Jane ignored the certificate and concentrated on what was important. His absurd accusation. " 'Course not." She pulled her tank away from the front of her body, fanned herself with the fabric. "I just have a lot to get done today. My to-do list for this fundraiser is huge, and I don't want to waste time stuck in a tin can with you."

"I'm your cochair. If you'd unclench a little and bring me up-to-date, I could help you with that list." He pushed a red button. "And you didn't used to feel that way. The backseat of my Chevy truck was a lot smaller than this, and you didn't have any complaints about 'wasting time' with me then."

Only the side of his face was visible, but it was enough for Jane to see the edge of his lips tipped up in a smile. Her chest burned. "I'll have you know—"

"Shh," he said, as a crackling noise came from a speaker in the panel. "Hello, anyone there?"

"This is Rajesh with Ford Elevator Company? We're registering that you're calling from elevator number two at the Regency Hotel in Pineville, Michigan. Is that correct?"

"That's correct," Chance said. "We're stuck between the first and second floors. Can we get some help out here?"

Silence.

Jane leaned forward to jab the red button again. "Did we lose them? Hello? Can you hear me?"

"Stop pushing that." He grabbed her hand.

"Ma'am, we can hear you," the voice from the speaker said. "I'm notifying the hotel now. Does anyone inside the elevator need medical attention?"

"No," Chance said at the same time Jane asked, "How long is that going to take?"

He shushed her. Actually shushed her. Placing her hands on her hips, she narrowed her eyes. "Don't shush me. We could suffocate in here, and you're having a nice little chat with the operator."

"We're going to be fine." He turned back to the speaker, dismissing her concerns.

"Air is a limited resource!"

Chance wrapped his arm around her waist, pulling her backside flush to his front. He covered her mouth with his hand, and her temperature spiked. He might have been able to pull that crap when they were kids, but he was in for a rude awakening.

She ground the heel of her shoe into his foot. Why couldn't she have been wearing spiky heels today instead of her Keds? Of course, he was only wearing loafers, and she wasn't exactly a lightweight. She should be able to inflict some pain.

Besides pulling her tighter against his chest, he ignored her assault. Leaning toward the call box, he said, "Everyone's fine in here, except for some mental instability. Just send maintenance, no emergency services needed."

Mental instability? Oh, hell no. Grabbing one of his fingers, she tried to bend it backward, tear it from her mouth.

He sighed. "Will you relax? I just want to finish my conversation with the operator. Stop acting out."

She'd heard him use that same condescending voice with Josh when he'd been misbehaving. She growled, incensed, but Chance ignored it. She couldn't beat him. Couldn't argue with him. So Jane licked him. It was just like they were teenagers again. The first time he'd muffled her, he'd been calling in sick to their high school, pretending to be Jane's father. She couldn't stop giggling, and he didn't want her to ruin their scam. She'd licked him then, too, just to be a brat. It had become a custom in their play fights, and here she was, falling into the same pattern.

She was ashamed of herself. Really, she was. But damn, he still tasted salty sweet, like honey-roasted peanuts. She remembered he tasted that way all over. A tingle started at the base of her spine, and she realized just how snugly she was pressed against the man behind her.

"Christ." He removed his hand and wiped it on her shirt over her stomach. Another holdover from childhood. His broad palm rested just below her breasts, and her breathing sped up. "We're adults now. You shouldn't be licking me." His body tensed. "Well . . ."

Jane jerked out of his grip. She didn't want him to finish that thought. Pulling the tank away from her heated skin, she scowled. "You started it. I could charge you with assault."

Chance twisted his lips, shook his head. "Janey-girl . . ." Hands on lean hips, he eyed the ceiling of the elevator.

She mimicked his stance. "Don't 'Janey-girl' me."

The speaker crackled. "The hotel has acknowledged our request for maintenance," Rajesh said. "If an emergency arises, please let us know. Otherwise, have a nice day." The speaker went silent.

Jane snorted. *Have a nice day?* Not likely. The walls on either side seemed to inch a little closer. "How long do you think it will take to get us out of here?"

Crossing his arms across his chest, he leaned back against the doors. "It depends on how responsive the maintenance crew is here at the hotel. Probably not long."

She cleared her throat. "Do you think . . . do you think we have enough air?"

He chuckled. Then stopped when he saw her expression. "You're serious, aren't you?" Pushing off the wall, he rubbed his hands up and down her arms. "Hey, we won't be here long, and there's plenty of air. We're not in an airtight box. We get air from the elevator shaft, too."

She swayed closer. Not close enough to touch, but enough so the warmth from his body soothed her like an old blanket. She hated herself for wanting that comfort, but she didn't move away. So what if he'd dumped her by leaving her a greeting card. He was here now, and he was a different man. In the past decade, he'd become a father, lost a wife, and embarked on a career that helped those in need.

Not that his dream of becoming a neurosurgeon wouldn't have saved lives. Chance had always wanted to help people. But the fact that he'd chosen a blue-collar profession surprised her. The McGoverns had been solidly upper middle-class, his father a pediatrician and his mother an accountant. A postgraduate education had been expected of Chance.

Jane liked his new career path. It made him more approachable.

She inched closer, his hands on her arms slowing from a brisk rub to a caress. Their eyes latched on to each other, and a shiver zipped down her spine. Heat flared in his chocolate eyes.

She took a large breath. This was probably a bad idea. A really bad idea. Kissing Chance would be spiraling backwards, and she'd long ago promised herself that she wouldn't live in the past.

He stepped closer, his chest brushing the tips of her breasts. Jane bit back a moan. Screw it. He was sexy, had been kind enough to try to comfort her, and even as a teenager had been one of the best kissers with whom she'd ever had the pleasure to lock lips. Tilting her head back, she waited, his soft breath brushing across her mouth. He leaned down.

With a jolt, the elevator screeched, rolled upwards. Chance frowned, looked over at the doors. When he turned back to Jane, she'd already stepped back. The doors dinged before sliding open.

"Saved by the bell, huh?" He shoved his hands in his pockets.

Voices in the hall stopped Jane's response, which was good, because she didn't have one. A maintenance man stood on the other side of the open doors, looking down the hall. "This one's working now, ma'am." He turned and smiled at Jane. "Sorry about the inconvenience."

"Do you know this elevator is eight months past inspection?" Chance stepped around Jane and pressed his hand to the doors to keep them open. "Who's in charge of maintaining them?"

"Uh . . ." The maintenance man scratched his head.

A feminine voice floated into the elevator. "Chance? What are you doing here?"

The shoulders under his polo hardened into boulders. Curious, Jane peeked around the doors, into the hall. A tall woman in a flirty floral dress and three-inch heels gave Chance a tentative smile. A wrap-sweater was tied with a bow around her waist, showcasing her trim figure. Its cream color stood in stark contrast with the swath of shiny dark hair that swung loose around her shoulders.

"I was hoping to see you today, but thought I'd have to track you down." The woman laughed, a musical tinkle. "Who would've thought you'd come to me?"

A muscle spasmed in Chance's jaw. "Annette. What in the hell are you doing here?"

The maintenance man grinned in delight. Anyone could sense a fight was brewing, and Jane could tell he was one of those people who relished having a front-row seat for the drama.

Jane ducked under Chance's arm and stepped into the hallway, taking a deep breath when she emerged out of the box. The tension rolling off of Chance had made the elevator even more stifling. Chance had just moved to Pineville. Did he already have an angry ex-girlfriend?

The woman's charming smile faded. Her mouth tightened, fine lines appearing around her lips. "You know why I'm here."

A dark flush crept up Chance's neck, mottling his face. He looked like he was about to blow.

Jane stepped close to Chance. Her hand itched to rub his back. She asked, "What's going on? Is something wrong?"

"Nothing's wrong." He glanced down at Jane, regret and resignation flickering over his face. Running a hand down his cheek, he sighed. "I was just hoping I'd seen the last of this woman for a good long time."

"Why? Who is she?"

He opened his mouth, but nothing came out. His gaze darted across Jane's face before settling back on the woman.

Annette stepped forward, raised her hand to shake Jane's. "His manners never were much to talk about. Hi. I'm Annette McGovern. Chance's wife."

Chapter Five

Jane's stomach plummeted to her toes. She shook the woman's hand in a daze. "I'm sorry, I must have misheard. I thought Chance's wife . . . I thought she was . . . uh . . ."

Chance cursed under his breath, and Jane knew she hadn't misheard. She was shaking hands with his wife, Josh's mother. She snapped her hand back. Putting on a cool smile, she said, "Jane Willoughby." She stepped away from Chance. "It looks like you'll be busy here. I'll go to the ballroom and meet with the manager."

She took two steps before his hand snagged her elbow. He swung her around to face him.

"Jane, it's not what you think."

She looked past him, not wanting to see regret in his eyes. Annette folded her arms across her chest and cocked her head, staring at the pair of them. She didn't seem upset that her husband was in a hotel with another woman. She looked curious. And amused.

Tucking his finger under her chin, he raised her face to his. "Just listen to me for a second."

Oh, hell no. He wasn't allowed to lie to her again and think an apology would cut it. "Oh? So your wife is dead? That woman there is just a crazy stalker?"

He swallowed, his Adam's apple bobbing up and down. "I never said my wife was dead."

Her chest felt tight, like the walls of the elevator were still pressing in on her. Chance's *wife* checked her watch, and the maintenance guy looked like he wanted popcorn with the show. She needed to get away. "My mistake."

She made it ten feet before he grabbed her again. "Why are you so mad about this? You've met Josh, you must know I had a wife." Running his hand through his short hair, he blew out a harsh breath.

Like this was her problem. Like she was the one being unreasonable. Heat rocketed up her neck to her face. She knew she must look like an angry tomato. "I don't care that you have a wife. You could be a bigamist and it wouldn't matter to me. Why I'm 'mad' "—she was too ticked to be embarrassed about using rabbit fingers around that word—"is that I thought you might have changed in ten years."

His eyebrows slammed together. "What are you talking about?"

"You're never honest," she hissed, leaning into him and poking his chest. "You should have just told me you were still married, like you should have told me you had another future planned out. One that didn't include me." She didn't know which was worse. That she was dredging up decade-old hurts like some pathetic woman clinging to her high school glory years, or that it felt so good to let him have it. She finally had her target in front of her.

"Jane." His voice held regret. And a tinge of pity.

She was surprised she didn't spontaneously combust. Heat and anger rolled off of her in waves. Time to pull it back from her hang-ups to his screwups. "You might not have outright said it, but you sure as hell implied that you were a widower. Are you even divorced?"

He hesitated. "Almost. Just waiting for the judge's signature."

She snorted.

Chance dipped his head, lowered his voice. "I was eighteen, and you're right. I acted like a jerk. This is a different situation. I wasn't hiding my wife, I just didn't want to talk about her. It hasn't been an easy divorce."

The pain in his eyes deflated her righteous indignation, like a nail to a tire causing a slow leak. He sounded so reasonable. She might have read more into his comment about his wife being gone than she should have. Maybe.

"Besides." Chance crossed his arms across his chest and narrowed his eyes. "I'm not the one who almost cheated on her boyfriend by kissing me in the elevator. My relationship with Annette is over. Yours with bailiff-boy still seems on."

And just like that her understanding evaporated. "*Leon's* and my relationship is none of your business. And I wasn't about to kiss you." Mimicking his position, she crossed her arms across her chest.

The aggressive stance didn't look as tough on her as it did on Chance. "I was feeling a little light-headed from the lack of oxygen."

"Uh-huh."

"Look." She dug in her purse, pulled out her spiral notebook, and made some notations. "You deal with your wife. I'll deal with the hotel." With a vicious yank, she tore her to-do list off, shoved it into his chest. "You wanted to be brought up-to-date? Here's what you have to do. You handle those, I'll handle the rest, and we don't have to talk to each other about it."

"Fine," he bit out.

"Good." Turning on her heel, she stalked off, his glare searing her the entire walk down the hallway. At the door to the ballroom, she forced herself not to look back. She didn't want him to see that he had the power to hurt her yet again.

The manager was waiting for her inside, and came toward her, hand outstretched. She put on a smile and made herself a promise. She'd get through this fundraiser with Chance. It was too important to let hurt feelings get in the way.

But once it was over, she'd make sure that her errands didn't take her past Firehouse 10 ever again.

Annette led Chance back to her room. Following her inside, he slammed the door behind them. Or he tried to. The damned thing was on some sort of hydraulics. It lazily hissed its way across the carpet, mocking his angry gesture.

"What the hell do you think you're doing just showing up here like this?" Picking her purse up off the desk, he tossed it on the bed and cocked a hip onto the empty space.

"I came to see Josh." She sat on the thin tan bedspread and crossed one slim leg over the other. "He's my son, too."

"Yes. And when I'm granted *permanent* full custody, I don't intend to cut you out of his life." He narrowed his eyes. "Aren't you supposed to be in rehab?"

Smoothing the skirt of her dress, she said, "It wasn't mandatory. I checked myself out."

"Of course you did." He didn't bother trying to keep the disgust out of his voice. A gambling addiction might be considered an illness, but he couldn't forget, or forgive, her actions.

"I was there for two weeks. I learned plenty and I'm doing better." Standing, Annette strode to the minibar, pulled out a tiny bottle of white wine. "Want anything?"

"Not from you."

Rolling her eyes, she poured herself a glass. Eyeing him over the rim, Annette said, "I met someone."

"Congratulations."

"We're getting married."

He crossed his arms over his chest, not liking where this was going. "Seems awfully sudden considering we only separated eight months ago. Were you having an affair?" He hoped she was. It might be one more piece of ammunition in his case to keep full custody of Josh.

Annette took a deep breath and walked to the window. "No. I met Edward after." Flicking the curtain open, she looked out. "God, how can you live here? When I drove in from the airport I thought I was in Mayberry."

"They had a job opening and it was two thousand miles away from you," Chance said. "Any resemblance to fictional towns is just a bonus."

"I'm suing for full custody of Josh." She turned from the window, her expression as cool as though she'd just said she wanted chicken for dinner. "My lawyer says that since I'll be married and able to provide a stable two-parent home for Josh, I have a good shot."

Rage flooded his veins, his muscles trembling with the effort it took not to throttle the woman. He took a deep breath, kept his voice even. "Stable? A bookie who was threatening your life came to our house. Spoke to Josh while he was playing in the front yard. You're not even safe for our son, much less stable."

She sighed. "Don't be so dramatic. And besides, I don't owe any bookies, and I've been to counseling. I'm not gambling anymore."

Yeah, she didn't owe bookies anymore because Chance had borrowed against his pension to pay off her debts. It had pissed him off, writing that check, cleaning up after the mistakes of a woman he'd stopped loving years ago. But it had been the best way to keep his son safe.

He fisted his hands so tightly, the knuckles on his right hand cracked. "I don't care what your lawyer says. You're not taking Josh."

"Edward said you'd say that." Her bright pink lips twisted. It was a mystery that he'd ever wanted to kiss that scheming mouth.

"I would say he's a smart man, but he's marrying you." He pushed off the desk. "I know Josh would like to see you while you're in town. When do you want to come over?"

"I thought I'd take him out to dinner," she said. "There's got to be some sort of pizza place that he'd like."

"No."

She cocked her head. "This pathetic town doesn't even have a pizza parlor?"

Moving to this small town had been a bit of a culture shock for him, too, but Annette's bitchy attitude was one more nail scraping down the chalkboard of his patience. "Yes, there's a pizza parlor, but there's no way in hell you're taking Josh out by yourself. If you want to see him tonight, you can have dinner at our house."

Narrowing her eyes, she asked, "What exactly do you think I'm going to do? Kidnap him?"

Chance remained silent.

"Christ," she muttered. "Fine. Dinner at your house. Remember, I don't eat red meat anymore."

"Got it." Steaks on the grill tonight. "How long are you planning on staying in town?"

"As long as I want to." She jutted out her chin. "He's my son, too."

Yes, unfortunately he was. And Chance understood her need to spend time with Josh. Respected it. But the way Annette was now, she could hurt their son more by spending time with him. Put him in danger.

Maybe it was a good thing she was marrying that Edward character. It might anchor her to the West Coast, keep her far away from Josh.

With a curt goodbye, and directions to his house, he left. Striding down the hallway, Chance kneaded the back of his neck. Now to find Jane. From one angry woman to another. Out of the frying pan, into the fire.

He punched the elevator call button, considered the metal doors in front of him, and turned for the stairwell. Jogging down the stairs, Chance knew the comparison between Jane and his ex wasn't fair. Jane *might* have a reason to be a bit pissed off. Technically, he hadn't lied. But he hadn't been eager to share the information that he was still married, either. He'd had too much fun flirting with Jane.

He pushed open the door to the hallway and followed the signs to the ballroom, quickening his step. It was strange, hurrying to see Jane again. Planning this fundraiser with her was causing déjà vu to crash upon him in waves. He used to trip all over his feet just to reach her side, a physical ache gripping his chest if he spent too long away from her.

As a teenager, everything had been life or death, a roller coaster of emotion from who'd win the Friday-night football game to what college he was going to apply to. But he wasn't a boy anymore, and he wouldn't die if he didn't see his girlfriend.

He hurried down the hall just the same.

And found an empty ballroom.

Frowning, he made his way back to reception. "Do you know where the manager is? He was supposed to be showing my friend and me the ballroom."

She smiled brightly. "Oh, they finished with that. Your friend left about five minutes ago."

"Left?" His voice rose above the soft classical music playing in the lobby.

The blinding smile dimmed. "Yes. Uh . . . maybe she's waiting for you in the parking lot?"

Nodding tersely, Chance strode to the spot where Jane had parked.

The empty spot.

Chance cursed, dug in his pocket for his phone. Scrolling through his contacts, his thumb hovered over Jane's picture. He'd snapped it without her knowledge, and it only captured about three-quarters of her face. The smile that had struck him as so sweet now looked devilish. Evil danced in those eyes.

He smacked his finger down on her smiling face.

The call went straight to voicemail, and Chance hung up, dialed another number.

"What can I do you for?" Chief Finnegan's hint of Irish met Chance's ear.

"Can you give me the name of a taxi service?" Chance asked. "I'm stranded at the Regency."

One quality Chance had come to appreciate from his new chief was that the man didn't ask unnecessary questions. "I'll come get you. I only live about ten minutes away."

"That's not necessary," Chance said.

"I'm off today. Got nothing better to do." Keys jingled over the line, a door shut. "Be there in a bit."

Chance ended the call and leaned against a minivan, settling in for the wait. Striking red cardinals flitted among the trees dotting the parking lot, but Chance couldn't appreciate their beauty. He was still too pissed off. Jane had no right to be that angry, to leave him without a ride simply because he hadn't mentioned his wife. His very soon to be ex-wife.

Jane always had been prone to overreacting.

Chance's shoulders were marginally less tense by the time the chief rolled into the lot. It was hard to stay angry when the sun was shining and a cool breeze was blowing. Chance thought about Jane ditching him again. Nope. Still ticked off.

"Thanks," Chance said, climbing into the passenger seat.

Finnegan grunted. "Where to?"

"My SUV's downtown at the Pantry, but Josh is at Edith Willoughby's apartment. Can you drop me there? Josh and I will walk to where I'm parked." If Josh wasn't going to be in the vehicle with him, he'd have tracked Jane down, expressing to her just how juvenile her actions had been. Demanded an apology.

Even his fantasy-self laughed at that. She wouldn't be apologizing anytime soon.

The chief pulled to the curb in front of the Apothic Gardens, climbed out with Chance. Chance raised an eyebrow.

"Thought I'd say hi to Josh," Finnegan said.

Chance shrugged. The chief hadn't seemed like he was a big fan of kids, but whatever. Finnegan's motives could remain his own. Chance had bigger fish to fry.

The door to the store was locked, and a little faux-clock in the window said the store would reopen at four. Chance and the chief took the staircase in the small alley next to the building, and knocked on the upstairs door.

Pans crashed, the sound muffled through the wall, followed by silence. Chance and Finnegan eyed each other.

Chance raised his hand again to knock, but stopped when Edith's voice called out, "Just one moment."

Some shuffling, a couple of bumps, and hushed whispers made Chance frown. He knew the sounds of trouble being covered up.

The door swung open, and Edith's long tunic billowed in the breeze. "Oh. Hello, Chance. Chief."

The smell of something sweet floated out the open door. "Baking something?" Chance asked.

"Just some granola." She tucked a lock of hair behind one ear. "And I'm burning a candle."

"Good." Chance moved inside, Finnegan a step behind him. "Because Josh can get really hyper with sweets, and his dinner's not far away."

"Of course." Smiling, Edith led them down a narrow hall. "I remember you telling me that." She raised her voice. "Josh. Your father's here."

The sound of running water cut off. Josh raced out of the bathroom, sliding to a stop in front of Chance. "Hiya, Dad. You done with your chores already?"

Edith stepped between the two, her back to Josh. Reaching back with her arm, she swiped at Josh's face, never taking her eyes off Chance. "Josh was a doll to watch. Anytime you need a babysitter, just let me know. If you and Jane want to go out, I'm available."

"That's mighty generous of you," Finnegan said, his voice low, aggressive. "I didn't know you had so much free time."

Edith narrowed her eyes. "I always have time for those who are important to me."

Chance gave Edith a weary smile. It would be nice to have a backup for when Katie was busy, although Chance had no illusions about needing a babysitter in order to date Jane. But she wasn't the only woman in Pineville. He might need a babysitter for a date with another woman.

He rubbed his chest. "Thanks." Reaching around Edith, he snagged his son by his shoulder. "By the way, you missed a spot." Chance wiped a smear of chocolate off Josh's cheek. "Frosting?"

"We made brownies." Josh jumped up and down and squealed.

"Oh boy." It was going to be one heck of a night.

Chapter Six

Katie popped a tablespoon of sugar-free vanilla ice cream into her mouth. “I can’t believe anyone would want to marry that train wreck,” she mumbled around her mouthful. Pushing the ice cream carton away, she wrinkled her nose. “This tastes like ass.”

“Nice language.” Chance looked over at his son. Josh was snapping plastic blocks together at the kitchen table, oblivious to their hushed conversation about his mother.

She leaned over from her perch on a barstool at the kitchen counter, darted a glance at her nephew. “I’m just saying, what kind of man decides to marry that W-I-T-C-H?” she asked.

He paused from stirring his marinara sauce, spoon raised. “You’ll spell out that word but say ‘ass’?” Shaking his head, he leveled the spoon at his sister. “She should be here in about half an hour, and you need to play nice. I don’t want Josh sensing trouble between us.”

“I know.” She poked at her ice cream, then looked up at him with a hopeful smile. “It will be easier for me to keep my mouth shut if you put real food in front of me.”

“Spaghetti and meatballs is real food.” He had backed down from steaks in the interests of keeping the peace, but no way was he giving up his meatballs. Annette could just push them off her plate.

She shrugged. “Yeah, that’s okay. But I’m tired of those funky-tasting shakes you keep buying and this fake-dessert crap you keep pushing at me.”

“Are you kidding me?” Adding chopped garlic to his sauce, he leveled his sister with his sternest big-brother look. “You got out of the hospital just yesterday because you screwed up managing your sugar levels. You’re already complaining about the diabetic-friendly food I’m serving?”

Shoulders rounding in on each other, Katie's lower lip trembled in a way that made him feel like the biggest jerk in town. But he wasn't going to back down on this. "I think we should come up with a food plan, maybe plan meals a week in advance."

She rolled her eyes. "You and your plans. I just need some time to adjust. I'll be fine."

"And when I'm on a three-day shift? What are you going to cook for yourself?"

Digging her spoon into the carton, she flicked a glob at him. "Can we stop talking about what I eat?" He stared at her until she glanced away. "I'll look at those recipes you printed out, okay?"

Tearing off a paper towel, he bent and wiped the mess off the floor, brushed at the stain on his apron. "I'm so happy I have a child watching over my son. And good."

"You know I'm grateful that you're letting me live with you guys, right?" Katie pushed a wedge of brown hair behind her ear. "If I had to live with Mom and Dad while I took my online courses, I think I'd lose my mind."

Chance snorted. "I hear that."

She poked him in the arm with her spoon. "And you're grateful that you don't have to hire a nanny, right?"

He kept stirring.

"Right?!"

Laughing, he leaned over and mussed her hair. "Of course, goober. We're lucky to have you."

"Dad, look at my castle!"

Chance put his elbows on the counter and looked over the blue, green, and yellow cube, giving it the attention and admiration of a tourist at Notre-Dame Cathedral. "That looks fantastic. Fit for a king."

"No, it's for a knight," Josh said, making a green plastic horse gallop around the structure.

"Can you put your knight's castle into the living room, buddy? We're going to be eating soon." Chance watched as Josh carefully picked up the cardboard square he had been building on, his small hands unsure with their bundle, and shuffled out of the kitchen.

His heart clenched. Josh was the best part of him. He couldn't lose him. Turning back to the stove, he told his sister, "Annette says she's going to sue for custody. That since she's getting married she'll have a better chance of getting him."

He waited for Katie to laugh at that idea. When she remained quiet, he turned to face her.

She chewed her lip. "Some judges might take that into account."

"Over the fact that she's a gambling addict who brought criminals into her son's life?" His gut still twisted every time he thought about that day he'd come home from work and found the strange tatted-up man kneeling on the front lawn talking to his son. It had taken all his self-control not to rip the guy's head off when the bookie had told Chance who he was. If Josh hadn't been watching, he didn't know that he wouldn't have.

"I don't know, Chance." Tapping the spoon against the counter, she shook her head. "If some doctor says she's better? And don't judges still think a child should be with his mother? I don't think this is something you should take lightly."

He added the cooked meatballs to the sauce and put the garlic bread in the oven. "I don't take anything having to do with Josh's safety lightly. That's why I moved back to Michigan."

Nose wrinkled, Katie asked, "I know Annette was less crazy in college"—Chance shot her a look—"but if it hadn't been for Josh, would you have married her?"

Checking that Josh was still in the living room, he sighed. "Annette was exciting, fun, and very supportive of my dream to become a doctor." She had been one hell of a study partner, doing unspeakable things as encouragement when he'd get the answers right. "But no. We wouldn't have married."

Katie nodded. "Good. I can respect that a lot more. I was fifteen when you brought her home to meet the family, and I thought you were a typical man, an idiot letting a piece of hot tail lead him around by the nose."

"Thanks, I guess." Josh raced back into the room, this time clutching a toy plane in his hand and making a noise that was supposed to sound like an engine. "Josh, I need you to set the table. There's going to be four of us tonight. Your mom's coming over."

"Mom's coming! Cool."

Katie slid off the stool. "I'll help. Come on, big guy."

Chance watched his son lay out the silverware, half of the pieces upside down. He smiled. No, he wouldn't have married Annette if they hadn't gotten pregnant. But he was damn glad she did.

Draining the noodles, he couldn't help but wonder how his life would be different if he'd been a little more discriminating over whom he had a child with. Running into Jane again, it was only natural. She'd be a great mother, he had no doubt.

Katie pulled out salad ingredients and brought down a large bamboo bowl from over the refrigerator. "I've got it! The solution to your"—she bobbed her head at Josh—"problem."

"What's that?"

"You need to get married, too," she crowed, as though that were the most obvious answer in the world.

"Is someone going to buy you as a husband at the ox-chin, Dad?" Josh crawled up onto the barstool.

"What are you talking about, buddy?" Chance mixed the spaghetti and sauce together and checked his watch. Annette was late. Why wasn't he surprised?

"The batch ox-chin." Josh swiped his hand under his nose. "Miss Edith told me about it. The firemen are getting sold to women."

Katie hooted. "That. Is. Awesome."

Chance's jaw hung open. Katie elbowed him in the side. "I think he meant a bachelor auction featuring you and your brothers."

"That's what I said. Batch ox-chin."

No. No way in hell. Jane would have told him . . . He bit back a curse. No, Jane wouldn't have told him. She would have thought it was funny as hell that he was left in the dark. Well, he wasn't going to do it. Being cochair of the fundraising committee was enough of a good deed.

"I'm not getting married," he told his sister. Raising an eyebrow at his son, he said, "And I'm not letting a woman buy me." He wiped at a smudge of God-only-knew-what on Josh's cheek. "Go wash up for dinner," he told his son.

Chance didn't know what to be more pissed about: Annette with her threats, or Jane trying to put one over on him with that stupid auction. "'Items for the auction,' my ass," he muttered, now understanding why she'd flushed such a pretty pink at their meeting. Like firemen were items.

He blew out a big breath, ignoring his sister's smirk. Okay, those problems were pretty easy to prioritize. Jane was irritating. Everything about her, from the way her eyes scrunched up every time she saw him, to her tight jeans, to the grudge she just wouldn't let go.

She was like an itch he couldn't scratch. Annoying, but he could live with it.

Annette was a threat. He couldn't live without Josh. Between Jane and Annette, it was like comparing a sparkler to a stick of TNT.

The doorbell rang, and Josh ran shrieking to the door, eager to see his mother. Chance tried to get his shoulders to relax as he joined his son. Time to face his dynamite.

Jane held Cyclops clutched tightly to her chest. She didn't know whether it was to protect the ginger cat or to use him as a shield. Probably a little bit of both.

"It'll be okay, Cy. He's more afraid of us than we are of him."

Cy's disdainful snarl told her he didn't believe it. Neither did she. One black hairy leg twitched before the spider raced up the wainscoting in her apartment. At the hip-level ledge, it paused, its thick body bobbing up and down, like it was doing its own version of push-ups.

"Gaaa!" Jane took another step back. That was the biggest spider she'd ever seen. She'd been sitting on her couch, calling around to the shops in town, trying to line up an item for the silent auction after one she'd been counting on had fallen through.

When she'd first felt the soft little brush against her toe, she'd thought it was Cyclops, playing around.

A shudder wracked her body, and she gripped the cat tighter. Just remembering those long legs prodding at her foot made her want to take a bath. In bleach. Cy hissed at the grip she had on him. It would have made a wide receiver proud. But the cat made no attempt to leap down. Coming across an insect half the size of his own head had turned even her bully of a cat into a coward.

The spider stopped its calisthenics and seemed to settle in place for a nap. Perfect. Just one more thing to make this day great. It was Sunday, supposed to be her day to lounge on a couch and read. Instead, she'd woken up to an apologetic phone call from the hot air ballooning company outside of town saying due to insurance concerns, they couldn't offer a free ride for the silent auction after all.

Chance had left two more angry text messages demanding she contact him about the bachelor auction.

And now she was being held hostage in her apartment by the Godzilla of spiders. She risked a glance toward her open kitchen window. The spider hadn't seemed amenable to her attempts to herd him outside using a greeting card as a prod.

The card in her hand was slightly crumpled, pressed as it was between her hand and Cy's haunch. It had seen worse. Over the nine years since she'd found it lying on her front porch, it had been jammed halfway down a garbage disposal before she'd changed her mind on its destruction, had come an inch away from a hot flame multiple times, and had more tear stains dotting its surface than craters littered the moon.

Her mother would have been appalled to know she still kept Chance's breakup card. It *was* rather pathetic. But she held on to it as a reminder. Even the guys who seemed so trustworthy could let you down. The card, with its sad clown face on the front and its printed message on the inside—*So sad, my bad, but this isn't going to work. Life moves on, we must be strong, and quit while we're ahead*—had clearly not been produced by Hallmark.

For reasons even Jane couldn't explain, her teenage self had searched, in a near frenzy, for the store that would sell such a card. She'd found it at a novelty store in downtown Lansing. It was part of a collection. There was even a card to end your marriage.

Jane hoped that one was merely a gag, that no one would be low enough to use it.

Chance, in his nearly indecipherable handwriting, had added his own message at the bottom. *Sorry Jane, but I'm going to college in California. Have a good life.*

Not even a "Love, Chance" to soften the blow.

Finding that horrible card on her porch that day, that day of all days, had devastated her eighteen-year-old heart. She and Chance had planned a summer road trip before driving to the University of Michigan and settling in. She'd been up half the night packing, so excited for two weeks alone with Chance. Her mom had given her a box of condoms and a ziplock bag full of homemade granola for the trip. She'd expected to find adventure, romance, and some good stories they could tell their future grandchildren.

She'd found the card on the doormat instead. For the most part, it had stayed tucked away in a shoe box along with photos of her and Chance. It was something she only pulled out when she needed a reminder not to raise her hopes. Since Chance had walked back into her life, all cut muscle and playful smiles, she'd needed that reminder so often the card had remained out of its box.

That card had been a big part of her life for the past decade.

But it was still too small, didn't give her fingers nearly enough buffer room to get that spider out of her apartment. Maybe it was time to move.

Someone pounded at her door. Sidling around an end chair to give the spider a wide berth, Jane sidestepped to the front door and flung it open, not taking her eyes off the hairy interloper.

"Why the hell aren't you answering your phone? Or responding to my texts?" Chance's angry voice was enough to drag her gaze off the wall. The chest beneath the faded AC/DC T-shirt was heaving and a tinge of red flushed his cheekbones. Both signs that he'd lost his temper.

She knew why he was ticked. His voicemails, accusing her of hiding the bachelor auction from him, had explained that very clearly. She'd hoped to avoid him until his wrath had calmed. But here he was, on her doorstep. She glanced at the spider, still unmoving on her wall, and back at the big firefighter filling her doorway.

Maybe she wouldn't have to move after all.

Cy wriggled in her grasp, and she let him jump down. He batted his paw in the air in Chance's direction, hissed his displeasure, and leaped onto the couch. Kneading the cushion, Cy glanced at the wall, remembered they had an intruder, and raced for the open kitchen window, yowling all the way.

"Your cat is nuts," Chance said, pushing past her into her living room.

Closing the door, Jane realized she still held the card, and shoved it down the back of her yoga pants, pulling the hem of her tank top down to cover the top of it. "It's so nice to see you. How've you been?" She circled around, keeping the couch between her and the spider.

"Cut the crap. I've been trying to get ahold of you for days." He rubbed a big hand up and down the back of his head, ruffling his hair. "Just so you know, I'm not doing it."

"Doing what?" she asked, distracted. The spider had crawled two more inches up the wall.

Chance shot her a disgusted look. "I'm not going to be sold like a piece of meat," he said, spelling it out for her. "I'm helping out as cochair. I'm not going to be a beefcake bachelor, too."

She snorted. "Beefcake bachelor? Nice alliteration."

He crossed his arms over his chest. "Chief came up with that one. It's accurate, isn't it?"

The spider zipped to the ceiling. Crap, how did it run so fast with those little legs?

"Sure, of course," she said. "I didn't expect you to." Jane shot him a sweet smile. "Chance, I don't suppose—"

His eyebrows lowered. "Why didn't you expect that?" He glanced down his body. "I might not be the best-looking guy in the department, but I could probably still raise some money."

She forced her eyes to remain unrolled. Did all men have such delicate egos? "I'm sure you'd make us a lot of money. More than anyone else. But Chance—"

"So you do think I should do it." He rested his hands on his denim-clad hips. "The other single guys keep razzing me to do it, and I want to help raise money—"

"But you're not single, are you?" The spider was momentarily forgotten as that old hurt clawed its way out.

"I'm legally separated, soon to be divorced. Single enough to be auctioned off at a charity ball."

She cocked her head to the side. "Wait. So are you arguing to be one of the bachelors or not? I'm confused."

Chance blew out a sigh, flopped down on the sofa. Staring at the ceiling, he muttered, "Join the club."

His throat was exposed, with his head leaning back on the cushion of the couch. He used to love it when she nibbled at his Adam's apple, and it took all her self-restraint not to straddle his hips and press kisses to his neck. She shifted, and the press of the card at her back brought her up short. As always, it was a good reminder.

Chance lifted an eyebrow. "Did you know there's a tarantula above your head?"

With a shriek, Jane flew to the door of her bedroom. She shook her head back and forth, hoping to dislodge the creepy insect in case it had decided to take up residence in her hair. Chance raised an eyebrow and pointed. She spotted the spider, still clinging to the ceiling.

She gulped down some breaths. "Can you get rid of it for me?"

"Maybe." Chance eyed her speculatively.

"It's not a tarantula," she told him, hoping that demoting the bug would encourage him to get rid of it for her.

"No. Close to the size, though." He threaded his fingers together behind his head and settled into the couch.

"Well?" She cocked a hip. "How do I get your maybe to a yes?"

He grinned. "Now that sounds like something I used to say to you." His gaze made a slow perusal of her body, and the comfy clothes she wore suddenly felt as revealing as a bikini. "It was never very hard to convince you."

"Forget it. I'll just call an exterminator."

"For one spider." Shaking his head, Chance rose to his feet. Moving to the kitchen, he said over his shoulder, "I'm doing this as a favor. Which means, when I want a favor from you, you reciprocate."

She watched as he walked back in with a paper towel in his hand. "What kind of favor?"

"Don't know yet." Reaching up, he quickly disposed of the spider. Not wanting to see its demise, Jane looked down, caught sight of the strip of skin exposed between his shirt and jeans when he raised his hand to the ceiling. His bronzed waist spoke of topless outdoor activities, and those chiseled indents that sat above the waistband of his Calvins made her mouth water. She'd never realized she had such a fondness for that part of the male anatomy, but whenever Chance raised his arms, her eyes were drawn to the spot.

Maybe she'd never realized it because none of the men she'd seen naked had that part of the male anatomy. None of them were as cut as Chance.

"There." He strode to the trash can. "The big bad spider is all gone."

She wanted to shoot back a snide response, wipe that patronizing look right off his face. But considering the fact that she didn't even want the dead spider in her trash can and was considering asking Chance to take it out for her, she kept her mouth shut.

"Now," he said. "About this auction."

"Look, if you want to be part of it, fine." Picking up an empty soda can and her Sunday paper, Jane tossed them in the trash. Maybe if she put enough on top of the smooshed bug, it would be okay. "If you don't, no problem. Just let me know before I set up the photographer."

"Photographer?"

"Yeah, a photography student from the community college is taking pictures of all the bachelors to go up on the website." She smiled. "I think some of the guys are even coming up with stripper names for themselves. Not," she added, "that there will be any stripping. This is supposed to be a classy event. Though what the guys decide to do on their dates is their own business."

Someone knocked at her front door. Chance raised an eyebrow. "Speaking of dates . . . you expecting someone?"

"No." She headed to the door, then slapped her palm on her forehead. "Crap on a cracker, it's Sunday."

"Is that supposed to mean something?" Chance asked.

Jane ignored him and opened the door. "Hi, Leon. Come on in."

The bailiff followed her into the living room. "Hey, you just about ready? Oh." He spotted Chance. "Hi. McGovern, isn't it?"

The men shook hands. "Call me Chance. You here to take our Jane out?"

She bristled at the use of the word "our."

"Yep." Leon rubbed his hands together. "It's game night."

"Leon"—she waved her hands up and down her body—"I forgot and I'm not dressed. Why don't we just do it next week?"

His brow drew down. "But it's game night. Tonight." Leon looked at her expectantly.

"Yeah, Jane." Chance smirked. "It's game night." His mocking voice scraped across her nerves. "Hop to it and get ready."

"Great." Leon plopped onto the couch, content it had all been resolved. "We should leave in ten minutes if we want to get a seat at a good table. You coming with us, Chance?"

Jane opened her mouth, but Chance beat her to it. "Sounds like fun." He sat next to Leon and clapped him on the shoulder.

She gritted her teeth. "I don't think that's really appropriate, Chance. Leon and I are on a date—"

"Oh no. The more the merrier," Leon said. He glanced at his watch. "About eight minutes now, Jane."

Fuming, she stormed into her bedroom and slammed the door. It was just like Chance to horn in on her non-date with Leon. There would be no chance in hell that he'd believe there was any sort of sparks flying between her and the bailiff if he spent the night shadowing them. He'd know she was going out on pathetic friend-dates when she'd rather he believed she was tearing up the sheets.

Not wanting Chance to think she was dressing up for him, and knowing he wouldn't believe she'd dressed up for Leon, she pulled on a pair of jeans and a lightweight sweater that covered her from collarbone to hips. Totally frumpy. Showed a complete lack of interest in looking appealing to Chance.

"Okay, let's go," she said and swept to the front door, waving the two men out. "Chance, you remember where the Legion is?" *Please say no.*

"Yep. I'll meet you two there." With a wink, he was gone. Damn, there went her fantasy of losing him on the way.

Leon hustled her to his car. "I think we'll get there in time to get a seat at the Dominion table."

And they did. Of course, Leon ran a yellow light or two. He took game night very seriously. Jane breathed a sigh of relief when she saw Chance hadn't yet arrived. Even better, the Dominion table only had two seats left.

Chance strolled in, a cup of coffee in his hand. He looked around, saw her at the full table and gave her that look. The one he had perfected as a teen that said *You may have won this round, but I'll still get you.* Taking a sip of coffee, he headed over to the poker table, took a seat.

The night passed painfully slowly. Her focus kept drifting to Chance, who wended his way from table to table, closing in on hers. She was always the first to lose, so she kept popping up to get herself and Leon drinks, diet soda for her and Rob Roys for him. She didn't need her mind muddled any more than it already was.

Chance's gaze pierced her between her shoulder blades, and Jane shifted in her metal seat. He was only at the next table. She looked at the clock above the American flag. God, when would this night end?

"Jane? Jane!?" The exasperation in Leon's voice told her he'd been trying to get her attention for a while.

"Sorry. What?" She tried to look suitably interested. But who was she kidding?

"I said, do you mind giving up your seat for Bob? He's been wanting to play Dominion all night and you, well . . ."

"Suck at it," she finished for him. Smiling up at Bob, a city councilman, she said, "Sure, no problem," and got to her feet.

A hand snaked around her elbow. "Jane can join us at this table," Chance said, and tugged her into the seat next to his.

She almost fell off the other side of the chair, and flung her hand out for balance. It landed on his hard thigh. "Sorry," she muttered and righted herself. "What are you guys playing?" she asked the three other people gathered around the table.

"Truth or Consequences," an older woman replied. "The person on your left asks you a question and you have to come up with three answers. Two you make up, one answer has to be true." She peered at Jane over red frame glasses. "It's the honor system, so make sure one is the truth. The rest of the players try to guess which one is the right answer, and those of us who guess correctly advance on the board." She pushed a carton of questions in front of Jane. "It's a great way to learn about the new guy in town." She nodded her head at Chance and waggled her Brillo Pad eyebrows.

He smiled. "My life's an open book to you, Maggie, my love."

The older woman's cheeks turned pink. "Oh, go on with you."

Chance pressed two dice into Jane's hand. "Your roll, Janey-girl."

"What am I rolling for?"

"The number you roll determines what question I ask you," Chance said.

"Oh." She blew on the cubes, and squealed when she rolled a seven.

Chance shook his head and reached for a card. "Calm down. This isn't craps." Reading the card, a slow grin stretched across his face, one corner of his mouth a little higher than the other. "Your question is 'Where was the first place you had sex'?"

Her lips pinched. "Pass."

"You can't pass," he told her. "It's not that kind of game."

"Pass," she told him loudly, glaring.

"Yes." Maggie shifted, her large frame making the chair groan with alarm. "We've been skipping the more personal questions. I think some cards from the couple's version of the game got mixed in. Give her another one, Chance."

Yet every question she rolled to, Chance asked her still more intimate questions. Questions where more often than not, he would be the answer. If she deigned to answer. Jane didn't know if he was palming the cards to the couple's version, or if he was making up the questions on the spot, but his impish smile told her he knew he was getting to her. After dodging more uncomfortable questions than she could count, she'd finally had enough.

With a tight smile, Jane stood. "It's been a long day. I'm going to head home. 'Night, everyone." She walked over to Leon. "Almost ready to go?"

He chewed on some ice. "Probably five minutes till I win this one." Belching softly, he picked up two cards.

"I'll wait for you outside." At his nod, she spun on her heel and strode away. She breathed the cool night air deeply, feeling her muscles relax for the first time that night. Footsteps sounded behind her, and just like that, her Zen moment was stolen. "Come on," she muttered under her breath.

"I'll give you a ride home," Chance said. "I already told Leon he could keep playing."

Narrowing her eyes, Jane turned to face him. "You shouldn't have done that. I came with Leon and I'll leave with him. You can head on home."

Chance dug his hand into his front pocket, digging for his keys. "Leon's had quite a bit to drink. Maggie's going to get him some coffee, but as of now he's not driving you anywhere." He took her hand with his free one and led her to his SUV.

She tugged away when he opened the passenger door. "Well, you're not taking me home, either."

Staring at the sky, Chance rolled his shoulders. Her own drooped. Yeah, that didn't sound like she wasn't still hung up on him. Crap, was she still hung up on Chance? She'd thought she'd grown past that teenage angst. She should have just thanked him, slid into his car, and engaged in polite conversation on the ride home. Like one person completely indifferent to the other. But something about Chance punched all her buttons. Not all of them in bad ways, she had to admit.

"Jane." His voice had a forced quality, like it was a struggle to keep it even. "Leon wants to keep playing. You want to go home. I have a car." His gaze lowered, his eyes pinning her in place. In the dimly lit parking lot, his normally milk-chocolate eyes had turned very dark. At least 85 percent cacao. "The math is simple."

Her mind raced, trying to think of a rational argument, something that wouldn't make her sound like a petulant child. He stepped closer, and her mind blanked. Even through the brisk chill, heat rolled off his body, causing parts of her to tingle. He placed his hands on the SUV's roof, his arms on either side of her head, probably to keep her from stalking back into the Legion. It just made her want to push to her toes, lean into him.

It had been so long. So long since she'd been in his arms. So long since she'd wanted to be wrapped up in a man. His aftershave was certainly different from the Aqua Velva he'd worn in high school. But the masculine scent underneath was still the same. He smelled of heated flesh, expensive spice, and her next mistake.

He sighed, seemingly unaware of the dirty thoughts roaming her mind. "I just watched Leon down his fourth cocktail. I repeat, you're not going home with him. Now"—he dipped his head, came nose to nose with her—"Get. In. The. Car."

Chapter Seven

Chance watched her face as Jane struggled with his demand, saw the exact moment when she gave in. She pushed her lower lip out the slightest bit. Those who didn't know her as well as he did would never know she was pouting.

As commander of his division in Cal Fire, he was used to his orders being followed. That Jane gave in to his command surprised the hell out of him, however. He knew he was a jerk for bossing her around. He didn't have the right. But he had followed her out of the building with the plan to get her home safely, and the more she'd fought, the more he'd dug his heels in to do just that.

Call it a character flaw.

Her tongue darted out, licked that bottom pouting lip, drawing his attention back to her lush mouth. God, he wanted nothing more than to suck that plump lip between his teeth. Did she still like a light bite? He frowned. No, he had to keep his mind from going there. This was Jane, the woman he'd done wrong, and who he suspected had dreams of castrating him.

Licking her lip again, Jane tilted her head. Bringing her mouth within a hairsbreadth of his. Everything inside of him lit up, like she'd flipped a switch. He should push away from her, give her some space. Really, he should.

Chance pressed his body closer, inhaled her delicate scent. She'd push him away soon enough. Any moment now . . .

"Chance," she whispered, her voice turning all throaty.

And that was it. All self-control gone.

Chance took that last inch, crushed his lips to hers.

Sweet. Damn, she tasted sweet. Sweeping his tongue along the seam of her lips, he moaned when she opened for him, welcomed him inside. Annette had never been a big one for kissing, preferring to just get to the main event. He'd forgotten the intimacy that was created when two partners sank into a kiss, the shiver that raced down his spine at the slide of a warm, wet tongue against his.

He lifted his hands from the SUV, brought one to the back of her neck, the other to the base of her spine. Pulling her closer, he took it deeper, held her head at just the right angle. A soft sound from the back of her throat encouraged him. He sucked on her tongue, used his teeth to scrape along the sensitive surface.

Her body melted into his, every inch of her, from chest to thigh, touching him. He needed more. Sliding his left hand down her back, he gripped her butt, pulled her snug against his erection.

Which, in hindsight, he realized was a mistake.

Jane stiffened, stopped dueling him with her tongue. It went from kissing a hot, eager woman to kissing an immobile blow-up doll. Not that he'd know what that was like.

Lifting his head, he stared down into her narrowed eyes. Her mouth was pressed into an angry line, as if she hadn't been right there with him in the doing. In the wanting. She could rearrange her face into all the expressions of disgust she wanted, but her heaving chest betrayed her.

"No?" he asked, nothing more articulate coming to mind. That kiss had reduced his brain to the basics.

Reaching behind her, she grabbed his hand off her ass. "No."

"Okay." Chance dragged in a shaky breath, took a step back. "Okay." Her puffy, reddened lips beckoned him to take another taste. "Any particular reason why?"

She snorted, seeming to have recovered much faster than he had. He ground his teeth together. "Do you want the list chronological or alphabetical?" she asked with so much sass if it had come from Josh he would have given his son a time-out.

The denim clinging to her curvy hips caught his eye. Maybe a spanking would be more appropriate. Before his mind could disappear down that delightful rabbit hole, she continued. "Can't decide? Well, I'll just start with the headliner then." She poked him in the chest. Hard. "You're married!"

Her face paled, and she turned and gripped the open door. "Oh God, I just made out with a married man."

"Legally separated!" Okay, he wasn't too proud of kissing a woman before the divorce papers came through. He hadn't planned on getting into another relationship until he'd recovered from his marriage. And with all the ups and downs with Annette, mainly downs, he'd thought it would be a long time coming. But that was before he'd found Jane again.

She shot him a scornful glare. "Don't bother threading that needle. It doesn't matter. We're not getting back together in any case."

And if that wasn't just a donkey kick to the gut. Chest tight, he growled, "I wasn't asking."

Hands on her hips, she made a sound that could only be classified as a snarl. Now he knew where Cyclops had learned it. "Good," she spat out.

"Fine." He crowded her against the SUV. "You know what your problem is?"

"Oh, please, do tell."

"You were always asking for too much," he said. "We were kids and you were plotting out our whole damn future, like it was just assumed we'd always be together." He ignored the flash of pain across her face, relieved when her chin tilted up defiantly. "And this was just a kiss, not me asking you to go steady."

"And *your* problem is you never offered enough." Jane's hands clenched her opposite biceps, her folded arms giving a boost to her lush breasts. The sight almost derailed Chance from the fight he was raring to have. "You weren't as serious about me as I was about you, fine. That happens. But you should have offered me some honesty. Some decency. A breakup card, Chance!" She turned her head, giving him her profile. He still caught the slight tremor of her lower lip. "That was a shit move. I thought better of you."

His heart did a belly flop. Onto cement. With that rebuke, Chance felt like he was eighteen again, uncertain and insecure. He hadn't broken up with Jane lightly. He'd looked over all his options and determined UC Berkeley was his best shot at achieving his goals. He planned to become the youngest neurosurgeon in history, and he knew if he and Jane remained a couple, she'd slow him down. Marriage and babies would have been inevitable.

Of course, that had happened anyway. And with a woman he hadn't been able to envision spending the rest of his life with, not the way he sometimes had with Jane.

He hadn't meant the card to hurt her, even though he'd known it would. He was just too much of a coward at eighteen to face her tears. Rubbing his chest with his knuckle, he bit back a bitter laugh. Fate was a bitch he couldn't escape. He had to face Jane now.

Except now she wasn't crying. Thank God. Chance had never been good with women's tears, and seeing Jane's would have slayed him.

"I can only say this so many times." He waited for Jane to look at him. "I'm sorry for what I did back then. Truly sorry."

She opened her mouth to say something, but changed her mind. She gave him a curt nod.

Wasn't the wholehearted forgiveness he'd hoped for, but he'd take it. "Now, unless you want to wait here an hour or two for Leon to sober up, I'd be happy to take you home."

She nodded again and slid into the passenger seat. Making sure all her bits were in, Chance shut the door and circled around to the driver's side. He didn't know when, but somewhere along the line tonight, his plan to reestablish a friendship with Jane had gone off the rails.

Probably when he had his tongue down her throat.

Sliding into his seat, he started the engine. He missed Jane as a friend. If they were going to live in the same town, he wanted that back. A new, mature friendship between two adults.

Chance squared his shoulders. So that was that. If he wanted to forge a solid relationship, one thing was clear.

From now on, hands off Dispatch Jane.

He glanced at her out of the corner of his eye, watched her breasts rise and fall beneath her thin sweater.

And lips off of her, too, he told himself sternly. And tongue. No touching her with his tongue.

She leaned her head against the back of the seat, exposing the long, silky column of her neck. His body tightened.

Christ. This friendship was doomed.

The clacking of pins kept beat with the pounding rock music coming from the bar. The Pins 'N' Pints was hopping for a Tuesday night, the bowling alley and bar combo filled with the raucous shouts of the patrons at the bar, on the dance floor, and down at the lanes. The local watering hole was popular with people of all ages and all walks of life, and the sawdust on the floor told anyone entering that the hotspot didn't tolerate pretensions.

Everyone was having a good time.

Everyone except Jane.

It was the night of her monthly girls' night out and she and her friends had opted for a fun night of bowling. Which Jane loved. She'd been whooping it up with the rest of her ladies, forgetting the mess that was her relationship with Chance, when the devil himself walked through the door.

Chance and four of his fellow firemen had sauntered across the wooden floor, chatted with the girl behind the shoe-rental desk, and taken a lane. Right next to hers.

Jane gritted her teeth. She just couldn't catch a break. She'd ignored her cochair's texts, which patiently explained why, if she couldn't accept their little kiss and move on, she needed to forget it happened. For the good of the fundraiser.

Glaring at Chance's back, Jane raised a bottle of beer to her lips. Little kiss? What the blasted man described as insignificant had shaken Jane's world, a veritable 6.0 on the Richter scale. Chance had been living in earthquake country too long if a kiss of that magnitude didn't register.

Maybe it hadn't been good for him. She darted a look out of the corner of her eye. Chance high-fived Martinez, laughed at something the young firefighter said. He'd probably been with a slew of women in college before settling down with his wife. Probably made out with the kind of woman who could knot a cherry stem with her tongue. To him, the kiss had meant nothing.

"Earth to Jane." Sharon waved a manicured hand in front of Jane's face. "Girl, it's your turn. If you throw at least a seven on this one, Sarah's buying the next round."

"Sorry." Putting her beer down, Jane moved to the ball return, found her red nine-pounder.

She reached for it, but another hand got there first.

"You never called me back," Chance said, keeping his voice low. "Didn't respond to my texts. Didn't even smile at me when I came in here. And I waved at you."

She grabbed for her ball, but he held it tight to his flat stomach. "I'm beginning to think you're giving me the silent treatment."

"The silent treatment?" Hands on her hips, Jane raised her eyebrows. "What are you, twelve? I just didn't want to talk to you."

His brows drew down. "You have to talk to me. We're cochairs of the charity ball."

"Was any message you left or texted me yesterday about the fundraiser?"

"Well, no—"

"Then I don't see the problem." She looked pointedly at her ball. "Do you mind? I'm up."

He slowly handed it to her. "Janey, it was just a kiss. We don't have to—"

Spinning on her heel, she stomped up to the top of the lane, not wanting to hear how unimportant their lip-lock was, yet again. He just had to keep pounding that nail home. It must be nice to be a man, able to easily separate physical intimacies from emotional ones. When Chance had kissed her, not only had it made her toes tingle, but it had made her feel reconnected to her ex. His kiss had told her he missed her. Wanted her.

His kiss had lied.

And she'd been an idiot for reading anything into it other than physical pleasure, even for a second. Her behavior Sunday night had been an aberration, a moment of weakness. She gritted her teeth. She was stronger than that.

Her ball skipped across the lane, knocking two pins off the end.

Sharon and their coworker, Sarah, booed, and Jane gave them a half shrug. Shuffling back to the ball return, she focused on the metal aperture, not on the man standing in front of her, arms crossed over his chest.

"Jane." His voice held a hint of warning, a thread of irritation.

Where was that damn ball? "Look, I'm fine. We're fine. What happened Sunday is already a distant memory. I won't let it affect our working relationship."

Putting his finger under her chin, Chance raised her face, his eyes examining hers. She tried for an expression of bored nonchalance, but feared her eyes whispered *I missed you* instead.

Whatever he read there, Chance didn't like. A furrow appeared between his eyebrows. "Okay." He hesitated, but whatever he was about to say next was lost in the rattle of the returning bowling ball.

Jane hefted it in her hands. "Gotta go." Rushing away, she stumbled, caught her balance, and tossed the ball down the lane, no longer caring about form or the score. Through sheer luck, her ball knocked down five more pins, and a loud groan emanated from behind her.

Sarah rose to her feet. "I'll be at the bar, putting in the order for our next round." She frowned. "Tonight's going to seriously deplete my shoe fund."

"Well, if you'd concentrate on your game instead of flirting with the firemen, maybe you wouldn't have to buy," Sharon said. "And I want a Corona this time. With a lime," she shouted after their friend's retreating form.

Climbing the steps to the bar, Sarah waved, one finger suspiciously raised.

"Did she just flip me off?" Sharon's red lips rounded in disbelief. "I think she just flipped me off."

Jane downed her beer, eager for the next round. It would have to be her last for the night, she was driving, but she hoped it would give her world a little haze so seeing Chance so close didn't hurt. At least for the next half hour or so.

Sharon nudged her in the side. "What's up with you tonight?"

Jane didn't want Sharon knowing what a fool she'd been, even though she was her closest friend. "Nothing. I think there's something on the bottom of my shoes, though. My feet keep sticking to the lane and it's throwing my form off."

"Uh-huh." Sharon raised a plucked eyebrow. "Well, let me see."

"See what?"

"Your shoes. Take them off." Digging around in the purse at her feet, Sharon emerged with a plastic packet. She tore it open, pulled out a small white cloth.

Mentally shrugging, Jane toed off her shoes. Sometimes it was just easier to go along with what Sharon wanted. Most of the time, really. She handed her the shoes and watched her friend scrub the soles with the Wet-Nap.

A tall figure drew her gaze. Chance paced to the front of his lane and smoothly released the ball, his leg sliding gracefully behind him. Bowling wasn't a sexy sport. Jane had never admired a man's form during the game before. But Chance's cotton chinos and T-shirt revealed every bulge and line of his muscles.

Shifting in her chair, Jane didn't see her friend's elbow until it was planted in her ribs.

"Ow!" Jane rubbed her side. "What was that for?"

"I was talking to you for a good thirty seconds before I realized you weren't listening," Sharon said. "Why don't you stop screwing that man with your eyes and go for it?"

"What?" Darting a look at Chance, Jane lowered her voice. "What are you talking about? I'm not screwing anyone with my eyes."

"Please." Cocking her head, Sharon ran her gaze over Chance as he sat back down on the plastic bench. "Not that I can blame you. You said you used to date that? Was he as good as he looks?"

Jane sighed.

Sharon whistled. "That good, huh?" She handed over the shoes, and Jane slipped them back on. "Well, what are you doing sitting over here moping? The way he's undressing you with his eyes, he looks interested. If all goes right, you could be playing tonsil-hockey by nine p.m."

Heat flamed up Jane's neck. "I think I'll go help Sarah with the drinks."

Sharon yanked her back down. "What did you do?"

"Nothing. I did nothing." Chance had done all the kissing. Well, she might have kissed him back a little, but he'd definitely started it.

"You wouldn't be that red if you'd done nothing." Sharon leaned back in her seat. "You and Chance already had s—"

"Keep your voice down," Jane hissed. Leaning closer, she said, "Me and Chance definitely did not have sex. It was just a kiss."

Sharon hooted, drawing looks from several of the men at the next lane. Chance stared at Jane instead.

"Details," Sharon said. "Give me details. Was there a little second-base action? He looks like he'd be good with his hands."

Jane stared at her friend for a moment. "You keep saying I need to go out on a real date. I think you're the one who's feeling neglected."

"Are you saying Fireman Hottie is available?" Sharon took a beer from Sarah. "Thanks." She nodded to the lane. "You're up. Loser goes first. Next round please buy me a coffee."

Sarah huffed. "Cocky doesn't look good on you." Flipping her long blond hair over her shoulder, she strutted to the ball return, pausing to chat with a fireman.

Sharon shook her head. "Everything looks good on me. Including dark-eyed firefighters." Giving Jane a pointed look, she said, "If you don't want him, I'm more than happy to take him."

Flexing her fingers, Jane took a deep breath. "Of course. If you're interested and he's interested, I have . . . I have . . ."

"Yes?" Sharon's smile was smug, but Jane still couldn't say she had no problem with Chance seeing other women.

"Fine." Jane unclenched her jaw. "I would prefer if you didn't go after him, okay? But only because it would be weird if you dated my high school boyfriend."

Sharon snorted. "Keep telling yourself that. So what's your plan here? Did you dress all slutty tonight to try to seduce him?"

Looking down at her clothes, Jane wrinkled her forehead. Her pleated skirt fell about an inch shorter than most of her hemlines, and her white silk tee did cling nicely to her curves, but she hardly thought her outfit qualified as slutty.

And she hadn't worn it for Chance. Quite the opposite. When she'd put her clothes on, she'd hoped to draw some attention from other men, to show herself that Chance wasn't the only game in town.

But when he'd walked into the bar, all the other men had faded from view. Her body was telling her that he was the only game she wanted to play.

"This is a perfectly respectable outfit," she said.

"Please." Sharon took a swill of beer. "Men love that knee-high-socks schoolgirl look."

Jane admired her green and red checked argyles. She did love showing them off.

Sharon continued. "And it's working. Your fireman can't keep his eyes off of you."

"That's only because he's mad at me," Jane said. "When I'm the one who should be ticked off. He kissed me when he's still a married man!"

Lowering her beer, Sharon leveled her with a shocked look, her eyes wide. "He's married? How did I not know this?"

Jane squirmed in her seat. She had kind of forgotten to tell her friend that detail. "He's in the process of getting a divorce, but technically he's still married."

"You've got to cut that shit out now." Sharon pinched her lips. "I was all for you fooling around with the hottie, but not if he's married. There's all kinds of potential for lots of people to get hurt." She glared at Chance. "And what kind of man kisses another woman when he's married? He's not good enough for you."

A chuckle escaped Jane's lips. Chance had been determined, ambitious, and smart. She used to feel unworthy of him. He was still all those things. His ambition had taken a different turn, but you didn't become an assistant fire chief at age twenty-seven by slacking off. Plus, he now had a drool-worthy set of abs.

Jane sucked in her stomach. She hadn't done a sit-up in years. Maybe she still wasn't good enough for him.

Jane downed some beer and gave herself a mental slap upside the head. She was smart, reasonably attractive, and had never lied about her marital status. She straightened her spine. Sharon was right. Jane looked across the lane. There he was, laughing with his buddies, not a care in the world. Probably already forgotten the feel of her lips.

"To hell with that," Jane muttered.

"What's that?" Sharon asked, as Sarah threw herself into the seat next to them, her turn over.

"I want to show him what he's missing," Jane said.

"What who's missing?" Sarah looked between her and Sharon. "What'd *I* miss?"

"Jane kissed the tall fireman, the married tall fireman, and now she wants to make him pay."

"Oooh. Drama in Pineville." Sarah lifted her hair off her neck and fanned herself. "It's about time something exciting happened in this town."

Jane didn't relish the idea of being the town's entertainment, but ignored that for the moment. "Sharon, help. You're the fashion guru. What can you do with what I already have on?"

Sharon stood, tugging Jane to her feet, and placed herself between Jane and the group of firefighters. Cocking her head to one side, she tapped a coral nail against her lips. "Roll the waist of your skirt two times."

Jane complied.

"We can't do anything with your hair, but . . ." She turned away, and Jane patted her head. What was wrong with her hair? Sharon twisted back, a plastic cup of water in one hand. "But we can work on that shirt."

Her friend started flicking large drops of water at her chest. Jane twisted, and Sharon barked, "Keep still."

"What the hell are you doing?" Sarah asked.

Jane wanted to know, too.

"Just making that shirt a little more interesting to look at." Sharon eyed her work, then splashed more at Jane's cleavage. Stepping back, she nodded with approval. "There. Not so drenched you'd be entering a wet T-shirt contest, but enough to get a man's attention."

Frowning, Jane looked down. In the dim lighting, her shirt wasn't see-through, not quite, but every curve was molded by the thin fabric, the lace of her pink bra creating a visible pattern.

Jane shivered.

"Oh, stop it," Sharon said. "It's not cold in here." She raised an eyebrow. "Although, it would help things along even more if you were cold."

Jane slapped her friend's arm. "Gross. I don't know why I asked you for help."

"Because you wanted to make Chance drool. And honey"—Sharon stepped aside, revealing Jane to the men—"that's what you'll get."

Chance didn't drool. But his eyes did get a funny glaze to them, and conversation at that lane stopped cold. His gaze flicked to her chest, her thighs, to her face, and then made the trip again.

Sharon pushed Jane's side, and Jane slipped a little, her shoes sliding on the waxed lane. "You're up," Sharon whispered. "Shake your stuff a little bit, bend low when you release, and that boy won't be able to string a sentence together."

Right. Shake and bend. She could do that.

"You do look hot," Sarah said. "Go get 'em." Her brow furrowed. "Or not get 'em, I guess. Go make him want to get you?" She shook her head. "I'm confused. Why doesn't she want to get the sexy fireman again?"

"I'll explain it to you later," Sharon said, and shoved Jane in the back.

Jane windmilled her arms to keep her balance. Shooting a dirty look over her shoulder at Sharon, she strutted to the ball return. Or tried to. Whatever her friend had put on the soles of her shoes had made the floor like ice. It was hard to look sexy when she was mincing along.

Chance was waiting for her and handed her the ball. "What happened to you?"

"Sharon spilled some of her drink." Jane tried to act nonchalant, as if she walked around with wet shirts on all the time. Puffing out her chest and sucking in her stomach, she added, "I hope it doesn't distract you from your game."

Martinez sidled up next to Chance. "Can I get you something to drink, Jane? Or what do you say we go dance instead of playing this stupid game?"

Chance stepped in front of the younger man, blocking his view of Jane. "Go back to your seat, Martinez." The other fireman hesitated. "Now."

Martinez stepped to the side, gave Jane an impish shrug, and strolled back to the guys. Chance's shoulders bunched to his ears as he turned back around to face Jane.

"Maybe you should go home and change your top. You're on your third drink, so I can drive."

Stepping onto her lane, she rolled her hips, making her skirt swish around her thighs. "You've had just as many drinks as I've had."

Chance circled around the ball return. "But I'm bigger. I can drink more."

"Regardless, I'm not going home to change my shirt. It will dry soon." So she'd better make the clingy wetness work for her while she could. She'd been bowling for years, knew how to make her form look good. In a short skirt, her leg extension when she released the ball should do the trick to make Chance drool.

"Now excuse me while I bowl." Pivoting, she enjoyed the quick breath he sucked in as her skirt twirled dangerously high. Maybe she should start dressing better, like Sharon said. The power it gave her was intoxicating.

With the eyes of four hot firemen on her, Jane wanted to make this throw good. A strike would be the cherry on top of her make-Chance-squirm sundae. Raising the ball to her chin, she eyed her target. She took her first step, her second, maybe a little more hip shimmy than was usually seen in bowling. She took her third and final step, her right leg sliding out behind her in a graceful arc.

And it kept right on sliding.

Her toes scrabbled for traction, but the slicked-up shoes gave her none. The ball flew out of her hand, bouncing into the next lane's gutter. Her legs folded into an awkward split, leaving Jane lying half on her side, half on her stomach.

A cool breeze drifted where no cool breeze should drift.

Jane reached behind her, clawed at the skirt that had settled somewhere around her waist. Her fingers scraped down bare skin, reminding Jane that tonight she'd decided to wear a thong.

"Holy crap on a cracker." Sharon's voice came from far away. It was hard to hear over the pounding of blood in Jane's ears.

"Jane!" Chance placed his hands under her arms, lifted her gently to her feet. "Are you okay?"

Staring at the faded decal on his shirt that read Cal Fire, Jane fought to hold back the tears. Her cheeks flamed, her inner thighs twinged from the unexpected stretch, and something that closely resembled defeat twisted her heart. "I'm fine," she whispered.

She tried to step back, but Chance kept a firm grip, as if afraid that without his support she'd go down again. He was probably right.

Her knees were shaking. She was so mortified she wanted to melt into a pile of goo, disappear from sight. What had she been thinking, trying to act sexy for Chance? She'd wanted to grab his attention and she'd succeeded. He'd seen more of her than any man had in over a year. Chance, and half the crowd at Pins 'N' Pints.

Eyes burning, she yanked herself from his grasp and carefully made her way back to her seat, not making eye contact with anyone. Her friends were waiting, varying levels of pity on their faces.

"Are you all right?" Sarah asked.

"That was rough." Sharon shook her head. "Usually I'm all for showing a little underwear to get the boys to sweat, but"—she pulled a face—"not like that."

Yanking off her shoes, Jane spit out, "What did you rub on the soles of these?" She waved them in Sharon's face. "Motor oil?"

Her friend's face fell. "It was just a little shoe polish rub I keep in my purse for emergencies. I didn't think it would make them that slick. Just rub the gunk off. I'm sorry."

Jane took a deep breath, then another. Snapping at Sharon wasn't going to rewind time, undo what had occurred. It wouldn't keep her from looking like an idiot in front of Chance. He must be thanking his lucky stars that nothing more than a kiss had happened Sunday night. If his wife was any measure, Chance liked his women polished and elegant.

She swallowed past the lump in her throat. "No, I'm sorry. It's not your fault I'm an idiot."

Sarah leaned forward. "It wasn't that bad. Except for the guys in the next lane, I don't think anybody saw. Everyone's too busy having their own good time to pay attention to us."

A waitress walked up to them, three shot glasses on the tray in her hands. "Bert and Clay send this round over with their compliments. Wanted me to tell you thanks. That was more action than they've seen from their wives in months."

Two middle-aged men at the bar raised their glasses in salute. Jane's cheeks flamed even hotter. Could a person spontaneously combust from humiliation?

"No one else noticed, huh?" Pulling her street shoes from underneath her chair, Jane shoved her feet into them.

"Okay, so maybe those two did." Sarah shrugged. "They're obnoxious and horny. It's no wonder their wives won't touch them. But in the grand scale of things, trust me, this wasn't a big deal. You're still the same Dispatch Jane we all know and love. Nothing's changed."

"I don't know if I'd say that." Sharon tried talking out of the side of her mouth, looking like she had a nervous tic. "Ever since your spill, your fireman hasn't taken his eyes off you."

All three women looked across at Chance. He raised his beer bottle to his mouth, licked his lips after taking a sip, his gaze never leaving Jane.

"I don't think he's blinking at all," Sharon whispered. "He's not even looking at me and his eyes are making me all"—she shifted on her seat—"flustered."

Yep, he could do that. Most of the time Chance was easygoing. So laid-back he was practically prone. But every once in a while, something would flip a switch in him, give him a singular laser-like focus that was nothing short of intense.

Her stomach fluttered. It was those times that turned Jane into putty.

She threw back her shot, grabbed Sharon's and tossed it back, too.

"Hey!" her friend protested.

Jane staggered to her feet, the alcohol already sanding down the edges of her rough night. "You can't drink any more. You're driving me home."

"What? Now?" Sharon replaced her bowling shoes with lime-green heels.

"Yes. I need to get out of here." Before Jane did something really stupid. Like crawl into Chance's lap. It would be easy to pretend he was still the man who gave her comfort.

"I'll take care of returning the shoes," Sarah said.

Jane gave her a hug. "Thanks. Sorry for ruining girls' night out."

Sarah patted her back. "Get some rest. By tomorrow, your fall will all be forgotten."

Nodding, Jane wobbled on her feet. Good thing she was wearing flats. God only knew what other damage she could wreak in heels. Chance stood up, took a step toward her, but Jane glared him back into place.

She didn't need his help. Or his soft married lips. Or his love-'em-and-leave-'em ways. She had her girlfriends. Slinging an arm around Sharon's shoulder, she shuffled to the stairs with her. "I love you, Sharon."

"Good God, you've already got to that stage of drunkenness?" Sharon huffed out a breath. "I'm glad you live close. You know I don't do sloppy drunks."

"I'm not drunk," Jane said. At least not drunk enough. She could still feel Chance's eyes pinned to her back, burning her like a brand. They followed her all the way to the door. Once outside, she took a deep breath of the cool night air.

It didn't help. She still felt him.

His presence was following her.

Nope, she wasn't nearly drunk enough.

Chapter Eight

Closing the door to Pins 'N' Pints behind him, Chance stepped into the blinding sunlight, squinted at his clipboard, and made a couple notations. Chief Finnegan had thought Chance, as the newest member of the Pineville Fire Department, should be responsible for making the annual inspections of the downtown businesses so he could "get to know his neighbors."

He rolled his shoulders. Because there was nothing to make people more welcoming and friendly than showing up at their doorstep with the ability to ticket them or shut them down.

He hadn't been in the place since Tuesday night, bowling with his new coworkers. Since Jane.

He scratched his chest through his work polo. His skin had been feeling tight lately. Itchy. As though it wasn't quite sure they were in the right place. Heaving a sigh, he slid his sunglasses on, a shield against the sun's glare. Itchy skin or no, this was where he'd settled and he was determined to make a good life for his son here.

It hadn't always been like this. When he'd first arrived in Pineville, he'd felt great. The traffic was minimal, the air was clean, and the streets were safe. It hadn't been . . .

He ground to a halt on the sidewalk, letting a hurried pedestrian brush past him. It hadn't been until he'd run into Jane again that he'd started to feel, well, off. Like he hadn't quite found his home yet.

Except when he was with her. She'd knocked him off balance, but when he was with her, actually in her presence, he was centered. Content. It was as if his body hadn't known what it'd been missing until she'd come along and reminded him.

All that skin she'd shown him a few nights ago after her tumble reminded him of a few other things. A smile stretched across his face. His Janey-girl never had been very graceful. Remembering just who else had seen the bits of Jane that should have been private turned his smile into a scowl. He'd almost knocked Martinez's dimpled face off his neck after Jane had left the bar.

Chance turned onto Main Street. He didn't have time for mooning over a woman who clearly wanted nothing to do with him. Checking the map he'd made of the downtown area, he headed for his next target. Luckily, only five businesses were up for inspections this month. And the next one was owned by . . . he blew out a relieved sigh. At least there'd be one welcoming face this morning.

A basket overflowing with pink flowers hung from a light pole, and the trailing petals brushed against his shoulder as Chance paused at the edge of the curb to check for traffic. The morning was dawning warm and bright, and Chance was thankful that this spring was mild. Moving from California, he was unprepared to properly outfit his son if a snowstorm arrived. A trip for parkas and boots could wait until next winter.

His target was three blocks up. Chance walked under a row of American flags and wondered if the store owners kept them as permanent decorations to their storefronts, or if this was in anticipation of Independence Day, still more than a month and a half away.

The store he stopped in front of didn't have a flag out front, but it did have a chalkboard written in a looping scrawl, announcing an ounce of essential oil was free with every visit to the aromatherapy bar.

Smiling, he pushed in, the tinkle of a bell announcing his entrance. Edith looked up from the register where she was ringing up a sale.

Her face lit up. "Hi, Chance. Come for that male-energy-boost powder we talked about?" She couldn't control her smile as she pushed the handles of a small brown bag filled with purple tissue paper into her customer's hand.

The young woman flicked an assessing glance at Chance. With a murmured thank-you to Edith, she strolled past him, an eye-wateringly strong perfume making his nose twitch. He fought back his sneeze as the woman sashayed out the door.

"Thanks, Edith. I'm always so pleased when people greet me with an insult to my manliness." Resting his clipboard on her counter, he scanned the room. Lots of dead plants hanging from the ceiling. Those would go up like tinder under a blowtorch, but would burn out quickly. He sniffed. They smelled pretty good, though. Reminded him of Jane.

She bobbed her head at the door that had just swung shut. "Just trying to save you from *that*. I hate to make judgments on anyone's sexuality, but trust me. You don't want that one coming after you. She chews up sweet men like you and eats them for dinner."

"And if she thinks I'm, uh, having problems, I'll remain unchewed?"

"Exactly." Edith floated to a reclaimed wood bar that held shelves of small brown dropper bottles above it. Pulling one down, she filled it with oil and added a couple of drips of something to it. "Here." She pressed the bottle into his hand. "A couple drops of this on your pillow every night and you'll be right as rain."

"You do know I don't actually have a problem in that area, right?" My God. He was defending his sexual prowess to Jane's mother. Something about that just wasn't right. "You just made that up, remember?"

"The oil isn't for that, silly. If you had that problem, I'd cook you up a mixture of ginseng and cayenne." Edith's long skirt swished over the wood floor as she tidied up her store. "You just look tired, and that's for a restful night's sleep."

Chance was about to protest. He didn't want to wake up smelling like a bouquet of flowers.

"And you know," she continued, "fatigue can lead to that other problem we were discussing."

Chance deposited the bottle in his pants pocket. A little aromatherapy never hurt anyone. Besides, he didn't want Edith having any reason to tell Jane he might not be able to perform satisfactorily.

He huffed out a breath. Jane and he weren't going to happen; she'd been all kinds of clear about that. He didn't need to worry about what she thought. He gripped the bottle in his pocket. Still, he didn't want to be rude to Edith and return her gift. He'd just hold on to it.

"So what brings you to the Apothic Garden?" Edith asked. "Looking for a gift for someone, or just wanted to say hello?"

"Neither. Although I always want to say hi to you," he hastily added. "But I'm here for work. It's time for your inspection." He held up his clipboard. "I have a list of things to check off and then I'll be out of your hair."

Rising up onto her toes, she patted his cheek. "You're never a bother, sweetie. Do what you have to do and holler if you have any questions. I'll just be in back."

Chance nodded, the tension he always seemed to carry in his shoulders slipping away. He'd always enjoyed Jane's parents, thought their carefree ways a refreshing change from his conservative upbringing. While Jane had been embarrassed by her mother's hippie ways, Edith had never failed to bring a smile to Chance's face.

Her wheat-germ granola cookies had been a baking abomination, but other than that minor flaw, Chance had been happy to enter the Willoughby house. He'd felt welcomed and respected, feelings not to be underestimated by a teenage boy.

Edith's presence in Pineville was another bonus to his relocation. Not as nice as if Jane had welcomed him with open arms, but a plus just the same. Chance looked at the wall of potions and wondered if Edith had anything to help a person forgive. He sighed. It would take time and hard work with Jane, but he'd get there.

He hoped.

Maybe after the inspection, he could convince Edith to put in a good word.

Jane opened her front door, and jumped back when her mom charged in. With a suitcase rolling behind her. "What's the matter, Mom? I think you woke up my upstairs neighbor with your pounding."

"Mr. Chu is fine. I, on the other hand, am furious." To emphasize her point, she kicked her suitcase. They both watched as it teetered and fell over.

Cyclops loped in from her bedroom and wound his body around Edith's ankles. She scooped him up, held him tight to her chest. "Hi, sweetie."

It was a mystery to everyone but Cyclops, but he adored her mother, the only human to whom he showed any real affection. Butting his head against her chin, he purred loudly, shut his one eye tight with delight.

"What happened?" Jane asked. "And why do you have a suitcase?" Uneasiness spiraled through her stomach. Luggage couldn't be a good sign.

"Your boyfriend—"

"Leon?" Jane asked hopefully. There was nothing Leon could do that would be so bad.

"No." Edith glared at Jane, kissing one of Cy's waving paws. "Your old boyfriend. The fireman."

"I really can't be held responsible for what—"

"Do you know what he did?" her mother interrupted. "He kicked me out! Of my own home. My store. I'm shut down until"—she reached into the top of her bra and pulled out a folded piece of yellow paper—" 'the following infractions are remedied,' " she read. A lengthy list of safety violations followed.

Snatching the paper from her mother, Jane ran her eyes down the checked boxes until she reached the signature. T. Chance McGovern. "That rat! I can't believe he cited you."

"And evicted. Don't forget about that." Edith swung her legs up on the couch and lay on her back, staring at the ceiling. "He said it wasn't, and I quote, 'safe.' "

Jane sank down onto the armchair across from her mom. "You need to call Colt McCoy. When you bought the building five years ago, you hired him to remodel the space. If there are safety issues, he's responsible."

"Well . . ." Her mother hugged Cy closer.

"Well what?"

"I might have told Colt not to bother with some of the electrical work. He almost refused to work in my space," Edith added, looking bewildered at the thought, "until I promised him that I'd hire a specialist just as soon as I could afford it."

Jane let her head fall onto the back of the chair. "And you never did."

"The time was never right!" Edith sat upright, crossed her legs Indian style. "I was running a business. I couldn't just shut down."

"Yeah, how's that working out for you now?" Jane held up a hand. "Sorry. I'm turning my anger on the wrong person. I can't believe he kicked you out instead of just giving you a fix-it ticket."

Edith shook her head. "Somewhere along the road, that boy turned into a real stickler for the rules. So sad."

Even though Jane *kinda* understood where Chance was coming from, her mom was now firmly on Team Jane, and that felt great. "I told you he was a jerk. People don't change their stripes."

"I think that's zebras, dear. Of course people can change." She stroked Cy's orange fur. "He was just so unreasonable, not giving me more time." She sniffed. "The past inspector always did."

Staring at the suitcase, Jane pursed her lips. "I only have the one bed, Mom. And that couch isn't comfortable to sleep on all night."

"Don't be silly. You don't have to sleep on the couch." Edith rose, stretched. "Your bed is plenty big for both of us." Carrying Cy, she headed for the bedroom, rifling through the woven bag that hung across her chest. "Will you bring my suitcase in here? I'm going to burn some sage. My aura is out of balance."

Jane wrinkled her nose. She hated burnt sage. It clung to her clothes, seeped into her skin. Chance would pay for this. She loved her mother, but one of her happiest memories was the day she'd moved out of her mom's house. They just weren't compatible roommates. And now they were stuck together in her one-bedroom apartment.

Oh yes, Chance would pay.

At least her mom would stop pushing her at Chance. Edith had finally realized that ship had sailed.

She walked into her bedroom to see her mother waving a bundle of smoking herbs in the corner of the room.

"Mom, you're going to set the fire alarm off." Jane opened a window. "We don't need another run-in with Chance right now. I think one of us would probably kill him, and I don't want to go to jail tonight."

Edith frowned. "You're right. I don't want to see that boy again anytime soon."

Nodding, Jane heaved the suitcase onto the bed. Finally, they agreed on something. Chance had just become their common enemy. No more insinuations about how good she and Chance were together, or how much Edith loved his son, Josh. No more sly winks over how good-looking Chance had become, how pretty their babies would be. No more lectures on forgiveness for past sins. After this ball was over, he could be forgotten by both mother and daughter.

"He has a damn fine ass under that uniform, however," Edith said, unpacking her clothes. "It might be worth a fire just to see that again."

Jane threw herself face-first onto her bed and screamed into her pillow.

Chapter Nine

Jane stomped up the driveway and charged into the firehouse. A quick glance showed that her quarry wasn't in the living room. Chief Finnegan, Martinez, and a new recruit sat at a long wood table playing cards; a long wall of trophies was displayed behind them.

Poor suckers. Unless they produced Chance, they'd be contending with her wrath today. With only three hours' sleep under her belt, Jane and reason had parted company sometime around breakfast that morning.

"Dispatch Jane!" Martinez waved her over, a smirk dancing around his lips as he looked her up and down. "You play Texas Hold 'Em?"

"Not today." She marched over to the men.

The chief laid down his cards. "You okay? You look tired."

Martinez leaned across the table. "I don't think you're supposed to say that to women," he said in a hushed tone.

Finnegan ignored him.

"I am tired." Jane placed her palms on the table. "I'm tired because your fireman kicked my mom out of her building. He kicked her out, and she's staying with me. In my bed. Until her electrical passes code. Do you have any idea how long that could take?"

A dog howled in the distance and Jane took her voice down a couple levels below screeching. "Several weeks. My mom called around for estimates this morning."

"You're sleeping next to your mother." Finnegan cringed. "That's rough."

Jane cocked her head. Tried to process that odd statement, but her mind didn't want to focus.

"I heard about Chance's decision. And even though your mom's not happy, I support him." The chief raised his hand. "She shouldn't have passed inspection last year, and I had some words with the man who passed her with just a warning." He frowned, and the Irish surfaced in his voice. "He'll be elbow-deep cleaning toilets for a long time to come, you can be sure of that."

The new recruit and Martinez flinched. The toilets here must be filthy.

"That doesn't really help me." She pushed off the table. "Where's Chance? Upstairs?"

"Hold up there." Finnegan got to his feet. "You hurting my number-two man won't help you, either. Besides, he did it because he was concerned about Edith's safety, and for her neighbors. He made the right call."

Jane's anger deflated a bit. "She could have had it fixed while she was living there. She's been in the building for five years and nothing's happened yet."

Finnegan's stare made her feel like she was back in grammar school.

"Jane?" Chance loped down the stairs two at a time. "I thought I heard your voice."

"Run, man," Martinez hissed. "Run fast, run far."

Finnegan sighed. "Martinez, go get lunch started."

Martinez backed out of the room, pointing at Jane, making choking motions and pointing at Chance. The newbie pursed his lips, pushed off the table, and sidled out of the room after Martinez, never saying a word.

Chance shifted on his feet. "I guess you heard about your mom's store."

"Heard about you evicting her from not only her store but her home as well?" She stalked up to him, poked him in the chest. "Yeah, I heard all about it. Between my mom harping on and on about what a rigid dill hole you are, and her kicking me all night in bed, I hardly got any sleep."

Finnegan nodded, rubbed his leg absently, and Jane glared at him, her anger hot enough to encompass any male in the vicinity.

"Look," Chance said. "When I pulled back a panel Edith had duct taped to the wall in her storeroom, I found several wires that were completely stripped of any insulation. Without taking down more of the walls, I had no way of knowing how extensive the problem was." Chance's voice was everything that was reasonable.

Fire licked in Jane's gut. No way did he get to be the voice of logic. "You kicked her out! My mom isn't rolling in dough. If she can't run her store for a month, she might go out of business."

Chance frowned. "It shouldn't take more than a week for those repairs."

"*If* a contractor was available immediately." Rubbing her gritty eyes, Jane sighed, the anger and fight draining out of her. Exhaustion took their place. "Unless she wants to pay an exorbitant sum of money that she can't afford, the earliest she can get someone out to her building is in three weeks."

Chance rested his hand on her shoulder. Even though he was the source of all her problems, the contact was warm and heavy and comforting. She leaned into his touch.

"I'm sorry," he said, his voice as soft as velvet. "It just wasn't safe. It looked like the electrical in that building was fifty years old. I didn't want anything to happen to her."

And how the hell could she argue with that? For all her quirks and her sleep-kicking, her mom was great, and of course Jane didn't want anything to happen to her either. She had stormed down to the fire station before her morning cup of coffee, all hellfired to really give it to Chance. Maybe that was her problem. She needed her coffee. Then she could figure out what to do about her mom.

She wrinkled her forehead. She had some savings she could give her mother, but she didn't think Edith would accept money. The woman never hesitated to give to charity, but accepting it was another matter.

Chance grasped her face between his two hands, his thumbs massaging the stress out of her temples. "I'll help you figure something out."

"What?" She should step away from him. His gesture was too familiar, especially in front of the chief. It would give him, and Chance, the wrong idea about their relationship. And in a couple of minutes, she would step back. She bit back a moan as his thumbs brushed a particularly sensitive spot.

"I can see what you're thinking," Chance said. "When your face gets all scrunched up, I know you're worrying about everyone around you. You never worry that much about yourself." He leaned in, and Jane inhaled his clean scent of soap and man. Pressing his mouth to her ear, he murmured, "Don't worry, Janey-girl. We'll think of something."

"I know some guys." Finnegan's gruff voice interrupted the spell she was falling under. With Chance pressed so closely to her, his smell, his strength enveloping her, it was hard for a girl to keep her head on straight. Digging down deep, Jane summoned up her willpower and pushed away from Chance, turning to the chief.

"What guys?" she asked.

"Electrical contractors." He scratched his jaw. "They're retired but still licensed. And they owe me a favor. And Chance and I and some of the other guys here can put the walls back up, slap on a new coat of paint, on our downtime. We'll have it looking like a brand-new place at very little cost." He crossed his arms across his burly chest, a patch of auburn hair curling above the vee of his polo shirt. "Edith deserves that much."

Chance also crossed his arms over his chest, but when he did it, he didn't look determined like the chief. He looked like a boy who'd just had his birthday present stolen.

Jane tilted her head to the side, lowered her brow. One second he was all *We'll figure something out. I just want to help you.* And the next he's ticked off because he had to help fix the mess he created? What the hell?

"I can find some guys." Chance faced off with the chief. "No need to call in a favor."

"I'm happy to help out Jane and her mother." Finnegan looked down his nose at Chance. "Besides, where will you be finding a contractor? You don't know anyone here, do you now?"

Chance cracked a knuckle on one of his fingers. "I know some guys in Lansing. I can handle it."

"Lansing's a couple of hours away. My guys are local." Finnegan took a step forward. "I think Edith would prefer my contractors."

Jane's mouth dropped open. It was like watching two junkyard dogs circling a bone. She'd woken up this morning with nothing but problems, and now she was listening to two men argue over multiple solutions. Her brain didn't want to focus, just wanted to go back to sleep. She didn't understand what was going on, and she didn't care.

She cut in before Chance could argue for his *guys* again. "Figure it out! I don't care which contractors you use, just get it done." Winding a key off its ring, she slapped it down on the table. "Here's the key for my mom's building. Give it to whichever contractor you choose, and tell him it's a rush job." She rubbed her temple. "I don't know how many more nights like last night I can take without snapping."

Finnegan's face softened in sympathy. "Aye. Don't you worry. We'll get it done as fast as possible."

Chance clenched his hands into fists, but nodded his agreement. "We'll sort it out, Jane. And if you need a good night's sleep—"

Jane put a stop to wherever that train of thought was heading. "Don't want to hear it." Her body offered up a token protest at her immediate refusal. That sounded like it could have been an interesting offer, one that could possibly make her body very, very happy. She told her body to shut up and promised it a nap during her break at work today. "Just call me when it's done."

Both men nodded. She didn't protest when Chance took her elbow, and led her to her car.

"You okay to drive?" he asked.

"Yeah." Jane unlocked her car. "My first stop will be Starbucks. I'll be fine."

"Okay." He settled her in the seat and leaned down. "Don't worry, Jane. I'll sort it out."

If there was an emphasis on the *I'll*, Jane didn't acknowledge it. She couldn't analyze the weird pissing match that had just occurred. She was just too tired to understand anything other than the fact that she didn't understand men at all.

Jane poked at the yellow piece of paper Chance was glowering at. "Right there. With the check mark. That was supposed to be your job!"

She, Chance, and Judge Nichols were holding an emergency meeting in her apartment after it'd been discovered that *someone*—she glared at Chance—hadn't secured the caterer like he was supposed to. Now it was two weeks before the ball and they had no food.

"There's a check mark by that number on the list," Chance growled. "Check marks mean it's already done."

"No, the check mark means I wanted you to do it," Jane said. "You said you wanted to help. I gave you the caterer and the florist." Leaning back on the couch, she sighed. "You haven't called the florist, either."

"No." Chance smacked his hand on the coffee table, picked up the to-do list, and waved it in her face. "Because there's a big fricking check mark in front of it."

She narrowed her eyes. Jane wasn't normally a violent person, but she really wanted to smack him. How could he be so dense? And now he was trying to blame her for his mess.

Edith poked her head in from the kitchen. "What did you expect, Jane? My place is one giant mess. If he can't organize one teensy rewiring, how do you think he's going to organize a fundraiser?"

Pinching the bridge of his nose between his thumb and forefinger, Chance sighed. "It's only been one day, Edith. It's going to look like a mess for a couple of days before it comes together."

She sniffed. "So you say." Picking up a cup of tea, she drifted across the living room. "I'll be in the bedroom taking a nap. No offense, Jane. But I just don't sleep well with you next to me."

Jane waited for the door to snick shut before biting down on her fist and stifling a scream. "I'm hard to sleep next to? The bags under my eyes would require oversized-luggage fees."

Chance smiled. "I don't know what Edith's talking about. I never had any problems sleeping next to you."

Judge Nichols coughed into his fist, and Jane glared at Chance. Reason number 212 to add him to her shit list. She knew the judge didn't think she was a virgin, but she still didn't want to fling her past love life in his face.

"Can we get back to the topic at hand?" she asked through clenched teeth. "Namely, your screwup and what we're going to do to solve it?"

"My screwup?" Chance inhaled deeply through his nose, let the breath out through his teeth with a hiss. "I'm not taking responsibility for this cluster fu—" Darting a look at the judge, he cut off the end of his tirade.

A flash of orange darted behind the couch they were sitting on. Jane watched as a bristly tail stalked around the corner, circling behind Chance. When Cyclops's tail got that twitchy, it wasn't a good sign. She smiled.

"Children," Judge Nichols said sternly, wiping the smile off her face right quick, "I expected better from the two of you. You were supposed to be working together."

"We were," she protested. "I gave Chance a list to do and I did mine." She spun on him. "Didn't you think there was anything strange when you went over the unchecked items and found that I'd already done them?"

He shrugged. "When I called the band and they said they'd already confirmed with you, I figured you didn't trust me and had decided to do everything yourself."

The judge interrupted Jane's fuming. "And you didn't call her to confirm that was the case?" The older man clucked his disapproval.

Jane smirked at Chance, and the judge turned on her. "And you didn't call to check in with his progress? You two are the cochairs of an important event. I expected better."

Jane lowered her chin toward her chest. "I'll call the florist. I know Paul pretty well since he helps with the Flower Rangers. If Chance will get a caterer—"

"So you two can still work separately?" Judge Nichols shook his head. "You need to learn to work together."

Jane poked her tongue into her cheek. Did the judge want her and Chance to make conference calls? That seemed rather silly. Besides, it would just be easier to do it herself. Chance obviously didn't know what he was doing as chair of a fundraising committee, and the less time she had to be around him, the better.

The hot kiss they'd shared after game night flashed through her mind. It was easier to work without him around, on a lot of levels. She darted a glance at him, and the tips of her breasts tingled. Even dressed casually in threadbare jeans and a polo shirt, he was hot as sin. She focused on the narrowed eye glaring at Chance's leather loafer from the foot of the couch instead.

She'd let Chance get too close, and she couldn't allow that to happen again. Working separately was better.

The judge's face cleared into a serene smile. "I'll handle the catering. I just left Allison's diner and I don't think I'll have any trouble convincing her to help us."

Jane wrinkled her nose. "I love the Pantry, and Allison's a great cook. But I don't think meat loaf and burgers is what we're looking for."

"Trust me." He rocked up onto his toes. "Allison is more than that. She'll do a great job."

At this point, they'd be lucky to get Colonel Sanders to cater. "Well, if you think you can get her on such short notice," Jane said doubtfully.

Chance sat forward on the sofa, not noticing the creeping bundle of fur stalking his foot. "Great. I'll get in touch with the florist—"

"You'll both talk to Paul. You can stop by his shop after you deliver the meal that Allison prepared for Saul Harraday. The dishes are in my car, but since I'll be back at the Pantry talking to Allison about the catering, I won't have time to deliver the food." The judge clapped his hands together, like the problem was solved. And for him, it probably was. Finding a caterer with only two weeks left was a cakewalk compared to going to Mr. Harraday's. The old man's tongue was filled with venom, and he used his cane more as a weapon than a tool to help him walk.

"You're taking food to Mr. Harraday?" Jane wet her lips with her tongue.

"Yep. Once a week Allison cooks him up something good, makes sure there'll be lots of leftovers so we know he's eating something solid, and I know he's still kicking. A safety check of sorts." He rubbed his hands together. "And this week you and Chance are the lucky people who get to deliver it to him."

"Great," she muttered.

"Sure," Chance agreed, oblivious to the danger. He was new in town and had no way of knowing the citizens of Pineville considered the old man their Boo Radley. He stood. "Jane and I . . . son of a—"

Chance lifted his foot, glared in outrage at Jane. "Your cat!" he spluttered.

"Run, Cyclops," Jane yelled. The cat didn't need telling. After delivering his revenge, the beast had sprinted for the kitchen, making his escape out the window. He paused at the sill, tail twitching, and Jane could have sworn the cat smiled smugly.

Chance advanced a step. "Your cat peed on me," he said quietly, only the flicker of a muscle in his jaw giving Jane warning.

She tried not to smile. From the fire that crackled to life in Chance's eyes, she knew she must not have succeeded.

"You can't blame Cyclops." She took a step back. "He's just defending his territory."

"I don't blame the cat." He stepped close enough to grab her, and Jane scuttled around the back of the couch. "I blame his owner."

The judge clapped his hands together. "Well, I'll just leave you kids to it." He started for the door.

"Wait!" Jane flew after him. "I'll just, uh, get that food from you." Chance stood behind the couch, gripping its back, his fingers white. Yep, leaving the apartment for a cooling-off period was a definite necessity. "I'll get the bag from the judge's car while you clean up." Snagging her keys from the bowl by the door, she added, "In fact, why don't you meet me downstairs?" Jane didn't want to come back to her living room to face him. Not when there were no witnesses. Being in public was a much better idea.

Grabbing her purse, she followed the judge out the door. "I'll see you downstairs," she said brightly, closing the door on his glower. She held back her laughter until she hit the sidewalk, then let it spill out.

Judge Nichols shook his head as he handed her the bag of food, but his lips twitched. "I'll see you two later. And Jane"—he rested his hand on her shoulder—"we can't let past hurts ruin this fundraiser. I don't know what happened between the two of you, but you need to work it out."

Easily said. But Jane nodded and waved as he drove off. Waited for Chance to come down.

And waited.

She was sitting on the trunk of her car when he finally emerged from her apartment building. The bottom half of one of his pant legs was wet and his one loafer was a darker shade of brown than the other. Holding the bag of food in front of her like a shield, she smiled. "Ready to go?"

"Yes." He snagged her keys from her hand, and climbed in the driver's side. Without holding her door open for her this time, she noticed.

Grumbling, she sat in the passenger's seat. "Took you long enough. It was just a little pee."

Chance jammed his foot on the accelerator, and her head whipped back. She gritted her teeth.

"I couldn't get my shin in your sink so I took my jeans off."

Whoa. Chance had been pantless in her apartment. She swallowed. His thighs looked really muscular now. Strong. Maybe she shouldn't have fled, but stuck it out in her place.

"And I used your hairdryer to try to save my shoe." They both looked down at his foot on the pedal. "I don't think it worked."

"They were old anyway. Had a good life."

He narrowed his eyes. "They're well-worn. Molded perfectly to my foot shape."

"And now one just has a couple of spots on it," she said. "Hardly noticeable."

His knuckles whitened around the steering wheel. "The smell is noticeable."

She'd hoped he was congested. Once they'd gotten into the enclosed space of the car, the odor had become pungent. Rolling down the window, she tried to force optimism into her voice. "I'm sure it will fade. You're going to want to take a left up here on Maple."

He followed her directions but remained silent. Pulling in front of Mr. Harraday's house, Jane gave up on her forced cheer. "Look, if you want me to buy you a new pair of shoes—"

"I don't." He turned off the ignition, pinned her with a stare. "I want your cat to not pee on me when I come over."

"The fundraiser will be over soon. You won't be coming over after that, so I don't think we have to worry about it." She tried to keep her voice light. What would happen after the ball? She'd sworn she never wanted to see the man again, but when faced with that prospect, she felt . . . Crap. She didn't know how she felt. But it wasn't warm and fuzzy.

Pineville was a small town. He was a firefighter and she worked in dispatch. They'd run into each other.

She rubbed at her tight chest. Was that what she wanted, or wanted to avoid? She was so confused she didn't know anymore.

Chance grunted and got out of the car. Grabbing the handles of the white plastic bag, she followed. He'd already knocked on the door by the time Jane joined him on the porch. They waited side by side a couple of minutes, Chance's arm brushing hers as he shifted.

"I don't think he's home," he said. Knocking again, Chance leaned sideways to look through the window. "It's pretty dark in there."

Jane peered through the window on the other side of the door. "He's an old man. He probably doesn't turn on the lights during the day, to save money."

"That's harsh."

Jane jumped off the porch and went to another window. "Remember your grandfather when he'd come to visit? He'd sit in that

BarcaLounger and shoot a rubber-band gun at me if I didn't turn the light off when I left a room."

Chance grinned. "I think he just liked hearing you shriek. Can't say I blame him."

Jane shot him a look.

"It's high-pitched and girly. Cute," he amended when she narrowed her eyes. Hands on hips, he looked at the small house. "Let's leave the food on the porch. He'll see it when he gets home."

Jane bit her lip.

"What?" he asked.

"Well, what if he's fallen? The judge said the man was expecting him." She tugged at the window, grunting when it didn't budge. "I'd hate to leave only to find out later that he needed help. Even if it is Mr. Harraday."

Chance pulled her away. "Breaking and entering isn't going to help. A neighbor might call the cops."

"I think Jerome's on duty. He'd help me break in to check on Mr. Harraday." Jane walked to the side of the house. A six-foot fence with a locked gate blocked her view.

"Meaning I won't?" Chance's breath was hot on her neck.

Stepping to the side, Jane gripped the top of the fence and tried to pull herself up to get a look over. She had about two seconds of hang time before scraping back down the wood to the ground. She shook her arms out. "Apparently you won't, since I'm doing all the work here." Besides a weed-strewn lawn and some rusty patio furniture, Jane hadn't seen much in her first jump.

She went for another. Clenching the top of the fence, she hopped up, trying to walk the soles of her sneakers up the side.

A hand on her butt took the weight off her arms. "Hey!"

Chance grunted and lifted her higher. "See anything?"

"No." Jane's hips dug into the wood, and she leaned forward, trying to shift her weight to a better position. "But I might hear something." She turned her head to listen. "A radio maybe?"

"Okay, get down." Chance shifted his hand from her butt to her hip. She knew he meant it to help, that he wouldn't let her fall. She knew it, but when that support that she'd been resting on disappeared and she started to slide backwards, her body went into panic mode, not trusting that the light grip on her hip would catch her.

She threw her upper body forward, hoping to balance herself.

And the light grip on her hip that would have eased her body back down the fence had no purchase to hold her as she toppled over the other side.

"Shit!" Chance yelled from the other side of the fence.

Jane lay on her back, disoriented from her ass-over-teakettle flop into Mr. Harraday's backyard. Chance's upper body sprang into view as he pulled himself up onto the fence and swung his legs over, leaping over in one smooth move.

She hated that men could do that so easily while she could barely clear ten inches in a jump. All those muscles flexing and bunching in Chance's body. Yeah, really hated it.

He dropped next to her. "Are you all right?" A crease appeared above his nose when she didn't answer. "What hurts?"

"Besides my pride?" She pushed his hand away and propped herself up on her elbows. Her rear end was going to be sore tomorrow, but he didn't need to know that. "I scraped my palm and banged my elbow, but I'm fine."

Chance didn't pay attention to her assessment and went into medic mode, running his hands lightly along her body, checking for breaks. "Follow my finger," he ordered, holding a digit up in front of her eyes, moving it back and forth.

Grabbing his finger with her own, she yanked it away from her face. "I'm fine. This patch of weeds broke my fall."

His face relaxed. Sighing, he ran his hands around her head, felt the contours of her skull. "I don't know why I'm even checking. Your head's too hard to get hurt."

Jane wanted to pull away, get up, but the head massage felt too damn good. She'd forgotten how talented Chance was with his hands. "I thought you used to say I was soft in the head."

His fingers paused. He looked down at her, the rim of his irises so dark they almost looked black. "That was your heart, Jane. You always had a soft heart."

That organ stilled before jumping into overdrive. She needed to keep her mouth shut. Something really stupid, something that would tell Chance more than she wanted him to know, was ready to tumble out, and she couldn't let that happen.

Dragging his fingers through her hair, Chance pulled his hand back, holding a dandelion. He put it before her mouth and smiled. "Make a wish."

Don't be an idiot. Don't let yourself get hurt again. There were too many wishes to pick just one. She puckered her lips and blew.

Don't lose him again darted through her head as the white seeds wafted from their stalk and floated to the ground.

She groaned. That was her wish? She was smarter than that.

Chance frowned. "You do hurt. Where?"

"I'm *fine.*" She extended her hand. "Help me up."

Chance's warm hand gripped hers, pulling her to her feet. She forced herself to let go. Brushing stray weeds from her pants, she nodded her head at the rectangle of cement that acted like a porch. "Let's knock at the side door. Maybe he just couldn't hear us before."

Nodding, he set off through the knee-high grass. The yard was wild, overrun, and green as a forest. Jane frowned. She wouldn't expect the elderly man to be out there mowing his lawn, but he must have someone who could help him.

"Hello? Mr. Harraday?" Chance pounded on the door.

Jane shaded her eyes, and tried to look in through the small window. She tugged at the sash, but it wouldn't budge.

Chance circled his arms around her, tried the window himself. "Now you've got me trying to break and enter."

She smiled. The role reversal was fun. She could understand why he'd always tried to push her into going outside her comfort zone in high school. Being the devil on someone's shoulder held a definite appeal.

For a worthy cause, of course.

"Maybe we should call the police," she said. "He had hip surgery last year." That Flower Ranger visit still sent a chill down her spine. Crotchety old men amped up on pain meds were just mean. "He really could have fallen. Or had a heart attack. Or a stroke."

Chance put his hands on her shoulders, turned her to him. "You don't need to list every possible cause of death. I'll walk around the house, see if there's any way I can get in. You keep knocking. If he still hasn't answered by the time I get back, we'll call the police."

Her shoulders released the tension she didn't know she'd been holding. That was why she'd gone along with his teenage schemes, why she felt comfortable clambering into someone else's backyard with Chance around. Whether it was skinny-dipping in Bonner's Pond or participating in Senior Cut Day, if Chance was by her side, she knew everything would end up okay. He could calm her with just one touch.

She watched him walk around the corner, trying to keep her eyes off his firm butt. *Focus*, she told herself. *Mr. Harraday*. Still watching the corner Chance had disappeared around, Jane raised her hand to knock on the door. The door that swung violently inward. She shrieked.

A cane that branched into four rubber-tipped ends poked out at her. She skittered back, stumbling off the cement slab.

"What the hell ya doing, poking round my backyard?" Mr. Harraday yelled.

Chance pounded around the corner. "What's wrong? You made your girly shriek."

"Nothing's wrong." She smoothed her hands down her sides. "Mr. Harraday just startled me. And I don't have a girly shriek."

Both men raised eyebrows.

Squaring her shoulders, she ignored the heat creeping up her neck. "Mr. Harraday, we brought you your meal from the Pantry. Why didn't you answer the door?"

"Huh?" He cupped his ear.

She gritted her teeth. "I know you have excellent hearing, Mr. Harraday."

He wrinkled his face like he'd just sucked a lemon. "None of your business why I didn't answer. Could've been on the crapper. Or maybe I just didn't want to see your ugly face."

"What?" Chance stepped forward. "What did you just say?" He sounded more perplexed than angry.

Jane patted his arm. The first experience with Mr. Harraday was always the hardest. "Judge Nichols asked that we deliver the food and make sure you're all right. The food is on the front porch and we can see you're just as . . . spirited as ever. We'll head out now."

"Sure. Breeze in, breeze out," the old man grumbled.

Jane hesitated. "Would you like us to stay for a bit? Keep you company?"

Chance's brow drew down and he shot her a look. He needn't have worried.

"Hell no! I don't need no damn babysitter." He shook his cane.

"You have a daughter in Ann Arbor, don't you, Mr. Harraday? Does she get out to visit you often?" She looked around the yard. If the daughter did come, yard work obviously wasn't on her agenda. Not that there weren't better ways to spend time with your father.

"What do I want her out here for?" Harraday asked. "Just another person bothering me, telling me what I can and can't do." He snorted. "All she does is pester me. Wants me to move in with her." Poking his cane in the air for emphasis, he hollered, "Well, I ain't gonna."

Putting a hand on her elbow, Chance pasted a placating smile on his face. "We'll get out of your hair." He leaned down to Jane. "You didn't tell me the guy is nuts."

"Not nuts," she whispered. "Just mean."

"I heard that!"

She sighed. "And definitely not deaf."

Harraday turned and smacked a button on a plastic box by the door. Odd. He didn't seem like the type to have a security system.

"Don't come back," he said over his shoulder. "Or I'll set the dogs on you." The door slammed shut.

"Does he have dogs?" Chance asked.

They moved toward the front gate. "Not that I've heard," she said. "But for us, I'm sure he wouldn't mind getting a couple of Dobermans."

Chance paused. "What's that sound?"

Jane cocked her head, heard several clicks. "I don't know. It sounds almost like . . . oh shit! Run!"

But it was too late. The sprinklers dotted around the yard had already popped their heads up and started spraying. Jane ran for the gate, felt water jet across her back.

Chance was right behind her. They pulled at the gate, not seeing the closed padlock in their rush to escape.

Jane flung herself at the fence. "Lift me over!" The back of her jeans clung wetly to her thighs.

"There's cement on the other side." Chance grabbed her around the waist, pulled her off the fence. "You'll split your head open."

He pulled her across the lawn to the back of the house, right into the eye of the sprinkler storm. Jane plastered herself to his side, got hit on the right by an arcing spray. Ducking under his arm, she dodged to his left.

"We're already wet," Chance yelled. "Stop bobbing and weaving. Let's just run for it." His hand slipped off her shoulder, and he stumbled. His legs caught in hers, and they tumbled to the lawn in a sodden heap.

Pressing up to her hands and knees, Jane turned to see if Chance was okay and got hit in the face with a spurt of water for her trouble. Chance's laughter drowned out the *snick-snick-snick* of the sprinklers. Jane glared at him, and he rolled on his back, laughing harder.

"Real nice." Jane pushed her hair off her face. "We're filthy and—"

Her sentence ended in a gasp as Chance wrapped an arm around her waist, pulled her under the stream of the returning sprinkler spray. She landed on his chest, her hand slapping into the earth beside him with a squelch. A slop of mud darted across his cheek.

This time Jane laughed.

Chance shook his head. "Be careful what you laugh at, Janey-girl." He trailed a finger down her face, and Jane felt the ooze of mud trickle down the path he made.

Digging her hand into the ground, she came up with a clump of dirt and crabgrass. Before she could make him eat it, Chance rolled and grabbed her wrist, pinning her hand to the ground. "Uh, uh, uh." His smirk dropped when she flicked mud at him with her other hand.

The maturity level went downhill from there. Jane shrieked when Chance shoved cold sludge down her shirt. She laughed when her own wiggling sent who-knows-what down the back of her jeans. They only stopped tussling when Harraday shouted out the window, "I'm calling the cops if you two don't git. Indecent is what you are!"

Chance grinned down at her, his chest brushing against hers with each breath, his eyes crinkling at the corners. "You heard the man." His gaze darkened when he looked at her wet shirt. "Wonderfully indecent."

His scrutiny heated her despite the wet and mud. Her pulse galloped, and the scent of grass swamped her senses. She'd forgotten how he made all her senses awaken, made her aware of the tingling in every nerve-ending in her body. When she was with Chance, she felt truly alive. She was a more exciting, interesting person when they were together.

Her fingers itched to reach up, thread in his thick hair, tug his head down to hers. She parted her lips in anticipation. Chance lifted one corner of his mouth in a move so familiar, it was a knife to her gut. This was Chance. The man who'd literally loved her and left her. Just because her body wanted him back didn't mean her mind was on board with that idea.

So she snorted, shook her head, and pushed at his shoulder. "You're a riot." She infused her words with a heavy dose of sarcasm.

He sat back on his haunches. "I like to think so."

Water slapped him in the face.

Jane laughed all the way around the house until they reached the sidewalk. Chance dripped next to her, tufts of chestnut hair sticking out in every direction. She only stopped laughing when he smiled evilly down at her and said, "I'm glad we took your car."

Looking at her filthy body and at the clean tan interior of her car, she sighed. No good deed went unpunished.

Chapter Ten

"Okay, everyone. I need ideas." Jane looked at the fundraiser committee, her hopes sinking at every blank face she encountered. They were all assembled at the Pantry, having agreed to make that their official meeting spot. Jane forked a flaky bit of cranberry-apple pie into her mouth. The desserts were just too damn good to go anywhere else.

Her mother wiped a smear of chocolate mousse from her lips with her napkin. "Are you sure the Regency can't host us? It was a big enough ballroom."

"We're sure," Chance butted in. A steaming mug of coffee sat on the table in front of him, the only person to forego a dessert. He'd been one of those freaks of nature who didn't really care for sweets, and Jane supposed he still was. If the trade-off was a chiseled set of washboard abs, it was probably worth the loss of Allison's baked deliciousness.

Jane laid a hand over her own softly rounded belly. She could make that trade-off, get in better shape. The half-eaten piece of pie beckoned, the tart cranberries a sharp contrast with the sweet apples. She shoveled in another mouthful, her eyes sliding shut. Nope. She'd just have to learn to live with the softness.

Chance kept talking, and she let him, because, pie. "The Regency had to close many of their public rooms for emergency renovations. At the time of our event, that ballroom will be torn down to the sheetrock." Frowning, he took a sip of coffee. "I'm not surprised they have a mold problem. With their lax attitude toward elevator maintenance, they probably make a habit of letting things slide. All in all, I think we're better off not holding the fundraiser there."

Jane paused, fork at her lips. She hadn't realized the problem at the hotel was so extensive. She'd just been told by the manager that the ballroom was no longer available. Chance must have called for more information. She chewed on her lip. Maybe his wife told him about it. Was she still in town? Had she been kicked out of the hotel, too, and if so, where was she staying?

Sneaking a sidelong glance at him, Jane thought about the encounter with the soon-to-be-ex at the Regency. Chance hadn't seemed pleased to see Annette. But she was Josh's mother. It would only make sense to let her stay at his house. She put her fork down, her stomach no longer a happy camper. Maybe they'd reconcile.

Which was a good thing. It was best for kids to have their two parents together. Placing her palm over her abdomen, she willed her intestines to stop twisting. The apple pie sat in there like a lead ball.

". . . don't you think, Jane?" her mother asked.

"What?"

Edith shook her head. "Your chakras are still all messed up. I said, what about the front foyer of city hall?"

"For the ball?" Jane asked. Her mother nodded. "It's not a big enough space. And there's only that one unisex bathroom. That would lead to problems."

"Okay." Edith raised her hands. "One reason was enough."

Judge Nichols brushed some crumbs off of his short-sleeved button-down shirt. Even though his clothes were hidden under a black cloak when he worked, he always wore pressed shirts and trousers underneath, the creases so sharp they looked lethal. No casual Fridays for this judge. "I was talking to the owner of Great Lakes Winery about their gift package for our auction. Jim over there mentioned their new cave. He said his daughter is going to hold her wedding reception there. If it's nice enough for a wedding, it should be nice enough for our ball."

"The Great Lakes Winery?" Jane had only been there once, when it had first opened. The grounds had been lovely, green fields with wildflowers next to the grapevines, a manicured area for bocce ball and croquet. But the actual tasting room had been tiny. But if they'd expanded . . .

"I'll check it out," she said. Next to her, Chance coughed. Rolling her eyes, she said, "We'll check it out." Jane lowered her voice. "Happy?" she asked him.

"Ecstatic," he replied, his voice as dry as Great Lakes Syrah. "But if I'd been along when you'd first looked at the Regency, I would have seen they were overdue for inspection. We wouldn't have wasted time assuming we would hold the event there."

"I'm sure the winery will love it if you go in there and act as a fire inspector." Jane tapped her fork against her plate. "They'll be just thrilled to offer us the space."

He leaned in close, his breath brushing across the side of her neck. The airy caress sent tingles all through her body. "I don't care if they like it or not. I'm not going to hold a function, especially one for the fire department, if the place isn't up to code."

Jane leaned back in her chair, needing to create some space before her body combusted. "I used to be the one who was a stickler for rules. What happened to you?"

He raised an eyebrow, looked thoughtful. "I became a father and a firefighter. Rules are important for both." Turning in his seat, he crossed one leg over the other. "What about you? When did Janey-girl learn to color outside the lines?"

She looked around the table. Now that a plan had been put in place, everyone was chatting and finishing up their desserts. Her mother nodded her head at Chance, then winked at Jane. Frowning, she scooted as far away from Chance as her chair allowed. She didn't want her mom to get the wrong idea.

"Jane?" he asked.

"I usually follow the rules." She took a sip of her iced tea. "But if no one gets hurt, I don't see the harm in doing what works best."

Chance smiled, and her heart stutter-stopped. He should be required to register that smile as a lethal weapon. "Your mom must be so proud."

A laugh burst out of Jane. "She still tries to press herbal remedies on me for my control issues, as she calls it." Jane smiled at her mom fondly.

Resting his arm on the back of her chair, he lowered his voice. "You and your mom. You're happy here?"

She knew what he was really asking. "Yes, I'm happy." His arm against her shoulder blades was warm. Solid. She eased away. "Getting dumped by my high school boyfriend didn't ruin my life."

Chuckling, he shrugged sheepishly. "Of course. I didn't mean . . ."

Jane thought he was too embarrassed to continue. But when his arm tensed behind her, she followed his gaze to the front door of the restaurant. Annette stood at the entrance, her gaze searching. Her eyes landed on Chance, and she made her way over. The belted wrap dress she wore clung to her slim curves, the strappy stilettos with their blood-red soles click-clacking across the linoleum.

"There you are." She stopped beside Chance, ignoring the rest of the table. "Your coworkers said you might be here."

"You stopped by the firehouse?" He stood and frowned down at Annette. "What did you say to them?"

"Just that your wife was looking for you." She bared her teeth. "They were ever so helpful."

"Great. Let's go outside."

Annette finally deigned to notice the rest of the table, every other conversation falling silent. "Aren't you going to introduce me to your friends, Chance?"

He took her elbow. "No."

Shaking out of his grip, Annette put both hands on the back of his chair and leaned forward. "Hi, everyone. I'm Annette. Chance's wife." At the collective inhale of air, she smiled. "Soon to be the ex–Mrs. McGovern, so you all can keep your panties on. Chance can still be a part of the bachelor auction." She shot her husband a malicious grin. "The boys at the fire station filled me in on that, too. Wish I could see it."

"It's in two weeks if you're still in town," Jane said. Chance was so clearly uncomfortable with Annette there that Jane felt almost friendly toward the woman. It was easier to keep poking at Chance than to analyze everything he stirred up in her. More fun, too.

"Jane, isn't it?" Annette asked. "You just keep popping up everywhere." Jane's warm feelings toward the woman turned tepid at the sarcasm in her voice. "You *good* friends with my husband?"

Jane didn't miss the innuendo, and she didn't particularly care for it.

Neither did her mother. From the end of the table, Edith said, "Chance and Jane have known each other forever. I caught that boy sneaking in her window more times than I could count." In the subtle game of one-upmanship, Edith obviously thought she'd scored a zinger. Crossing her legs, she waved a hand in dismissal.

"In her bedroom?" A furrow creased Annette's forehead before her mouth fell slack. "Oh my God. You're that Jane."

"Annette." The warning in Chance's voice was unmistakable.

His soon-to-be ex ignored it. "Is this why you came to this Podunk town? To be with her?"

"Uh . . ." Eyes wide, Jane wanted to shut this, whatever this was, down fast. "We just ran into each other a couple weeks ago. If he'd known I was here he probably would have chosen another town to settle in." The truth of that statement dug a little crater in her heart. She might never have seen Chance again if the Pineville FD hadn't been hiring.

"Oh, I doubt that." Annette shook Chance's hand off her elbow. "An opportunity to reunite with his one true love? My husband wouldn't miss that for the world."

Hands gripping the steering wheel, Chance risked a glance at the woman in his passenger seat. Jane's lips were still pressed into a hard line as she sat, elbow up on the window, head resting in her palm, radiating pissed-off.

Which he didn't get. Just because Annette ran her mouth off and said some stupid shit, he didn't understand what Jane had to be angry about. Still, he was happy enough that their trip to the winery included a detour to pick up Josh. She couldn't tear him a new one if he had his kid with him, right?

The silence in the SUV was oppressive. Tugging at the neck of his shirt, he shot her another look. "I never told Annette you were the 'love of my life.'" He snorted, but it came out sounding like the snuffling of a dying pig rather than the derisive exclamation he'd intended. "The few times your name came up, I might have said you were my first love. She misunderstood."

Annette had always seemed to have an attitude about his former girlfriend. Her snide little retorts had never failed to both irritate and bewilder Chance. For the first time he questioned his part in her petty jealousy. Had he mentioned Jane more than he should have? Jane had been such an integral part of his young life that any childhood story he told would of course include her.

Continuing to face front, she shrugged. "I really don't care what your wife"—at his growl she held up a hand—"your soon-to-be ex-wife has to say. It doesn't matter anymore."

"Right." He nodded, feeling like a bobblehead. "Of course." Then why did she look as though it mattered? Jane held herself as stiff as a board. Blowing out a deep breath, Chance gave up. He'd never understand women.

Silence descended again. He beat his thumbs against the steering wheel until her narrowed gaze stopped it.

"So." He cleared his throat. "Josh shouldn't be a problem. I told him if he's a good boy today we'll have pizza tonight. Unfortunately, bribery is my most reliable parenting tool."

"I told you, it's fine."

Chance waited a beat. "Katie has a doctor's appointment so she can't watch him."

Jane finally looked over. He wished she hadn't, not if she was going to purse up her pretty lips like she'd just tasted day-old fish. "Yeah, I got that the first time you said it."

Chance's shoulders slumped with relief when he turned onto his street. If there was anyone who could relieve awkward silences, it was his son.

Josh stood on the front porch, bouncing up and down in his red sneakers. Warmth spread through Chance's chest, just like every time he saw his son. The kid was just so damn cute. When he wasn't driving Chance nuts.

He pulled into his driveway, and Josh raced to the SUV, a small pack slapping against his back. Stepping out of the car, Chance grabbed Josh in a bear hug. "Hey there, buddy. How's it going?"

"Aunt Katie made me grill cheese for lunch, and we builded a moat for my castle, and . . ." Josh chattered away as Chance strapped him into his car seat.

Testing the belts, Chance said, "Can you take a breath and say hello to Jane?"

"Hi, Jane," Josh said. Like a rocket, he was off again, describing his day, minute by minute.

She raised her eyebrows and smiled at Chance. "Hi, kiddo."

Josh didn't hear her. Chance shut the back door, enjoyed a moment of silence before getting in the SUV, and waved goodbye to his sister at the front door. Settling himself behind the wheel, he wondered if perhaps he'd been too hasty in wanting to escape the awkward silence with Jane.

"Buddy, why don't you show Jane your new action figure?" Chance looked in the rearview mirror, watching his son root around in his backpack.

Jane leaned over to him. "I don't need to see—" she whispered, then broke into a big smile when Josh shoved a green turtle-man between the seats. "Hey. That's cool."

"Yeah, he is." Josh ran the figure over the seats and up onto the window, making kung fu fighting sounds in his imaginary battle.

"And that's why I told him to show you his toy," Chance said in a low voice. "That should keep him occupied for a good ten minutes." It kept Josh occupied the entire drive to the winery, about twenty minutes outside of town. The rows of vines bordering the dirt drive came as a surprise to Chance. He knew a winery must grow grapes, but it seemed out of place in Michigan.

"I wonder how good the wine can be here." Chance parked next to another car in front of a small building designed like an Italian-style villa. "This isn't exactly prime wine country."

Jane hopped out of the SUV. "We have two wineries in the area. The chamber of commerce says if we get two more, they're going to declare a wine trail." She looked down, eyes wide, when Josh grabbed her hand. "And the merlot is very good. You can grow grapes anywhere now."

Chance took his son's other hand and Josh immediately started swinging between the two of them. He was too big for it, his knees nearly scraping the ground when he dropped to hang between the two adults. But Jane held her own, hefting her half of Josh's weight with little problem.

"I didn't mean to sound like a wine snob," he said. "But I lived near Napa. I know what type of climate is good for grapes." They passed under a lattice archway blanketed with bougainvillea. He stopped for a moment to let his eyes adjust to the tasting room's dim light.

A woman behind a reclaimed-wood bar smiled warmly at them. "Hi, folks. You here for a tasting?" A man and woman stood across from her, noses deep in bulbous wineglasses.

Jane stepped forward, bringing Josh and Chance along with her. "We'd like to speak to someone about possibly renting out your new cave for an event. Are you the manager?"

"I wish." The petite blonde gave the couple a generous pour. "I could do a much better job at it than the owner."

"I heard that!" a disembodied voice bellowed from a back room.

The woman grinned.

A half-open door behind the bar banged open, and a large man filled the opening. "Hi. I'm Jim. Can I help you?" Tugging at the polo shirt stretched tight across his round stomach, he rounded the counter and stretched out a hand. "Did I hear that you have an event coming up?"

"Yes." Jane shook his hand. "We're organizing the Pineville Fire Department's charity ball and we're in a bit of a bind. Our location fell through, and Judge Nichols said you had a space big enough to hold your daughter's wedding. Congratulations on that, by the way."

Jim gave her a proud smile. Thirty seconds later, he and Jane were huddled over his smartphone, oohing and aahing over his daughter's engagement photos. Chance shook his head. Jane just had a way about her, got everyone to open up.

Josh tugged on his hand. "Daddy, can I have it?"

An automatic *no* rose to Chance's lips, and he looked where his son pointed. A basket of rubber chickens in a rainbow of colors had caught Josh's eye. Chance walked over and picked one up. It was odd, even for a tasting room gift shop.

"That's one of our biggest sellers," Jim said. He strode over to Chance and flipped the bird over. "It's a corkscrew. You turn the chicken's head and the screw comes out of his . . ." He shot a glance at Josh. "Well, you know, and the wings act as the levers. Pretty fun, right?"

Chance murmured an agreement, hiding his chuckle at Jane's horrified look. If this chicken was Jim's style, Chance didn't hold out much hope that the cave would be nice enough to hold their ball.

But a couple of minutes later, Chance was surprised. The room wasn't technically a cave, but a lower level dug into the side of the hill. One long wall was floor-to-ceiling glass, giving the room plenty of natural light. The concrete floor was painted to look like slate, and the exposed wood beams of the ceiling were draped in strands of white lights. Wine barrels dominated the large space.

"For events, we roll most of the barrels into the storeroom, but keep some for character," Jim said. "It can hold up to two hundred and fifty people, twenty-five ten-person tables, and along that wall is space for a stage."

"Is two-fifty the permitted capacity?" Chance ignored Jane's eye roll.

"It is." Jim flipped a switch and recessed lighting in the dark wood walls gave the room a warm glow. "And of course we have a wine and liquor license."

Josh tugged on Jane's hand and whispered something in her ear when she bent down. He knew his son's hair would darken with age, but right now it was closer to Jane's whiskey-colored hair than his own. They looked like a matched set. Rubbing a knuckle across his chest, Chance turned back to Jim and asked a couple more questions.

Jane straightened. "Josh needs to go to the bathroom. Is there one down here?"

Jim nodded. "But the grout is still drying on the floor tiles. Both restrooms will be ready for business in a day or two, in plenty of time for your event. But for now, you can use the one up the stairs off the tasting room."

Chance held out a hand. "I'll take him."

"I want Jane," Josh said. He pulled her forward a couple of steps before she regained her balance.

"Buddy, it's not Jane's job to—"

"It's okay. I can take him." Jane led Josh to the staircase. "You finish up here with Jim. Be sure to ask about his rates. And Jim"—she paused and shot the owner a sweet smile—"remember, it's for a good cause."

Jim watched the two climb the stairs, his brows drawn together. "I'm donating a basket for the auction worth two hundred dollars. I'm happy to give you a good rate, but I can't just donate the space. I don't want you to think I'm not civic minded."

Smothering a grin, Chance nodded solemnly. Jane's comment had clearly put the poor man on the defensive. "Women. Nothing's ever enough." He clapped a hand on Jim's shoulder and peppered him with questions and compliments on the winery until the man's good humor was restored.

After shaking hands on the deal, he emailed Jeremy with the new location so the volunteer could update their website and notify the ticket holders of the different address. Then Chance went looking for Jane and his son. He found them outside playing bocce ball, smudges of dirt marking their cheeks. Jane tipped her head back and laughed at something his son said, sunlight reflecting off her hair.

Satisfaction pooled low in his gut. Seeing the two of them together just seemed... right. They looked so natural together, like they fit. Like they were family.

Rubbing a hand up and down the back of his head, Chance blew out a disgusted breath. Just because his marriage had failed didn't mean he should start seeing substitutes wherever he looked. Jane squatted, grabbed Josh around the waist, and promptly fell over onto her butt. Josh squealed, and Jane burst out laughing.

Chance strode over to them, wanting in on the fun. He couldn't help but think that Annette had never gotten dirty with their son. She wasn't a bad mother, gambling addiction aside, but she wasn't the kind of mother Chance wanted for his son, either. No sharing milk and cookies and stories after kindergarten for Annette.

"Hey. Who's winning?" he asked, taking Jane's hand and helping her to her feet.

"I am!" Josh picked up the hard ball and chucked it shot-put style. It bounced across the sand until it butted up against the lawn.

"I'm impressed, Josh," Jane said. She brushed sand off her pants. There was a line across her left butt cheek that she missed. Chance resisted the urge to help her out. "You can tell you're winning when we're not even keeping score."

Josh missed the sarcasm. "Yep." He ran after the ball and hurled it again.

"How do you play?" Chance asked.

Jane laughed. "Who knows? We were taking turns making up rules, but after Josh said the ball needed to bounce ten feet in the air before we rolled it, I decided that wasn't such a good idea." She pursed her lips. "That ball doesn't really bounce."

A smile pulled at his cheeks. "I love that you tried."

Josh lay on his stomach and pushed the ball along the court. Military crawling to catch up, he pushed it again. "Dad, can we get this?"

Chance sighed. "My son has become very materialistic. Anything he sees he wants me to buy."

"I'm sure that's normal." Jane brought a hand to her mouth to cover her laugh when Josh somersaulted, kicking sand up in the air, only to have it land on his face. He spit it out and kept rolling. "He certainly has a lot of energy."

"You have no idea." Looking at the rectangle of sand, Chance considered his own backyard. Unlike the roller coaster his son wanted to put in, a bocce court might fit. It might be fun. Plus, less grass to mow.

He would have to find out how to actually play the game. Until then, Chance took Jane's hand and walked over to his son. "Do I get to make up a rule?"

Chapter Eleven

"That has got to be the tastiest thing ever." Sharon licked her spoon clean, her eyes pinned to the large glass window of the Apothic Garden.

"The soup here is fantastic."

Sharon shot her a disgusted look. "I'm not talking about soup. I'm talking about that hoard of delicious half-naked men pounding away in your mother's store."

It hadn't taken much arm-twisting on Sharon's part to get Jane to take part in her reconnaissance mission. Spying on the men of Firehouse 10 was a hobby for the women of Pineville, and when her friend had heard the firemen were going to be hammering nails in her mother's store, well, it was on.

Behind her sunglasses, Jane darted a glance up and down the sidewalk. The pair sat under the umbrella of a sidewalk table at Soup's On, the hole-in-the-wall eatery next to her mom's store. Still no sign of her mother.

Jane tried to relax. She shouldn't be there. Her mom and the owner of Soup's On, Mr. Kane, had previously had some differences of opinion on Mr. Kane's contribution to the downtown society's beautification project. Or lack thereof. Every other business owner on Main Street had donated to the project. Her mother had decided to never patronize that "free rider's" restaurant again.

And she'd decided Jane should join the boycott. Jane lifted her spoon to her mouth and sighed, her stomach doing a happy dance. She'd missed the soup.

Fabulous food, a great show—two firemen held up a large section of sheetrock while a third hammered it to the studs—it was a perfect afternoon. If her mom didn't catch her supporting the enemy.

"Did you see that young one with the tattoo?" Sharon fanned herself with her hand. "Whoo boy. I wouldn't kick that one out of bed for eating crackers."

"Martinez? He's barely twenty." Jane swirled her spoon in her split pea. "Don't be that."

"What?"

"A cougar," Jane said. "There's nothing wrong with a little May-December romance, but Martinez is still a kid. Mentally anyway." She wrinkled her nose. "That's just not right."

"Cougars are in their forties." Sharon pinned her with a glare. "Do I look forty to you?"

Shaking her head, Jane kept her mouth shut. Opening it now could be dangerous.

Her friend returned her gaze to the construction crew. "For a shot at one of those guys, I might admit to being a bobcat, though."

Jane snorted. Sharon was beautiful, and any one of those guys would be lucky to spend time with her. She just didn't think her friend would appreciate a date of fast food and video games, something Jane knew from local gossip that Martinez specialized in.

"You need sunglasses," Jane said. "Behind them at least you could pretend that you aren't drooling over our firemen. This is downright embarrassing."

"Sunglasses mess up my hair," Sharon said, her focus never wavering. Jane discreetly glanced at said hair. The bangs were still cemented two inches straight up. Only a sledgehammer could mess up that hair.

"Besides," her friend continued, "I've noticed your eyes taking in the man scenery once or twice. Don't act so high-and-mighty."

Jane sipped at her tea. "I only peeked to see what progress is being made."

Sharon rolled her eyes. "So I guess you wouldn't be interested in knowing that a certain assistant fire chief just took his shirt off."

Whipping her head around, Jane zeroed in on Chance. He still wore a white tank top, but the Pendleton he'd discarded now hung off the back of a folding chair. The front of the tank top clung wetly to his chest, and when he turned and hefted a stack of plywood, *sweet Jesus*, his shoulders rippled and bunched.

Jane's spoon clattered to the table.

Sharon laughed. "Yeah, you're not interested at all."

Heat streaked up from Jane's chest until she thought she could fry an egg on her forehead. "That's not . . . I wasn't . . ."

"Uh-huh." Sharon picked up her cup of coffee. "Keep telling yourself that." She ignored Jane's frown. "I don't know why you're embarrassed to ogle that fine piece of meat. He's one of the tastiest of the bunch."

Jane shook her head. "What is it with you turning men into food? Tasty, delicious. Are you hungry? You should have ordered more than a cup of soup."

"My hips can't handle more than a cup of soup," Sharon grumbled. Pointing her spoon at Jane, she added, "And you're deflecting."

"Not deflecting." Jane settled back in her chair and adjusted her sunglasses. "Just not interested." She held up a hand. "I'm not saying I don't find Chance attractive. You'd have to be blind not to. But a lot of men are attractive. I can admire them aesthetically, and move on. Besides"—she twisted in her chair to face Sharon, a metal spoke in the back digging into her side—"I thought you were anti-Chance."

"That was before I got the full scoop." Catching the waiter's eye, her friend made the universal *check, please* hand gesture. "He's legally separated, just days from finalizing his divorce, and his soon-to-be-ex is Bitchzilla. That man could use a nice woman."

"How do you know she's Bitchzilla?"

Sharon peered into her empty soup cup and frowned. "She's gone into a couple of stores in Pineville. Let's just say the shopkeepers aren't fans."

"While that makes me feel sad for Josh, I'm not going to throw myself at his father as a sympathy prize." Reaching into her purse, Jane pulled out her wallet. "If you, *and my mom*, want to find Chance a nice second wife, look elsewhere."

Breaking open a packet of crackers, Sharon munched on one and shook her head. "I'm not talking about settling down with the hottie. But that man is remodeling your mom's store. On a valuable day off when he could be off doing something fun. He's practically offering himself up on a platter to you. You could do a heck of a lot more than *admire* him. You could get down and dirty, have some fun."

"That kind of fun leads to trouble."

"That's the best kind of fun." Crossing her legs, Sharon leaned back to enjoy the show.

Jane sipped her tea. Chance used to say that, too. But trouble with

Chance now wouldn't consist of getting caught trespassing at Old Man Riley's pond. Now if he caused her trouble, it meant a broken heart. She wasn't willing to risk that again.

So she was decided. Definitely not interested in her former boyfriend. Didn't mean she couldn't enjoy the show. Turning, she sat side by side with Sharon, tilting her head to avoid the beam of sunlight reflecting off the window.

Chief Finnegan held up a section of wall while Chance hammered nails down its side. Chance's biceps flexed enticingly, and a faint tan line told Jane he spent most of his days in T-shirts. Finnegan wiped a bandana across his forehead.

Jane leaned her head toward Sharon. "You know how you said Chance was helping with the store because of me?"

"Yeah. I just said it like five minutes ago. Of course I remember." She drained her coffee.

"Smartass," Jane muttered. "My point is, why is Chief Finnegan so involved in this? He organized his guys coming down here. We saw him order Martinez to take down a section of wall that wasn't hung perfectly straight. What's his motive?"

Sharon put her elbow on the table. "You think Finnegan wants you, too?"

"What?" Jane looked at the neighboring tables, hoping no one had heard. "Of course I don't think that. I'm talking about my mom. Do you think the chief likes her?"

"Oh." Her eyebrows drew together. "I don't think your mom is really the chief's type. She's a little more laid-back than he is. But who knows? Opposites can attract." She scooted to the edge of her chair. "Tattoo boy took his shirt off. Red alert. That boy's got some guns. And a six-pack. I think I'm in love."

Jane squinted. "How far down do you think that tattoo goes?"

Sharon just looked at her, eyebrows raised.

"Why don't I go get us some dessert?" Jane asked. "It could take us at least another hour to eat it."

Sharon grinned. "Who's drooling now?"

"So what do you think?" Chief Finnegan asked. "We added a trim of sage green that complements your wall color, but otherwise left everything how you had it. Now you just have a fresher coat of paint, and a safe building."

Edith and Jane were touring the restored Apothic Garden, having already inspected the apartment above. Everything looked sharp and clean and Jane was eager to start restocking the shelves. The sooner her mother was moved back in, the sooner Jane would have her apartment to herself.

"I already have too much green as it is, with all the herbs and plants I sell," her mother said. "The trim is a little much."

The chief crossed his arms over his wide chest. Jane stepped between the two. "It looks great. I think what my mom meant to say was 'thank you very much.' We both know how hard you and the guys worked, and we really appreciate it." Turning to face her mother, she pinned her with a stare. "Isn't that right, Mom?"

Edith sniffed. "It was kind of you to do the work."

Jane knew that was all the gratitude her mother was going to show. She still hadn't forgiven the firemen for kicking her out of her apartment, and the fact that the chief had supported Chance's decision hadn't endeared him to Edith.

Jane sighed. Whatever hopes she might have had for her mom and Chief Finnegan evaporated. Her mother seemed to turn up her nose when the man walked into a room, and any tender feelings the chief might have had couldn't survive such obvious disdain. It was a shame. The chief was one of the good guys, a steady influence someone like her mother could use.

"Well, it's safe for you to live in, if nothing else," he said. "As fire chief, that's my only concern."

"Is it safe for me to breathe in all these paint fumes?" Edith asked, tucking a lock of salt-and-pepper hair behind her ear. "Do you know how many chemicals go into one gallon of the poison you slapped on my walls?"

The knuckles curling around his biceps whitened. "You weren't using organic paint on your walls before, Edith. You survived that chemical attack just fine. You'll make it through my onslaught alive, as well."

"My onslaught" came out sounding like "me onsloot," and it took Jane a moment to interpret. Her mom must really be getting under the man's skin.

"It looks great, Chief. Really," Jane said.

He gave her a tired smile.

"It smells like paint," Edith said. "I can't live here or open to the public yet."

"I'll open some windows," Jane bit out. Putting action to words, she raced around the space opening every window she could reach, then took the stairs in the back two at a time and did the same for the apartment. When she came back down into the shop, it looked like her mother and the chief hadn't moved an inch in her absence. Or said a word to each other.

With a bright smile, Jane tried to ease the tension. "Well, that's all done. I'm sure by this evening it will be all aired out. And when we hang your lavender and burn some oils, it will smell great."

"At least someone has a plan," Edith muttered. The chief narrowed his eyes.

"Mom, didn't you say you had some things you wanted to pack up at my place?" Jane herded the two toward the front door. "Why don't you go do that and when you come back we'll get your store ready to open. It should only take us a couple of hours."

The chief blew out a sigh. "I'd offer to help you, but I have to get back to work."

"You've done enough, Chief." Jane locked the door, and turned to look up at the man. The sun made her eyes water. She flipped her sunglasses down from the top of her head onto her nose.

"More than enough," Edith said. Jane looked at her mother sharply, but the woman smiled sweetly.

"Miss Edith!"

The trio turned. Josh was running toward them down the sidewalk, dragging his father along behind, his small hand swallowed up by Chance's. "Hi, Miss Edith! And Jane. And Chief. Look, Dad, they're all here."

"I can see that." Chance smiled a hello at them, his gaze lingering on Jane's face. "Josh wanted to come by to see your place all fixed up, Edith. Maybe help you restock your inventory."

"Is that right?" The look she gave Chance said all wasn't forgiven, but when she turned to Josh, her face lit up. "That's real sweet of you. I bet you're a good helper."

"Uh-huh." His eyes widened, as if a thought had just struck him. "But not for cleaning. I'm not good at that."

Jane bit the inside of her cheek.

Shaking his head, Chance said, "You only have to clean up messes you make, Josh. Not the ones I do."

"So you admit you made a mess?" Edith asked. "That you should have handled this differently?"

"There are a lot of things I should have handled differently." Chance stared straight into Jane's eyes, and she was glad she wore her sunglasses. He could read her too well. She still didn't know what she was feeling around the man. She didn't want Chance figuring it out before she did. Before she could make a decision on those feelings.

"A lot of things," he continued. "But declaring your building uninhabitable until the wiring was fixed isn't one of them."

"Dad says he saved your life, but you're too stubborn to rec'nize that." Josh rolled up onto his toes. Jane didn't know whether he was proud of his dad or happy that he remembered some big words, but he was adorable just the same.

Edith didn't agree. "Did he now?" Steel laced her words, a warning to anyone with half a brain that it was time to back down and placate.

Chief Finnegan loosed a deep belly laugh.

Jane inched backwards. The man might be an expert at saving other people's lives, but he obviously didn't know how to protect his own. Her mom was an easygoing, live-and-let-live kind of woman—to a point. When pushed over a certain threshold of aggravation, one that teenage-Jane had tried many times to pinpoint, her mother changed from a peace-and-love flower child into the harpy from hell.

Chance tucked Josh into his side. "I said fixing your wiring *could* save your life." He frowned down at his son. "And you weren't supposed to be listening to that. I was talking to your Aunt Katie."

Jane squared her shoulders and leaned close to her mother. "Don't blow with Josh standing right here. He doesn't need to see you yelling at his father."

Edith patted Jane's cheek, a little harder than necessary. "Don't worry. I wouldn't waste my breath arguing with our fine fire department." Bending down so she was at eye level with Josh, she said, "I have to go right now, but come back later if you want a tour. There might even be a cookie or two in the cookie jar upstairs with your name on it."

Josh hopped up and down at that information. Chance grimaced. He must remember her mother's cookies. Jane shook her head. It was so sad to disillusion such a young boy that all cookies were not created equal. But everyone had to learn that lesson someday.

"Look!" Josh pointed across the street. "There's my friend Tony with his mom and dad and grandma and granddad." He looked from his father to Jane to Edith and the Chief. "Looks like us."

The adults all gaped, eyes wide like deer caught in headlights. "Not like us," Chance said quickly.

"Completely different situation," Finnegan said gruffly as Edith repeated, "Not like us."

Jane shook her head but kept her mouth shut. Something pinched behind her breastbone, and she rubbed her knuckle against it. Of course that happy family across the street was nothing like the motley group around her. But Jane saw what Josh did. Potential.

And that potential scared the crap out of her.

Chapter Twelve

Jane folded her umbrella and climbed into Chance's SUV. This was the last day of his three-off, and she was determined to collect all the outstanding auction items while he was around for the heavy lifting.

She wasn't surprised to see Josh in the backseat. On Chance's days off, he and Josh were practically attached at the hip. "Hi, Josh. How was school today?"

"Miley has chicken pox. Noah said she had big spots all over her face." He drew his brow down in a look that left no doubt that he was Chance's son. "Noah said 'cause I played with her I'll get it, too."

Jane reached back and felt his forehead as Chance slid behind the wheel. "Do you feel sick at all?"

He shook his head.

"And you're not hot. I'm sure you'll be fine."

" 'Kay." Josh went back to playing with his ninja turtle.

"Okay?" Chance flicked on the blinker. "When I told you you'd be fine, you didn't believe me. But Jane says it and you take it as the Bible's truth?" Shaking his head, he pinned a stern look on Josh through the rearview mirror. "Not cool."

Josh giggled. "Jane knows more than you."

"What?!"

"Have I ever told you how much I like your son?" Jane asked. "He's the smartest kid I know."

Chance shot her a dirty look.

"That's what momma says," Josh continued. "That girls know more than boys."

"Is that so?" Jane fought her smile. She wasn't a self-esteem expert, but that probably wasn't the best thing to tell a little boy. But considering the man she was sitting next to, Jane wanted to echo that sentiment wholeheartedly.

Chance scowled. Yep, he thought that fell under the heading of crap parenting, she could tell.

She tried to be diplomatic. "I think it depends on the girl and on the boy. Between your father and me, you're right, I know more. But I bet you know more than a lot of girls in your class."

Chance's eyes turned dark. She shifted away in her seat. Diplomacy wasn't her strong suit.

Pulling into the driveway of a split-level ranch house, Chance turned in his seat. "Well, tonight, just remember that Mrs. Harper knows more than you. You do what she says, and remember to say please and thank you."

"'Kay." Josh unsnapped his seat belt and wriggled from his seat. Chance picked up an overnight bag and led him to the front porch, giving him a big hug when a woman and young boy opened the doors. The boys bounded inside, and Chance and Mrs. Harper laughed about something.

Jogging to the SUV, Chance opened the door and got in. He stared at the house.

"Problem?"

"No." He turned the ignition but still didn't back out. "It's his first sleepover. He might get scared tonight in a strange house."

"Ah." She didn't have many friends with children. She didn't know if she should tell him not to worry or sympathize. "He can always call if he has a problem, right?"

"Yeah." Looking over his shoulder, he backed into the street. "He'll be fine. So where to first?"

"There are four shops on Main that are donating items, and two more on Thurgood and King." She consulted her list. "Why don't we start on Main?"

"Got it." Chance turned on the radio, and they drove in companionable silence for the five minutes it took to reach downtown. Parking in front of the address, he looked at the pink awning with the words Glam and Glow written in elaborate italics. "What's this?"

"A spa. You can stay here. I'm just picking up a gift certificate."

He looked relieved not to have to go into the feminine store, a haven for Pineville's women. And some men, too. It wasn't everywhere you could get a massage, wax, facial, and haircut.

Jane hurried back out ten minutes later. "Sorry. Janine's chatty. Also, I set up an appointment for the morning of the ball." Looking at her list, she chewed on her lower lip. "My mom's store is up next."

"Okay." Chance pulled into the street. "So. You're going to get all girlied up for the ball?"

That *sounded* like a casual question, but Jane wasn't buying it. "Yeah. Why?"

"No reason." He tapped his thumbs on the steering wheel. "I've been meaning to talk to you about that."

Jane shifted her butt on the upholstered seat, turning to face him. "About what? My personal grooming habits before a ball?"

"What? No." He cleared his throat. "I was just thinking that since we're the cochairs and we're both going alone, it would make sense for us to go together." He blew out a breath, as if that was a weight off his shoulders.

"I'm not going alone."

"So if you want, I can pick you up at—" He snapped his head around. "Wait. What?"

"I'm going with Leon." Crossing her arms over her chest, she narrowed her gaze. "And it's a little insulting that you'd assume I didn't have a date."

"Leon." Chance spat out the name like it was Bozo the Clown. They approached a stop sign and he stomped on the brake harder than necessary. "But it's not game night. Whatever will Leon find to entertain himself?"

"Don't mock him. He's a nice guy who just happens to like games." He'd given her a giant book of sudoku puzzles for Valentine's Day. "Okay, he *really* likes games. But Leon and I have been dating for a while now"—*Jesus, did Chance just growl?*—"and when we decided to hold the ball, of course I asked Leon to go with me."

"Of course." A muscle throbbed in his jaw.

"Hey." She grabbed his arm. "You're driving past my mom's place. Stop up here." She tapped her small notebook against her thigh. "Although I wouldn't mind having to pick up her donation another day." Or not at all.

"Why do you sound like that? You two get in a fight?"

Jane rolled her eyes. "What am I, ten? No, we didn't get in a fight.

I'm just worried about her contribution to the auction. She's donating a gift certificate for a free feng shui consultation, and I don't think anyone in Pineville cares about that sort of thing."

"Yeah." He shot her a sympathetic smile. "Can you convince her to give away some of that smelly stuff she sells? I think people would like that better. I know I enjoy the way you smell with her stuff."

She didn't quite know where to go with that one, so she remained silent. Did he prefer the aromatherapy oils to her normal perfume? Did she smell and he was encouraging her to cover it up with layers of oil? And why was she being so defensive? First the spa question and now this.

"Um. She's really excited about the feng shui consultation." She pressed herself against the door and took a sniff. She wasn't wearing any oil today. All she smelled was soap, and she sighed, relieved.

Chance waited for a car to pull out of a diagonal parking spot near her mom's store. "I'm sure someone will want it. If for no other reason than to help out the charity."

Resting her fingers on the door handle, Jane hesitated before climbing out of the SUV. "Can you bid on it? You know, if no one else does? I can't do it because she'll know I have no interest in feng shui and only bid because no one else would. But you just moved into a new house. If you say you don't like the layout of the furniture, she'll buy that. I'll pay you back."

"Of course I'll bid on it. And no, you won't pay me back." He opened his door. "Now let's go in. I want to say hi to your mom."

Jane's shoulders relaxed, and she followed him in. Even her mother's pointed looks between her and Chance couldn't darken her mood. She took the gift certificate, kissed her mom on the cheek, and left the store, her heart so light it felt like it was floating.

For the first time in a long time, maybe since her dad died, she felt like someone had her back. Her mom loved her, but her support came more in the form of burnt sage cleansings instead of solid action. Her father would have gone to the mat for her, and she missed having that. The only other person in her life that she'd known would fight for her was Chance.

A part of her said that she was an idiot, that Chance had only been good at appearing to care. When the chips were down, he'd hurt her more than anyone. But having him back in her life, as a friend, was like being wrapped in a favorite blanket. She was tired of denying herself that comfort.

"What the hell is that?" Chance asked. They were at their last stop, a home furnishings store with an eclectic mix of boho chic and country casual. He toed the cast-iron sculpture and cocked his head.

Jane elbowed him in the side. "Shh. Mr. Cranston might hear you." Waving at the old man behind the register, she said out of the corner of her mouth, "His son's an artist. He made this. Just smile, tell him thank you, and let's get it out of here."

Following orders, Chance stretched his lips across his face. He spoke through gritted teeth. "Why are we talking like ventriloquists? Mr. Cranston is as deaf as a bat. He can't hear us."

Speaking normally, she bent and grabbed one side of the sculpture. She assumed it was a concept piece, because the five waving tentacles curling out from an oblong mass looked like nothing Jane was familiar with. Maybe a stylized sun? "Let's just get this into the SUV."

With a grunt, Chance hefted the sculpture, taking most of the weight. The iron was smooth beneath Jane's fingers, and she had to keep switching her grip to keep hold of it.

Chance pressed the sculpture between his thigh and the side of the SUV and reached for the keys in his back pocket. "Just a sec and I'll get the back door . . . hold up, wait . . . son of a—!" Chance loosed a torrent of curse words, hopping up and down on one foot.

Squatting beside the fallen artwork, she ran her hands along its side. "Thank God. I didn't dent it."

"You dented my foot!" Leaning against the side of his car, Chance cradled his left foot and glared at her.

"Big baby," she muttered.

"What was that?" He put his injured foot down, took two limping steps toward her. He must have been trying to look intimidating, but he was about as terrifying as Boris Karloff's mummy, dragging his leg behind him. At least he was putting some weight on his foot. It couldn't be broken.

"If you wore grown-up shoes instead of those loafers, this wouldn't be a problem."

Squatting next to her, Chance lifted the flap on his canvas sneakers. "I see blood!"

For a firefighter, the alarm in his voice was a little sad. She rolled her eyes. Men could be such whiners. "Look, we're not far from my apartment. Let's go and I'll patch you up." She put her hands under the sculpture. "Get that side and—"

He brushed her hands away. "I'll get it. Just open the door for me."

She wasn't going to argue if he wanted to break his back instead of hers. After he settled the piece in the back, she held out her hand. "Keys. I'll drive. What with your horrible injury and all."

His eyes narrowed and she could almost see the wheels turning in his head. He didn't want her driving him around for some stupid reason only known to men, but he also didn't want to let go of the righteous indignation that limping around on an injured foot could give. He smacked the keys into her palm and hobbled around the hood to the passenger's side, playing it up, she was sure.

She didn't object, however, when Chance tossed an arm around her shoulders and leaned on her going up the stairs to her apartment. His muscles were hard beneath his thin T-shirt, and when they pressed against her, heat swept through her body. Who had ripped muscles in their side? What were those muscles even called? Lats?

"Here we go." Jane kicked open the door, sighing when an orange blur streaked into the bedroom. Cy had yet to warm to Chance. Pushing Chance onto the couch, she picked up his left leg, his calf muscle firm and warm even through the denim. She dropped it on the coffee table.

"Gentle," he warned.

She ignored that and strode to the bathroom for the first aid kit. Taking a look at her flushed face in the mirror, she wet a hand towel and placed it on the back of her neck. How young could early menopause set in? Surely that was a more logical explanation than her getting all hot and bothered over his leg. And his side, she reminded herself. The side of his chest had pressed against her breast, which was, she had to admit, more action than she'd seen in over a year.

She threw the washcloth into the sink with a wet smack. Wasn't that just frigging pathetic?

"Did you get lost? I'm bleeding out here," he bellowed from the living room.

Pulling the plastic kit from under the sink, she huffed out a disgusted breath. It was a good thing he was a whiny baby or else she'd be on him like fudge sauce on ice cream. She walked back into the living room. Chance leaned back on the couch, his hands linked behind his head, exposing a strip of tan midsection and a trail of dark hair that disappeared into his jeans.

A sexy, whiny baby.

She squared her shoulders and sat on the coffee table. Her knees encased his uninjured leg, and she widened her legs so as not to brush against him.

Chance had taken off his loafer, and she examined his foot. An inch-long stretch of skin was scraped, but only a quarter of that scratch was deep enough to draw blood. A thin trickle ran down the arch of his foot.

"Wow. I think you'll need stitches. Do you feel light-headed?"

He narrowed his eyes. "Smartass. Are you going to use those Band-Aids before I bleed on your table?"

Tearing open an antibacterial towelette, Jane dabbed at his foot. God help her, even his feet were sexy. Long and narrow, with neatly trimmed toenails.

She bent over to blow the area dry. Raising his foot, he placed it on her upper thigh. A lazy smile curled his lips. "So you don't have to bend down so far."

He brushed his other leg against the inside of her thigh, and Jane bit back a moan. Running through the list of names she'd called him over the years—dipshit, heartbreaker, asswipe—she wanted to remember just why this man was off-limits. It was like that saying: Fool me once, shame on you, fool me twice . . .

Chance shifted, his heel digging into the crease where her leg met her torso. His eyes were glued to her tank top. Jane had a sinking feeling she knew why. She risked a glance down. Yep. Her arousal was on full display. It really was shame on her.

But she didn't feel shame. Judging by the heat in his stare, Chance was just as affected as she was. She held just as much power over him as he did over her. Was it so wrong to let herself want him?

She was older now, didn't equate sex with love like her teenage self. He was older now, a father. It wasn't possible he could still be so immature.

Curling his toes into her abdomen, Chance brought his gaze to meet hers. His eyes were heavy, dark. The air between them thickened, each breath she took a struggle to suck into her lungs.

"Chance," she whispered. It came out a question. A wish. Above anything else, it was a plea that he not hurt her again.

Not breaking her gaze, he dropped his foot to the floor.

"I didn't put a Band-Aid on it yet." Jane leaned forward.

"Don't care."

A slow smile stretched across her face. "Don't you want me to kiss it and make it better?"

A growl erupted from deep in his chest. He sat forward on the couch, leaned in until his face was a hairsbreadth away from hers. "Baby, other areas need your attention first."

Chapter Thirteen

Her stomach clenched. She was in so much trouble. Chance closed the distance and pressed his lips to hers. He nibbled at her bottom lip, and her eyes closed in pleasure.

Trouble made life a lot more fun. He'd shown her that in high school. She was more than happy to let him reteach her that lesson.

Opening her mouth, she let him in. His tongue tangled with hers, then scraped over the roof of her mouth, sending a shiver straight down her back. Threading his fingers into her hair, he tilted her head to the angle he wanted. His fingers dug into her scalp, like he was scared she'd disappear if he didn't hang on tight.

Tentatively, Jane placed her palms on his chest. God, he felt good. She ran her hands to his shoulders, feeling the definition of his muscles, reveled when they shuddered in response to her caress. His shirt was soft, thin. She hated it. Even that small barrier was too much, standing between her and what she wanted. She dragged her hands down, and fumbled for the hem. She'd just inched her fingers underneath, felt his searing flesh, when he grabbed her around the waist and lifted her off the table to settle in a straddle over his lap.

Her hands were pinned between their bodies, unable to explore, and she moaned in protest. When he moved his hips, she stopped complaining. This was a much better position.

Holding her firmly in place, Chance deserted her mouth, using that talented tongue to trace the rim of her ear instead. Bliss arced through her body. She tugged her hands free and tucked her hair behind her ear, giving him full access. His teeth tugged, his tongue lashed, and his hot breath blew soothingly over the abused flesh.

She was ready to come, and he hadn't even gotten to the good bits yet.

Digging her fingers into his hair, she scraped her nails up and down the back of his neck. His moan told her he still liked that. It was strange, being in his arms again. She had come to know Chance's body better than her own, he was that familiar. But the years had wrought changes on his frame, and she had a lot of territory to relearn.

She paused. The years had made a difference on her body, too. She was softer in areas, sagged a bit more in others. Would the adult Chance like what he saw?

"Wherever you just went," he murmured against her neck, "come back."

"Huh?"

"I can practically hear those gears turning in your head." He bit into the tendon above her collarbone. "If you're thinking about the fundraiser, your job, or how big an asshole I was a decade ago, I want you to stop." He sucked at the hollow of her throat, then lifted his head to stare into her eyes. "All I want you thinking about is how good I'm going to make you feel."

She melted into him. He might have guessed wrong about where her thoughts had wandered, but his remedy was spot-on. She wasn't going to miss a second of the joy he could bring her by worrying about how she looked. She was going all in, and she was going to love every minute.

Just as soon as she rid herself of her last concern. "Chance? I want . . . oh God that feels good . . . I want to make sure we're on the same page."

Sucking at the tender skin of her throat, he curved his hands around her butt. "I'm positive we are," he murmured.

Letting her head fall back, Jane stared at the ceiling, her gaze unfocused. "You're still not divorced and I'm not looking for serious." Serious with Chance had the potential of leaving her seriously hurt. "So we're just having some fun here, right?"

Chance lifted his head. "If that's what you want."

What she wanted was for Chance to get on with it. He was going to kill her with foreplay. His hands hadn't stopped moving, his fingers gliding lower and lower around her butt until—

Okay, no more talking. She whipped off her tank top, smiling at the slackening of his jaw, the heat in his eyes as they took their fill. Wrapping her arms around him, Jane reclaimed his mouth with her own. She supped on his lips, fed him kiss after kiss, until even being plastered chest to chest, hip to hip, was no longer enough.

Gripping the hem of his shirt, she tugged it up, scratching his stomach in her haste. She leaned back, needing to catch her breath, wanting to examine the skin she'd exposed. She ran her fingertips over his chest, the muscles hard beneath her touch, the light matting of hair soft as baby's down.

"You're beautiful," she said.

His cheeks flushed. "You don't say that to a guy. Call me sexy or hot or something. You're the one who's beautiful."

Flicking her thumbs over the flat discs of his nipples, she trailed a row of kisses down his chest. "You are hot and sexy. But that's not what I want to call you."

His chest heaved beneath her mouth. "Baby, you keep doing that, you can call me anything you want."

Lips curving, she trailed lower.

"Changed my mind." He threaded his hands in her hair and tugged her head back. "Go any lower and I'm going to blow. Need you now."

He rolled, taking her with him until her back pressed into the couch cushions. Kneeling above her, Chance attacked her pants. His fingers fumbled. "Why are there so many buttons?"

"They're sailor pants," she explained. "Two rows of . . . hey!"

"Well, that's one less," he muttered, tugging at the fabric again.

She put her hands over his. "I'll get mine, you get yours. Deal?" She liked those pants. She didn't want to spend her evening sewing buttons back on.

Chance grinned and climbed to his feet. "Deal." His hands flew to his fly. "But leave your underwear on. Those are mine to take off. I've been fantasizing about peeling your panties down your long legs for a couple of weeks."

"Have you now?" Jane shimmied out of her pants. Resting her head against the arm of the couch, she bit back a moan at the view in front of her. Six foot two inches of packed muscle. After nine years, he seemed bigger. Everywhere.

Settling on top of her, Chance nuzzled the crook of her neck. He scraped his teeth where her neck met her shoulder. "You taste good. You always did. Like my grandma's Christmas spice cookies."

Jane hadn't heard that before. "Like her pfeffernuss?"

"I don't remember the name." He traced the swell of her breasts with his tongue. "I just remember the taste. Just like you."

Arching, she tried to increase the contact. She was burning up from the inside out, as if she had a pool of molten iron at her core. Her lace bra chafed against the tips of her breasts.

It also chafed Chance's chest. He groaned, the sound low, guttural. "I hope you're ready, baby. It's been too damn many years, and I can't wait a minute more."

Not bothering with the hooks, Chance slid his thumbs under her bra and pulled it off over her head. Her panties joined the bra on the floor. Prowling over her, he took her mouth in a deep kiss.

"Tell me that Band-Aid box has condoms in it."

"No, it doesn't have condoms," she said. "It's a first aid kit, not a booty-call pack."

He swore. "If we don't take care of this soon, I'm going to need some first aid."

"Bathroom." She pushed at his shoulders. "In the cabinet behind the mirror."

His lips bruised hers, took her breath away. "Too far." He stilled. "Wait. My sister."

Jane's hands stopped roaming across his back. "What? Be careful what you say next. It could be a mood killer."

Reaching for his jeans, he tugged out his wallet. "Katie gave me a celebration condom when my legal separation came through. She's a little twisted that way. I put it in my wallet and forgot about it."

Jane helped him sheath himself. "Thank God for twisted sisters."

He laughed, and it was like a bottle of fizzy champagne burst in her chest. She remembered this. How much fun she could have in bed. She'd never laughed with another partner the way she had with Chance.

And then the time for laughing was over. His gaze turned scorching, every inch of her skin that it touched coming alive. His lips tugged at her own as he settled between her thighs. Pressing in, he swallowed her gasp.

The stretch felt so good. He filled her like no other man. Opening her thighs wider, she lifted her hips, drew him all the way in. It was a perfect moment. Chance buried deep, his warm body a comforting weight. "Heaven," he whispered in her ear.

Her heart soared, and she needed some way to keep herself grounded. *This is Chance, the man who broke your heart. Don't make more out of this than it is.* The reminder didn't work. That stupid organ still leapt around like a deranged rabbit in her chest.

His body moved over hers, lighting up all her nerve endings. She had no problem living in the moment, accepting just the physical pleasure he gave her. But a little part of her whispered, *This is Chance. The man you thought you'd be with forever.*

It was easier than she'd thought it would be telling that part of herself to shut up. The man above her had learned a lot between the sheets, and she melted around him. Chance 2.0 was a new and improved lover. He made it easy to separate the moment from her memories.

But when he grabbed her hips and moaned, "I missed you," she believed him.

Chance knew he had a lot to make up to Jane for, and he intended to start repaying his debt one orgasm at a time. But it was hard to keep his head in the game. His hips had a mind of their own, and sweat rolled down his back at the restraint it took to keep from pounding away to a quick finish.

So much had changed. He'd changed, and so had Jane. This wasn't the awkward fumblings of two teenagers.

She'd been his first. Chance had thought he'd understood the mysteries of the universe after that first time he'd been with a woman. Cocky-ass punk that he'd been. But so much time had passed that this should have felt like a first time with a new woman.

But it felt like coming home.

Shifting his hips, he slowed down and took her lips. He couldn't get enough of them. They parted so sweetly for him, accepted what he gave her. He tangled his tongue with hers, swallowed up her breathy moans. When she lifted her hips, tried to speed things up, he resisted and slowed down even further.

It was killing him. She was killing him. But it was the sweetest death he could imagine.

"Please." She tugged his head away from her mouth. "Please."

A drop of his sweat fell to her collarbone, and he licked it away. "Please what, baby?"

"Faster. Now." Her eyes were closed and a flush swept every part of her body that he could see. He reared back onto his knees. And he could see a lot.

"Not yet." Jesus, how many times had he thought of Jane, what he'd left behind, the warm slide of her body against his? Now that he was actually here, like hell he'd rush it.

She scraped her nails down his spine, his body instinctively arching away from each delicious inch she clawed. His eyelids drooped. Patience. He didn't know whether the advice was for himself or for Jane. Curling his hands into fists beside her head, he grasped for control. He was on the razor's edge, but this was Jane, and he was going to make it great.

She moved, did something with her body that had his eyes rolling back in his head. Any idea of control evaporated like water from a garden hose on a five-alarm fire.

His body bucked, pistoned. Mindless, he threaded his fingers in her hair and held tight, his body seeking its release. The throaty little mewling noises Jane made in his ear told Chance that she was right there with him. His muscles coiled tighter and tighter, his breathing became labored. His body screamed with need.

Wait, wait, wait, he chanted to himself. Wait for his Janey-girl. She threw her head back and moaned. For a split-second of time, Chance's world stopped. He wanted to frame this moment, capture her bliss as she came apart in his arms. Mouth open, eyes closed, she was a picture of beauty. Her abandon was stunning, and it humbled him.

But his body wouldn't wait. The pressure grew too great. With a roar, he tipped over the edge and joined her in surrender.

Chapter Fourteen

"This. Is. Awesome." Wonder filled the young photography student's voice as she looked at the group of firemen huddled in the corner of the station. She leaned over to Jane. "I almost feel like I should pay you for this." *This* being taking shots of ten of the station's hottest bachelors. "Almost."

Jane smiled wryly. The teacher at the community college swore Sammie was his top student and would have no problem providing professional quality head shots for the fundraiser's website. The girl didn't dress to impress, wearing stretchy yoga pants and flip-flops. Hopefully she could make the bachelors look better put together than she did.

Which shouldn't be difficult. Jane turned toward the men who stood joking around with each other as they waited to be photographed. They rippled with muscles, their blue T-shirts, with the Pineville FD logo over their left breast, stretched taut. Every lovely shade of skin was represented, from vanilla to mocha to dark chocolate. Pineville FD was the twenty-one flavors of masculinity. It was enough to give a woman heartburn.

Jane sought her favorite flavor and found Chance near the back of the group. He was nodding his head at something the chief said. When he'd learned that Chief Finnegan was going to be one of the bachelors up for auction, as a show of solidarity, Chance had agreed to be sold off as well. A sacrifice he'd been reminding Jane of for the past two days.

"Okay, guys. Let's get this show going." She pointed to the photographer. "Sammie has set up a backdrop for the shots and I'll call you forward one at a time. Hopefully we'll be done and out of your hair shortly."

The chief stepped forward. "Until the next call comes in, we're all yours."

"Great," Jane said. "And since you've come forward, why don't you go first."

Chief Finnegan didn't look thrilled, but moved into place in front of the draped blue sheet, stoic.

Sammie stepped behind her camera. "Okay, I'm not shooting you with a gun, just taking your picture. Try not to look like a martyr."

He bared his teeth.

"Oookay." Sammie stepped back. "Imagine I'm a little kid that you're rescuing. You don't want to scare me. Give me the smile you'd give the kid."

With some more prodding, the chief relaxed, his smile becoming easy. For a man his age, he really was quite good-looking. And definitely fit. With his soft brogue and burly good looks, women were probably lined up to date him, but Jane hadn't heard of any relationships. In a small town like Pineville, that meant he was either very discreet or had been living like a monk.

Jane pursed her lips. It really was a pity he wasn't her mother's type. Her mom deserved a good man in her life.

The chief twisted to the right and back, posing at Sammie's commands. The guys hooted, but kept their trash-talking to a minimum, something Jane was sure had more to do with the power the chief wielded to make them pull KP duty rather than any sense of decorum.

The next firefighter up was in his early twenties. When he got in front of the camera, he whipped his shirt off and flexed his pecs.

Sammie pressed the shutter without aiming, an involuntary reflex, her mouth open wide. "That's . . . wow. I mean, yeah, hold that pose."

Jane stepped forward amid the catcalls. "Frankie, that's not the look we're going for. We're doing head shots."

Sammie glared at her. "You wanna make money on your auction? That's the look you want. Trust me." Before Jane could tell her no, Sammie clicked away, while Frankie preened like a peacock.

Jane rocked back on her heels. The girl was probably right. If that . . . *Holy hell, what sort of muscles in your butt do that?* Jane licked her lip. Yeah, if that didn't get the ladies of Pineville to whip out their checkbooks, nothing would. So she sat back and enjoyed the show. Each young buck tried to outdo the other, one even going so far as to flip into a handstand. Topless, of course.

"Like what you see?"

Jane jumped. Chance stood behind her, arms crossed, face tight.

"Um, no, of course not. They're all hideous." Her gaze was dragged to a firefighter who'd donned his turnout pants and was snapping the suspenders against his chest. Topless.

Putting a finger under her chin, Chance drew her face back to his. "It's only been two days since we were together and you're already looking at other men. I think I'm insulted." The edges of his eyes crinkled, telling Jane he was teasing. Mostly.

"Two days is a long time, especially considering you won't be going off shift for another two. A girl's memory can only stretch so far." She ran a hand over his abdomen, then snatched it back before anyone saw. "I *think* I liked what was under here. But the memories are fading away."

He narrowed his eyes. "Janey-girl, it sounds like you need a reminder." Grasping the neck of his shirt, he dragged it up and over his head.

Her breath stuck in her throat. "Crap. I really had forgotten. I'd convinced myself there was no way you could actually look this good."

"And that's not even the best part." He pressed his shirt into her hands. "When my shift ends, you'll be getting a refresher course, have no worries."

Frankie paused, his flirtation with Sammie momentarily forgotten. "Whoo-hoo, look at the new assistant chief. I thought everyone from California was supposed to be tan and fit. What happened to you?"

Jane almost objected. Sure, Chance wasn't as dark as Frankie's natural olive skin tone, but his golden flesh had obviously been kissed by the sun. But it would be stupid to defend him from a little light razzing. That would start the gossip up, and by noon, everyone in Pineville would know she and Chance were sleeping together.

Chance walked to the backdrop, throwing his shoulder into Frankie along the way. "Didn't your mama teach you to respect your elders? Now, step aside and let me show you how it's done."

That drew a rousing chorus of boos.

Unlike the over-the-top muscleman poses the other firemen had flaunted, Chance stood naturally, hands in his pockets, a panty-melting smile on his face. Topless. A trickle of sweat wended its way down Jane's spine. The rest of the firefighters faded from view.

She didn't like to think of herself as shallow. Looks were fleeting; character was what mattered. Chance turned his body to the side, caught her looking at him, winked. She blew out a shaky breath. But even if Chance had been the devil himself, she didn't know if she could have resisted all that. She hoped she would.

Following Sammie's instructions, Chance crossed his arms across his bare chest, his pecs bunching. Jane bit back a whimper. Nope, she would have been toast.

Sammie thanked him, and Chance swaggered back toward her, his gaze trained on her face, pinning her in place. She shoved his shirt at him. Jane was seconds away from dragging him behind the fire engine. He needed to cover up, stat.

Trying to keep her voice casual, she told him, "I think that photo shoot went well. The auction will be a big hit."

He whipped the shirt over his head, smoothed it down his flat stomach. Bending close, he said, "Are you going to bid on me?"

She chuckled. Now that he was fully clothed again, the laugh sounded mostly normal. "I'm organizing the auction, not participating in it. That would be too cliché, even for me." Finding a stray thread on her red sweater, Jane plucked it off, kept her eyes lowered. She found the concept of a bachelor auction embarrassing, and if it hadn't been for the statistics she'd read about top moneymakers for fundraisers, she never would have agreed to the idea. But deep inside, the idea of buying Chance for the evening, marking him as hers, sent a thrill racing through her bones.

She wasn't proud of it, but there it was.

Clearing her throat, she changed the subject. "The bachelor auction needs to raise a lot of money. Judge Nichols was telling me this morning that we're a couple items shy on the silent auction end of the fundraiser. The hot air balloon company that was going to donate a free ride changed their mind, and a couple other items fell through."

He frowned. "Can't we get replacements?"

"Of course we'll try. But the economy isn't great and businesses have a hard time giving away their goods." Making her way to the backdrop, she started taking down the draping. "And time is running short."

Chance reached over her head, unsnapping the fabric from the pipe it hung on. "I'll make the rounds in town, see if I can get something." He smiled down at her. "Women seem to like firemen wearing their blues. Maybe I'll get lucky."

Jane narrowed her eyes.

"Getting donations," he hastily added. He took one edge of the sheet, Jane the other, and they folded the ends together, meeting in the middle. Eyes crinkling at the corners, he said, "Really. Jane, you need to get your mind out of the gutter."

He was too tall for the noogie she used to give him when they'd first become friends, so she punched him in the arm. "I'm not the one who just put on a striptease."

His lips brushed her ear. "You can put one on for me anytime."

"Just grab the lights." She shook her head and managed to keep the smile off her face.

"Jane." He shifted on his feet, a floodlight balanced on one shoulder. "What color dress are you wearing to the ball? I, uh, thought I might get a matching pocket square."

His flushed cheeks would have been adorable if Jane hadn't been so confused. "Why would we go to the ball as a matching couple? I think Leon would feel weird about that."

"Leon?" He dropped the light with a clang on the cement floor. "What the hell does he have to do with it?"

Jane frowned. "What do you mean, what does he have to do with it? He's my date. He won't want me matching some other guy."

"You're still going with that moron?" His growl cut through the bay like a chainsaw. Sammie's and Frankie's heads whipped around to stare at them.

Jane pasted a smile on her face. "Sammie, I'm sure you can get Frankie and the other guys to help you carry your equipment to your car." Grabbing Chance's wrist, she dragged him away from the crowd onto the driveway of the fire station. "What is your problem?" she hissed. "We already had this conversation. I told you I was going with Leon. And he's not a moron."

"That was before." He stepped into her space.

She tilted her head, looked up. "Before what?"

"Before we slept together." Running a hand up and down the back of his head, Chance huffed out a breath. "That changed things. You can't go out with another man."

Can't? Jane planted her legs wide, her muscles quivering. "So what would you have me do? It's less than a week until the ball. I'm supposed to tell Leon—*Sorry, find someone else to go with, I found someone new*?"

"Yes." He jutted his jaw out. "Besides, he probably doesn't even want to go. A silent auction doesn't have the same thrill as Jumanji, or whatever the hell it is he likes to play. Tell him there aren't any games there and he'll be happy enough to stay home." His brows drew together. "You're not still going out to game nights with him, right?"

"Uh . . ."

"Are you?"

"Honestly, I haven't even thought about game night." Jane blew out a breath. "But do you really think it's fair to Leon to break a pre-existing date because you and I are . . . ?" She flicked a hand between the two of them.

"Yes." Mules had nothing on his stubbornness.

"Well, I don't." She crossed her arms over her chest. "I'm not breaking the date to the ball with him."

"And what about game nights?"

"You know those aren't real dates." Teenage Chance hadn't been so demanding. This new Chance was starting to tick her off. "You saw that Leon and I are nothing more than friends, so I don't know what your problem is."

"My problem"—he stepped in so close his toes touched hers—"is that I don't share. I'm not saying I know where we're going, but while we're going there, I expect us to be exclusive. I'm not going to date someone who's seeing someone else. Even if that someone is an asexual tool."

"And I'm not breaking a date I made months ago. It would be rude."

He smiled, but there was nothing friendly about it. "You want to see rude, how's this."

And he turned on his heel and walked away without another word.

* * *

For the eighth time that afternoon, Chance grabbed the waist of his son's pants and pulled him back down from the rock wall in Washington Park. It was day one of a three-off, and he and Josh had spent it together. First an early lunch, then the latest Disney movie, and now what should have been a relaxing afternoon in the park.

If his son didn't keep risking life and limb trying to scale the twenty-foot-high climbing wall. It was meant to be attempted using rappelling gear.

"I told you. When the man with the climbing gear isn't here, you can only climb as high as I stand. You try to go higher one more time, and we're done here." His son loved to push his limits. A quality he admired in adults, but one that scared the hell out of him when it came to his child.

"But Dad," Josh whined. "I'm a good climber. I can go all the way to the top."

"Maybe you can"—Chance raised an eyebrow, pinned his son with his stern-father look—"but you won't. I'm the grown-up. My rules."

Josh heaved a dramatic sigh. Squinting, he cocked his head and looked Chance up and down. "You're really tall. Much bigger than Joey's dad." Joey was Josh's new best friend. Chance didn't know why he'd worried about moving his son across the country. Kids adapted quickly.

"You're as tall as that one, right there." Josh pointed to a blue plastic handhold at least ten feet higher than Chance's eye level. "I can climb to that one, right?"

"Nice try." He knocked his knuckles on a green knob about six feet off the ground. "No higher than this."

"Fine." Josh stuck his fat bottom lip out, a move he could only have learned from his mother. It looked a hell of a lot cuter on a five-year-old.

Chance settled onto a bench where he could keep an eye on Josh. After about thirty seconds, he could tell that Josh had gotten over his sulk, determination and joy writ all over his face. If only adults got over their temper tantrums as easily as kids.

One adult in particular.

Jane wasn't answering his calls or responding to his texts. As if she were the offended party and not him. Okay, maybe he could see her point about not ditching the bailiff after they'd already set up the date to the ball. Maybe. He bet that if he laid it out to Leon that things had changed between Jane and Chance since she'd made the date, the guy would be fine stepping aside.

Yeah, for all his stupid game playing, Leon seemed like a reasonable man. He'd be cool with it. Jane's reaction, if Chance interfered, wouldn't be so cool. Somewhere along the way, his sweet and quiet little Jane had turned into a hothead. A quality he could appreciate when it wasn't directed at him.

Chance rolled his shoulders. Why was he making himself nuts over Jane? Since he'd moved to Pineville, he'd had one night in her bed. Just one. Hardly a lifelong commitment. The way the mother sitting on an opposite park bench was eyeing him, Chance knew he was attractive to women. He had options. If Jane was too bullheaded to agree to even the simplest of requests, he could look elsewhere.

His chest tightened. She could look elsewhere, too.

Josh had reached the green knob. With a glance over his shoulder, his son prodded the red wedge-shaped handhold above it with a grimy finger. Chance stared him down. Blowing out a dramatic breath, Josh reached for the knob to his right instead.

Rubbing a knuckle over his breastbone, Chance sighed. Yeah, he could look elsewhere. But he didn't want to. He wanted Jane.

A shuffling noise was his only warning. A cane slapped his shin, and Chance bent over to rub his leg, a frown covering his face when he turned to Mr. Harraday. The older man eased into a squat over the bench, kicked out his legs and plopped onto the seat next to Chance.

"What're you doing here watching the kiddies?" Harraday asked, massaging his knee. "You one of them pervs?"

Chance gritted his teeth. "That boy over there is my son." He pointed. "I'm not a pervert. But if that's the only reason you can think why a man would be in a park, what, exactly, are you doing here?"

"My daughter dropped me off while she runs errands." Squinting one eye, Harraday nodded at Josh. "Your boy looks squirrely. I wouldn't trust him to deliver my paper."

A kernel of heat popped open in Chance's gut. What the hell did he mean Josh looked squirrely? Who even used that word anymore?

"It's a good thing Josh isn't a paperboy then." Chance leaned against the bench's arm rail, distancing himself from Harraday as much as possible. "I don't think kids even get those jobs anymore. Adults do it."

Harraday snorted. "That's what's wrong with the world today. Everything's changing. Jobs that kids used to get, adults with college degrees take. And kids try to act like parents to their own moms and dads." Laying one blue-veined hand on the bench between them, Harraday leaned close. "Like my daughter. She thinks she knows what's best for me. Trying to kick me out of my own house!"

Josh streaked across the playground, ignoring a group of kids huddled at the slides, to swing on the monkey bars by himself. Shouldn't he be interacting with the other children? Aside from Joey, had his son made any other friends? Blowing out a sigh, he turned back to Harraday. "I'm sure she's just worried about you," he said.

"Worried about me?" Harraday poked at the air with his cane. "Worried about her inheritance, more like. Always cleaning up my house, trying to see what I'll leave for her."

"Or maybe she just wants her father to live in a clean home." Chance took a deep breath. Whoever this man's daughter was, she must be a saint to put up with his crap. Chance had only spent five minutes with the man and already wanted to wrap his cane around his chicken-like neck.

Ignoring Chance's comment, Harraday rambled on. "And now she keeps pressing me to sell the house, move in with her." He slapped Chance in the shoulder. "Do I look like I want to live in Ann Arbor with my daughter's hoity-toity husband and her hoity-toity kids?"

A girl with uneven pigtails raced up to Josh, showed him something in her hand, and they skipped over to the swings. Chance took a deep breath. Good. His son wasn't a social outcast. His shoulder stung from another slap.

"Are you listening?" Harraday asked.

"Unfortunately, I heard every word." Pushing his sunglasses onto his head, Chance stared at the old man. "You're bitching that you have a daughter nice enough to open her house to a grumpy old man when she could put you in a home instead. She's cleaning for you, running errands for you, and all you're doing is complaining. Did I get that right?"

Harraday gaped at him like a guppy. Finally, he pinched his lips tight. "You don't know what you're talking about." Pointing a bent finger at Josh, he said, "Just wait until your boy starts telling you how to live your life, takes your keys away, starts making decisions for you. This ain't no damn walk in the park."

Chance closed his eyes, blew out a breath. He was being an idiot, letting the old man get to him. So what if Harraday was rude. Getting old must be hell.

Chance looked at Harraday, trying to keep the pity out of his expression. "All I'm saying is that it sounds like your daughter cares about you, which is more than a lot of other people in your situation have. You shouldn't be so hard on her."

Pushing his lower set of false teeth forward, then snapping them back with a clack, Harraday stared at the children. "She's a good girl," he admitted grudgingly. "Although she wasted the college education I paid for, quitting her job when she had her first baby." Happier now that he had another complaint to add to the list, Harraday settled into the bench seat. "Foolish, if you ask me. When those kids grow up, she won't have an easy time getting another job."

Harraday narrowed his watery eyes. "What do you do? Out here in the middle of the day, I bet you're an unemployed grifter. That woman you were with when you broke into my backyard, she your wife? You let her make the money while you watch the kid?"

The idea of Jane as his wife wasn't as shocking as he expected. Not even fully free of the shackles of his first unhappy marriage, he'd thought it would be a long time before he'd want to jump back into that institution. But with Jane . . .

Her sweet smile drifted across his memory.

Eventually he might take the plunge again. With the right woman. But he couldn't let the second part of the old man's harangue go unchallenged. "I wouldn't let a woman support me. I'm fully employed, as a firefighter. And Jane isn't my wife." Chance rubbed a knuckle on his breastbone.

"A fireman." For the first time since Chance had met Harraday, the old man looked interested instead of angry. He leaned in toward Chance. "I thought about being a fireman when I was young. All the ladies love a fireman."

"The saving lives part is fun, too," Chance said dryly.

Harraday waved a dismissive hand. "Yeah, that's all fine and good. Hey." He lowered his voice as if imparting state secrets. "You got one of those dogs that rides with you? You know, them black and white numbers."

"No, no Dalmatian. Although one of the guys sometimes brings in his standard poodle." Chance watched Josh shuffle his feet through the sand pit, and sighed. He'd need a hose-down before getting in the SUV.

"A poodle?" Disgust dripped from Harraday's words. "Well, at least you still get to ride in the fire truck. You do still have that, right? You're not strapping those hoses to the top of some Prius, are you?"

"Still have the trucks." Chance's stomach rumbled. Movie popcorn just didn't tide you over. "Still have an axe and climb up the ladders, too."

Harraday nodded. "Well, at least there's that." Whipping his head around, he watched a faded blue Acura pull into the parking lot. "My girl's here. I bet she got that smelly thing that sprays lilac blossoms at me whenever I walk past. I told her not to."

"Yeah, she sounds like a monster." Chance put his hand under the man's elbow, helped him rise to his feet. "Be nice to your daughter. She might be family, but she doesn't have to put up with your crap."

"Yeah, yeah." Harraday hobbled off, moving with surprising speed for a man with a cane. He'd have to keep himself spry to set the sprinklers off on unsuspecting do-gooders without getting wet himself.

Chance waved at Josh, tapped his watch.

Josh jumped off a swing, his arms and legs pinwheeling wildly before landing on the ground in a crouch. He raced up to Chance. "Can we come back when the wall man is here? So I can climb high?"

"You bet, buddy." Chance took his hand, the feel of his son's small, warm grip making Chance feel content. He headed for his SUV. "Maybe I can set up some time for you on the rappelling wall at our training facility. We can ride in a fire truck over there. It can be like junior firefighter day."

"Can I wear the hat, too?" Josh's body wiggled in excitement.

His son loved acting like a fireman. He thought about Harraday. It wasn't just his son. Everyone, from young to old, dreamt of riding in that truck, fighting fires. Chance paused, his key fob aimed at his vehicle. Mind whirling, he settled Josh into the child seat, a plan formulating. The fundraiser needed more silent auction items. He was pretty sure he could get the chief's okay on his idea. And the guys would be happy to help.

Settling behind the wheel, Chance nodded his head. It could work. But he wanted to tell Jane about it first, get her opinion.

If only the blasted woman would call him back.

Chance looked in the rearview mirror at his son. A smile crept across his face. The woman might not want to see him, but she should know by now a person doesn't always get what she wants. Throwing the SUV in reverse, he headed toward the courthouse. He didn't even mind when Josh asked for his phone and blasted the teenybopper music he inexplicably liked, going so far as humming along with the insipid tunes.

Much as her eyes might threaten it, Jane couldn't cut off his balls and feed them to him if he had his son with him. Nope, she'd feel obliged to be polite, sweet even, in front of the boy. Reason number 882,000 why he was thankful he had a son.

"You want to have dinner with Jane?" Chance asked.

"Yeah!" Josh threw a small fist in the air as he bopped to the music. "Can we go to the Pizza Pit?"

A place where a kid could run around for hours playing games, leaving adults to talk. Good choice. Still. "We'll have to ask Jane. She'll be our guest and it will be her choice."

Chance found a spot near the ivy-covered two-story brick courthouse. Across the street in the town square, a weekly farmer's market was in full swing. He was torn between taking Josh across the street to look for some flowers for Jane and staying put in direct view of the exit. He didn't want to chance missing her, so he and Josh staked out the entrance.

They didn't have to wait long. At 5:32, Jane and that friend of hers from the bowling alley, the woman with the startlingly high hair, exited the building, having a laugh at something together.

So Jane wasn't as torn up over their fight as he'd been imagining. He grunted. He didn't want her crying in her cornflakes, but a little gravity would be appreciated. Holding Josh's hand tightly in his own, he approached the women. To be fair, it was more of a disagreement than a fight. And the happier she was now, the easier it should be to convince her to have dinner with them.

"Jane," he called. The two women stopped. Jane narrowed her eyes. The other woman pursed her lips in a silent whistle. Stopping in front of them, Chance tugged Josh closer. "Hi, Jane." He nodded to her friend. "Josh and I were hoping to take you out to dinner. Your friend is welcome of course."

Remembering her manners, Jane said, "This is Sharon. She and I work together. Sharon, this is Chance and Josh." Squatting down to Josh's level, she held out a fist. "How you doing, Josh?"

"Good." He bumped her fist with his own. "We're going to the Pizza Pit. You'll love it."

Chance frowned at his son. Not exactly the polite choice his son should have given her.

"Well, as delicious as that sounds," Sharon said dryly, "I have other plans. But thanks for the invite."

Chance fought to hide his relief. Not that he didn't want to meet Jane's friends. Just not tonight. "Another time." He held his hand out to the woman. "It was nice to meet you."

"Same here." She gave Jane a quick hug, whispered something in her ear. Jane frowned at Chance over her friend's shoulder. Sharon pulled back. "See you later."

The three stood in silence for a minute. Jane didn't look angry, not really, but she also didn't look easy in his company. She shifted on her feet.

"How've you—"

"What have you—"

They spoke at the same time, then relaxed into chuckles.

"How have you been?" Chance asked. "I wanted to talk to you about"—he glanced down at Josh—"the firehouse. And apologize."

"Me too." She tucked a wisp of hair behind her ear. "I, uh, wanted to tell you that I talked to Leon. I told him I can't go to game nights with him anymore."

Chance nodded. A pressure he hadn't even realized was on his chest eased, and he took a full breath. "So what do you say to dinner? It doesn't have to be pizza, but I'd love for you to join us. And I have an idea for an auction item I'd like to discuss with you."

Josh pulled at Chance's hand. "Jane likes pizza. Don't you?" he asked her.

"Well, of course—"

"See!" He grabbed her hand, too. "It's all settled."

Jane's eyes crinkled at the edges. She held Chance's gaze above Josh's head, a smile dancing around her lips. "I guess it's all settled."

Josh led them to the SUV, practically pushing Jane into the passenger's seat before clambering into the back.

"He takes pizza very seriously," Chance explained. He really would have to talk with his son about manners.

"Pizza is important," she agreed. "You do it right, and it's got all the food groups together in one slice."

"Yeah," his son agreed. "All six food groups."

Chance shook his head, got behind the wheel. The Pizza Pit was across town, by the highway, and Chance sketched out his idea for the auction item to Jane on the way.

"Your training wall is what, four stories high?" Jane asked when he'd finished.

"Eight."

"And you want to strap someone into a thin fabric harness and tell them to go out a window at eight stories high and climb down the side of a building?" She shook her head, eyes wide. "And you expect someone to pay for this near-death experience?"

Chance smiled. "The training exercises are a hell of a lot of fun. But that's just a part of it. I think we should promote it as a day as a firefighter. We'll show the winner around, demonstrate all the equipment, let him slide down the pole, ride in the truck, and experience some of the training we have to go through. Not only will people pay for that, but it's a great way to raise awareness of what firefighters do."

Chance swung into the parking lot. "In fact, I think we could open this item up to a group of winners. Maybe the top five bidders can get a day as a Pineville firefighter."

She still looked skeptical.

"And we'll barbecue them a nice lunch."

She opened her door. "Well, I know you guys can cook, that's for sure."

Chance unstrapped his son and joined her in front of the car. He narrowed his eyes. "Which of the guys has cooked for you? Did you date one of my men?"

She gave him a little smile and took Josh's hand. They walked ahead into the restaurant. Chance couldn't complain at being left behind. She was wearing those jeans again, the dark blue ones that hugged her every curve, and the view from behind was fantastic. The high-heeled ankle boots she wore gave her steps a little more strut than usual.

Chance swallowed, his mouth suddenly dry. He did some quick calculations. He usually read a story to Josh at around eight thirty, bed by nine. After that, he could spend hours with Jane and still be home before Josh woke up at six. Thank God his sister lived with him.

Crap. His sister. He sent off a text telling her that he and Josh were going out to dinner and not to wait for them, then followed Jane and his son into the building. Inside, it was chaos. Kids screaming, bells on the game machines ringing, and a loud thumping beat coming from invisible speakers.

Jane was digging in her purse. She gave his son a handful of quarters. "Have fun," she told him. "We'll order the pizza and . . ." But he was already gone.

Chance slung an arm around her shoulders. "Don't worry. He'll find us when the pizza comes. He has an amazing ability to know just when we get served." They walked to the order line. "You still like pepperoni with bell peppers and onions?"

"Yeah." She snuggled into his side, and his chest ballooned. "I guess my tastes haven't changed much since high school."

His pulse pounded in time to the music. Chance hoped she was right. Because *he'd* been to her taste in high school, and the more time he spent with Jane, the more he wanted to.

His back pocket buzzed. He pulled out his phone and read the text from his sister. Frowned.

"What's wrong?" Jane asked.

"Nothing. My sister says she has plans tonight, too."

"And that's a problem because . . . ?"

"No problem. She deserves to go out more. Have fun." He stepped up to the register and placed their order. Looking for an empty table, he led Jane through the crowd. It kept gnawing at him. "But she doesn't know anyone here," he burst out. "Just her doctor. And if she's going out with that married sixty-year-old, there's going to be a problem."

Jane wrapped her arm around his waist and squeezed. "Katie is young, friendly, and attractive. I'm sure she's met lots of people since you moved here. Even as a kid, she had a good head on her shoulders. Don't worry so much."

He snorted. "That person with a good head on her shoulders passed out a couple of weeks ago because she couldn't be bothered to test her blood-sugar levels." His shoulders tensed. "Maybe she should go out with the pervy doctor. At least he'd keep her from eating a hot fudge sundae."

Jane pulled him onto the bench seat next to her. She rubbed her hand on his thigh. She meant the gesture to be soothing, he was sure, but it had the opposite effect on him. And since they were in a pizza parlor surrounded by children where he couldn't do anything about it, he rested his hand over hers and held it tight.

"Katie's an adult," she said. "You can help her and give her support, but ultimately the choices she makes are her own. It sounds like this is all new for her. I'm sure it's a hard adjustment to make." Resting her head on his shoulder, she sighed. "When you're in your early twenties, you think you're invincible. She found out her body isn't indestructible. That's rough."

Her hair tickled his cheek. Her shorter hairstyle suited the woman she'd become, spunky and sexy. He breathed in the vanilla scent of her shampoo.

"How old were you when your dad died?" he asked.

"About Katie's age."

He pressed a kiss to her hair. "I'm sorry, baby. He was a good man. Always treated me fairly." His lips tilted up. "Considering what I was doing to his little girl, he treated me better than I deserved."

She laughed, and the sound lightened his heart.

A teenage waiter placed a pitcher of cola on the table with three glasses, then came back with the pizza. Right on cue, Josh raced up to the table. He crawled onto the seat next to Chance. With Jane on his right and his son at his left, Chance was pretty much exactly where he wanted to be.

"Can I have some pop?" Josh asked.

Chance raised an eyebrow.

"Pleease?"

He set his son up, and made sure Jane's glass was full. "Dig in, everyone."

Jane ate a couple of bites. "Chance, this idea you have for a firefighter's day. Don't you think the liability will be too big? What if someone gets hurt?"

"No one's going to get hurt. We have lots of safety measures.

And we won't be simulating a burning building." He nudged her with his elbow. "Just because you obviously aren't interested in my job," he teased, "doesn't mean other people aren't. People love this stuff."

"Dad's going to let me climb the building," Josh added.

Jane's eyes rounded in horror.

"See? I wouldn't let my son do it if it wasn't safe." He reached for another slice. "Tell you what. I'll show you what I have planned. If you still don't think it's safe, and you have legitimate reasons for your concern, we won't do it. Deal?"

She eyed him warily. "What all will this demonstration entail?"

He grinned. "You'll find out."

Meal finished, Josh scooted off the bench. "Jane! Jane! You have to come do dance move with me."

"Dance move?"

"It's a game," Chance said. "You have to copy the dance moves on the screen in front of you."

"I'm not much of a dancer." Jane shook her head. "I don't think I'd be good at it."

Josh batted his eyes. "Pleease?"

Chance stood, pulling Jane up with him. "He said the magic word, Jane. You can't refuse him now. What kind of lesson would he learn?"

She narrowed her eyes, a cute little growl escaping her lips. Turning a sweet smile to Josh, she held out her hand. "Let's go, kiddo. Just don't expect too much from me."

Chance maneuvered himself into a good location to view the fun. No way was he going to miss Jane bouncing up and down. Just to make sure she had plenty of time to shake her stuff, he slid a five into the machine. That should give them several games.

He wasn't disappointed. The cotton shirt she wore did little to hide the slide of her breasts as she hopped from one foot to the other. And when the screen showed her a move to turn to one side and wiggle her ass, Chance's whole body hummed.

She watched the screen with a singular focus, intent on following each move exactly. After two games, Josh left the raised platform, his chest heaving and feet dragging. Jane was just getting started.

A young girl who looked about ten joined Jane on the floor. She gave a flip to her long brown hair. "I have the high score on this game," she said.

"Really." Jane pulled off her ankle boots and tossed them to Chance. "Let's see what you've got."

Chance laid a hand on Josh's shoulder. Leaning down, he said, "I think you've created a monster."

Chapter Fifteen

"Is he asleep?" Jane asked.

"Yes." Chance propped the screen door open with his shin, snuck an arm out, and pulled her into his body. "And you don't need to whisper. He sleeps like a rock."

"Then why are you whispering, too?"

Grinning, he bent his head down until their mouths were millimeters apart. "Peer pressure?" His breath danced across her lips.

She rested a hand on his pec. It twitched beneath the thin cotton tee. "You never succumbed to peer pressure." Jane, on the other hand, had fallen for whatever line Chance had thrown her way. A smile, a raised eyebrow, and she'd been wrapped around his little finger.

"Must be succumbing to something else then." Closing the distance, he kissed the corner of her mouth, nibbled on her bottom lip.

"Katie—"

"Isn't home. Her car's not here and she texted me not to wait up. Now stop talking, woman."

Jane sighed and sank into his hold. She tipped her head back, and Chance obliged her unspoken request, moving his mouth to her throat. "Chance?"

"Hmm?" His mouth vibrated against her skin, and she smiled.

"What are we doing?"

Raising his head, he looked down at her, his dark eyes glittering from the porch light. "Well, if you can't tell, I must be doing something wrong." He tugged her inside, let the screen door snick shut. "And I'm tired of giving the neighbors a show. Let's go upstairs and I'll show you, in great detail, what we're doing." He kicked the front door closed and advanced on Jane.

The heat in his eyes just about melted her into a puddle, but this had been weighing on Jane's mind for a while and she wanted some sort of answer. She held up a hand, and he walked right into it, pinning her hand to his chest under his own broad palm. "I'm serious, Chance. I know I said I didn't want anything too serious, and I still don't"—*liar*—"but I also don't want to be your post-divorce hookup. I have to live in this town, and I don't want to be embarrassed."

He dropped his hand. "Why would you say that? Why would you even think that?"

Jane wrapped her arms around her waist. "We're just getting to know each other again. You've lived a whole life without me. I'm not sure what's going through your head."

"And I embarrassed you once before, right?" A layer of granite lay under his words. "This is still about that damned card."

Jane blinked, her eyes burning. "You left me like I was nothing. You obviously meant more to me than I did to you. I don't want to make the same mistake twice."

He moved so fast Jane would have jumped back if Chance's arms hadn't wound around her, pulled her close. "Don't ever think that you didn't mean the world to me. You were my best friend, Jane. I loved you." Pulling back, he gripped the back of her neck, forced her to look him in the eye. "But the love of an eighteen-year-old isn't worth a whole hell of a lot. At least not this eighteen-year-old. I wanted to experience everything, and I didn't think I could do that if I was settled down with the girl that I'd known since I was fourteen."

"I believe you." She cupped his cheek, his day-old stubble scratching her palm. "That still doesn't take away the hurt. I would have followed you anywhere. But that was just me being foolish. You always were smarter."

"Bull." Resting his forehead against hers, Chance closed his eyes. "Can't we just agree that we were on different wavelengths back then? We needed different things. But we're both older and hopefully wiser. I will never intentionally embarrass or hurt you."

It was the intentional part that was a sticking point for Jane. Yes, Chance was older and wouldn't pull the same teenage crap he had before. But he had his own life, a career, and a son that he had to look out for. He'd cut her out of his world if she interfered with any of those three. He might not want to, but he could still rip her heart in two.

Something had changed for her at dinner that night. Playing with Josh, eating as part of their family, a shift had occurred. She'd never spent much time around children, and now she felt like she'd been missing out. Josh had become special to her.

No matter how she might fight it, she wanted the McGovern boys.

And there was no way in hell she could let Chance know.

So she kissed him, ending the conversation. It started out sweet, she and Chance trying to reassure each other. He kept his lips soft as he ran his hands down her back to the curve right above her bottom. Clenching his fists, he dug his fingers into her shirt, pulling it tight across her stomach, making Jane feel that he was desperate to hold on to her.

She didn't care if it wasn't true. Thoughts of the future evaporated from her mind like mist in the morning light. Chance was in her arms now, and that's all her body cared about. Hopes and regrets were for the morning.

Wrapping one arm around his neck, she threaded her other in his hair, deepening the kiss. She plunged her tongue into his mouth, felt his dance across hers. A shiver raced down her spine as he took control, explored every corner of her mouth, and nipped at her bottom lip with his teeth.

Jane whimpered. His chest was rock hard beneath her achy breasts, and he smelled of soap, pizza, and man. It felt like his hands were everywhere. He possessed her entirely, and it had never felt so good to lose herself.

He smoothed his hands down her backside, lifted her up against him until she had no choice but to wrap her legs around his waist. Taking the stairs two at a time, Chance sucked her earlobe into his hot mouth.

"Oh shit." Jane's body was an exposed wire.

"Shh," he whispered in her ear. "Josh is just down the hall."

There was no way she'd make it to his room.

"Then don't do that," she moaned as he pressed her against the wall inside his bedroom door, every part of him lining up perfectly with her.

"What?" He rocked his hips into her. "That?"

Coherent words were beyond her. She took his mouth again, only releasing it to pull his T-shirt and her top over their heads. "Bed. Now."

"Yes, ma'am."

He laid her down over the soft comforter as if she were as fragile as a piece of crystal, and she blinked back tears. He kissed her, softly, sweetly, all down her body as he dragged her pants and underwear off her legs. She could barely gasp past the lump that sat heavy in the base of her throat. Every action screamed that he was making love to her.

The soft brush of his fingertips across her stomach spoke of tenderness. The drag of his nose from her collarbone up her neck, his sigh as he inhaled her scent, expressed his desire for her in a way no words ever could. Unless she was reading him all wrong, Chance was as crazy about her as she was about him.

Please don't be reading this wrong.

Reaching under the bed, he pulled out a small box and placed it on the duvet before shucking his pants. He settled himself over her, face to face. Tracing a path from her temple to her chin with his index finger, Chance never took his eyes off hers.

She could drown in those eyes. Already she found it hard to breathe, each inhalation ragged, shaky. She knew he must feel the rapid pounding of her heart, because she could feel his, the strong beat steady against her breast.

The urgency of the front porch had disappeared. Chance seemed to have all the time in the world. He nuzzled her neck, sucked at the patch of skin below her ear, and scraped his teeth down to that sensitive spot where her neck met her shoulder.

His bite was light, but Jane felt the possession straight to her core. "Oh God," she whispered.

His lips curved against her skin. If he wasn't making her feel so good, she would have chewed him out for smiling at her weakness. It wasn't fair. On this bed, she was completely at his mercy.

He continued his path down, nibbling here, licking there. His tongue was lethal, his lips sinful. He found a particularly sensitive spot, sucked, and her eyes rolled back in her head.

Clenching his hair in her fists, she begged. "Sweet Jesus, please. Please, Chance."

He ignored her pleas. He'd taken that children's story about the tortoise and the hare too much to heart. But his slow and steady wasn't going to win any races, it was going to kill her. When her eyesight had grown dim except for the flickering splashes of light dancing across her retinas, when her lungs burned with the strain of sucking down air, finally, finally he reared up, taking mercy on her.

Sheathing himself, he settled into the cradle of her hips. He tugged her hands from his hair and threaded his fingers with hers, pressing them down beside her head. "Jane . . ." A furrow appeared between his eyebrows.

Terrified of what he might say, knowing it could destroy her, Jane lifted her head and closed her mouth over his. She thought he might pull away; Chance was never one to be silenced. But his mouth was hot and eager. He devoured her, pressing her head down until she was pinned between the pillow and Chance's lips. He only let up on his oral assault when he gave a soft grunt and pushed his way into her body.

Her core softened, allowed him deep, until they were hip to hip. His gaze held hers, his eyes as hot as paper when it catches fire, the brown edges turning darker until Jane only saw black. She was on fire with him, her body melting like wax, her skin so heated she thought she'd combust.

She wanted to touch him, feel the slick muscles of his back, but he held her hands firm. She could do nothing but accept him. Accept his pace, accept his control, accept his love.

So she did. She stopped worrying about how much she might mean to him, stopped wondering if he'd end up hurting her, and reveled in the feeling of being cherished. As he rocked into her and the heat grew, so did the intimacy. She'd never felt this close to anyone before, not even the eighteen-year-old Chance.

The world around them faded, and Jane hoped Josh was as good a sleeper as his father promised. Because she didn't think she could keep quiet. Chance brought too much feeling up in her, a flood of emotions that she couldn't suppress. They needed an outlet. The peak he drove her toward was like a seething caldera, waiting to erupt.

Lowering his head, he covered her mouth with his. The kiss was slow, deep, a sweet contrast to the determined pistoning of his hips. She couldn't contain the cry that tore from her throat.

He swallowed down the sound, never breaking their kiss even as her screams turned to whimpers. He stayed with her, devouring her mouth until he reached his own completion, rasped out his own muttered curses, groaned deeply.

Chance executed a neat roll, pulling her to rest on top of his heaving chest. Sweat slicked his flesh, and Jane traced the curve of his pec, the ridges of his abdomen as she came down from her own high. She was wrung out, physically and emotionally, as if she'd just finished her first marathon.

Only Chance could do that to her.

He slid his hand around the curve of her bottom, and squeezed. "Janey-girl, that was . . ."

"Yeah."

They listened to each other breathe for a minute.

"Chance?"

"Hmm?"

She wrinkled her nose. "You keep your condoms under your bed?"

His rumbling chest jostled her. "You don't like that decorating style?" he asked. "Don't worry. It's temporary until I get a bedside table."

She looked around his room for the first time. Aside from the bed, no other furniture dented the thick carpet. Half-packed boxes littered the room, a small television perched precariously on top of an upended cardboard box.

"I made sure to get Josh's room and the rest of the house organized, but I let my own room slide. I didn't think anyone would see it." Wrapping his arms around her waist, he hugged her close, and breathed deeply. "I'll get it put together soon."

The front door banged shut. Jane tensed. Her escape route just became more complicated. "Katie's home."

" 'Bout damn time," Chance muttered.

"How late does she usually go to sleep?" Jane asked. "I know she's an adult, but she's still your little sister and I'd prefer to avoid her on my way out of your bed."

He trailed his fingers up her spine, eliciting a shiver from her sated body. "She can be a real night owl. But she likes to sleep in late. Probably be better if you stayed until morning."

"How convenient," Jane said.

"Isn't it though?"

"Well"—she pushed up to her elbows and stared down at him—

"if I'm stuck here for the night, you'd better make it worth my while."

A wicked smile curled his lips. "Trust me. Tonight is going to be worth both our whiles."

He rolled, lightning quick, and proved just how right he was.

Chapter Sixteen

Jane heard a sound in the living room, a shuffle, and she changed course from the front door and darted into the kitchen. Her fingers were wrapped around the back-door handle when Katie called out from behind her, “Morning, Janey-girl.”

Cursing under her breath, Jane turned, shoulders hunched under her ears. “Good morning. You know I only let Chance call me that. Please don’t say it again.”

Katie’s grin only widened. “It’s five a.m. and you’re sneaking out of Chance’s house. It’s like déjà vu.”

Jane’s shoulders sagged. She hoped Katie was wrong. Jane didn’t want to repeat old patterns, not when she knew the outcome. When she’d woken that morning in Chance’s arms, it had felt perfect, like she’d found her own piece of heaven.

And that had made her nervous as hell.

When she couldn’t calm the horde of butterflies fighting a cage match in her stomach, she’d eased out of his bed and made her escape. Or tried to.

“I’m not sneaking,” Jane said, holding her head high. “I just didn’t want to wake anyone up. Especially Josh.” Kids were great. Not only was Josh a lot of fun, but he made a handy excuse for her bad behavior.

“Uh-huh.” Katie raised a mug to her mouth. The sweet aroma of brewed coffee teased Jane’s nose, and she tried not to drool. She darted a glance at the half-full coffeepot on the counter. Did she want a cup, or did she want to get out of the house more?

Cocking a hip against the counter, Katie crossed one slim ankle over the other. “So what exactly is going on between you and my brother? A quick bang for old times' sake? Or are you picking up where you left off?"

Jane's spine snapped straight. She bit back what she wanted to say, that Katie should watch her damn mouth. The woman had probably been twelve years old last time Jane had seen her, and the impish smile and turned-up nose still reminded her of that little girl. Instead, with as much reserve as she could infuse in her words, she said, "That's really not your business."

"I disagree." Katie sipped her coffee, her dark eyes staring at Jane over the cup's rim. "Chance is my brother and he's been through a lot lately. And as you pointed out, Josh is now involved. They're my family and I protect what's mine. So if you're messing with Chance out of some perverse idea of revenge, I'm going to find out about it. And that wouldn't go well for you."

Jane gaped. She didn't know which surprised her more. The fierceness in little Katie's voice. Who obviously wasn't so little anymore. Or the idea that she could hurt Chance. The implied threat she ignored.

"You think I'm sleeping with your brother as an act of revenge? That's kind of a weird way to go about it."

"Not really." Katie placed the mug on the counter. "It's what I would do. Make the man who left me fall in love with me, then dump him so he knows how it feels." Crossing her arms over her chest, she pinned Jane with a glare. "I'd understand if you wanted that. I'll rip your spine out and clean my teeth with it if you hurt either Chance or Josh, but I get it."

Jane blinked. She used to play Strawberry Shortcake with Chance's sister. She didn't remember her being so bloodthirsty.

"I'm not here working some plot for revenge, so take it down a notch, would you?" Jane shook her head. "You must scare the hell out of men. I bet none of them mess with you."

Turning her back, Katie washed out her mug in the sink, but not before Jane saw a flicker of pain on her face.

Jane stepped forward, tentatively put a hand on Katie's shoulder. "I'm sorry. I didn't mean it like that. I just meant that you're strong, and a man would have to be an idiot to toy with you."

"It's okay. Men *are* afraid of me."

"Why do you say that?" Jane asked.

Katie shrugged.

"What, do you slap them around? Sit on their backs and hold their faces in a puddle of mud?"

Smiling, Katie turned around. "That was awesome. Chance sulked for weeks."

"He didn't talk to me for months." Jane leaned against the counter. "For the record, I did that before we started dating. He and Jason Toombey were laughing about seeing up Mary Jo Hannover's skirt when she fell on the tennis court, and it ticked me off. He deserved it."

"He did deserve it." Katie narrowed her eyes. "Carter deserves worse."

"Who's Carter? Is he the reason you're awake at this ungodly hour?" Jane didn't want to think about what Chance would do if some man hurt his baby sister. She was pretty sure blood would flow.

Katie ducked her head. "I wasn't feeling well," she mumbled. "I had to come down and eat a piece of fruit."

"Did you test your glucose levels?"

"Yes." Heaving a sigh, Katie rolled her eyes. "Before and after the apple. I'm fine now." She hunched her shoulders. "I can take care of myself. I don't need you, or Chance, or Carter"—she spit his name out—"telling me how to live."

Ah. Now they were getting to it. "Carter's the man you were out with last night?"

Katie nodded.

"And he doesn't like some of your lifestyle choices?"

"Lifestyle choices." Katie snorted. "As if I have choices anymore. He told me, told *me*, that I was tired and that it was time to go home. Even after I said I was fine." Picking up a sponge, she scrubbed viciously at the counter. "So I told him fine, but I wasn't going home with him. Not ever again."

Jane cocked her head. "And a couple of hours later you were sick. Maybe he saw something you didn't."

"I know my body better than anyone," she said hotly.

"And most guys your age would believe that. Would have agreed just to keep spending time with you." Jane plucked the sponge from her hand, tossed it in the sink. "It sounds like Carter really cares about you."

Katie chewed on her lip.

"And it definitely sounds like he isn't scared of you," Jane added.

"No." Katie was silent a moment. "He's the first guy who didn't get all bug-eyed when I told him about what me and my girls did to the one and only boyfriend who cheated on me." She shot Jane a look. "That's sort of a test I have for guys. It lets them know that if they treat me badly, I'll make them pay. But Carter . . ." Worrying the hem of her shirt between her fingers, Katie sighed. "Carter just smiled and took my hand and walked me to his car."

"You really like this guy."

"Do you think I was too hard on him?" Katie asked.

Jane shrugged. "Only you can know that. But if you got mad because he was concerned about your well-being, then, yeah, probably. It's okay to let someone else take care of you."

The ceiling above them creaked, as if two large feet had just plopped onto the floor above.

Digging in her pocket, Jane made sure she had her keys. "Well, gotta go. Don't want to be late for work."

Katie arched an eyebrow. "Your shift starts this early?"

"Well, I have to shower and eat and all that." Jane took a backward step toward the door, reached behind her for the handle, and grabbed air. "By the time I get my coffee, I'll practically be late." Cool metal finally met her hand, and the tight vise around her lungs eased the smallest bit. She didn't want to face Chance right now, have him plop a casual kiss on her cheek, like they might be nothing more than friends with benefits.

She couldn't take that, not after last night.

"We've got coffee here," Katie said. "Chance will be down for his morning cup any minute now."

"Josh—"

"Sleeps till seven." The edges of Katie's lips tilted, making her look every bit as mischievous as Josh. Jane's heart squeezed. The resemblance among the family was uncanny.

A foot landed at the top of the stairs.

Jane pulled the door open. "Cyclops needs me. My cat," she explained, backing out. "He gets grumpy when I don't feed him on time. I'll see you around, Katie." She fled, praying Chance wouldn't see her through the windows as she circled his house and ran for her car.

The man had her all knotted up. Feeling high on love one minute and terrified the next. Sliding behind the steering wheel, she rested a hand on her stomach. He was going to give her an ulcer. She put the car in drive and fishtailed onto the street.

Rolling her shoulders, Jane slowed down and forced herself to take deep breaths. She glanced in the rearview mirror, half expecting to see Chance running after her car. Of course, he wasn't.

She'd made it out of his house without having to talk with him. She should be relieved. Slumping in the seat, she leaned against the headrest. Relief wasn't what she felt. Shame was more like it. She was acting like a coward. A fool. She'd just spent a wonderful evening with Chance and run away the next morning.

She had no right giving Katie any dating advice. The woman she needed to work on was herself.

Jane listened with half an ear to her mother's chatter over lunch. They were at the Pantry noshing on items from Allison Stuart's proposed catering menu. That was definitely one of the better perks of organizing the fundraiser. The café was packed, the little bell above the door dinging every couple of minutes. A girl next to her at the counter slurped at the remains of her strawberry shake, trying to lift the cherry at the bottom of the large glass with suction power.

She should have invited Chance to join them, wasn't quite sure why she hadn't. The past couple hours had given Jane some perspective. She'd texted an apology to Chance for rushing out that morning, and promised herself that she'd stop being so scared.

Chance was in her life again, and everything was good. Memories of last night drifted through her mind. Life was very good.

The amazing food also helped buoy her mood. The spicy orange glaze that coated her chicken skewer was delicious. She licked a dab off her lip. Imagined licking it off of Chance's rock-hard stomach. Or his biceps. She loved his biceps. Could really sink her teeth into—

"I swear, you haven't heard one word in ten of what I'm saying." Edith poked Jane in the sleeve with her fork. "While I'm all for encouraging daydreaming, it should only be to escape the tedium of work or bad company, not when you're having lunch with your mother."

"Sorry," Jane said sheepishly. Her mom was right. Not only was she being rude, it was completely inappropriate to be having the kind of daydreams she was having while sitting next to her mother. It was like having naughty fantasies in church. Just not done.

"This appetizer is delicious," she said, trying to get the lunch meeting back on track. "I definitely want it at the ball."

"I agree." Edith made a note on her small spiral notepad. "And I can't wait to try that dessert Allison was talking about. The one with the fudge sauce. Might be too messy for a cocktail party, but I still want to try it."

Fudge sauce. Jane bit her lip. If she trailed a bit down her neck, she'd bet she could get Chance to do that wicked thing he did with his mouth that she loved so much. Jane shifted on her seat.

"You're doing it again!" Edith clucked in that disapproving way all mothers seemed to know.

"Doing what again?" Allison lowered a tray of food to the counter, the scents of rosemary and lemon making Jane's mouth water. Mini–pot pies with lattice tops made with delicate strands of pastry beckoned.

"Daydreaming about sex," her mother said. In her normally brash voice.

"Could you say that any louder?" Jane darted a glance at the table next to them. The four older women didn't look her way, but Jane didn't think it was her imagination that they all leaned closer to the counter where she and her mother sat. "And I was not," she lied.

Allison ignored that. "Who are you having sex dreams about? That singer you like? Or that actor we were talking about last week?"

Edith shook her head. "Not fantasies. A real man. Someone she was seen with just last night having a pizza date."

Picking up one of her pastries, Allison took a bite and stared at Jane speculatively. "You and Leon finally getting serious?" The distaste in her voice should have offended Jane. Leon was a perfectly nice man. But the idea of getting serious with Leon left a bitter taste in her mouth, too. "And you're daydreaming about sleeping with him?" Allison asked. "Does Leon have a hidden wild side I'm not seeing?"

"Eew, and no." Jane picked up a pastry before dropping it on her plate and blowing on her fingers. "Jesus, that's hot. How can you eat it?"

Allison shrugged. "I'm a chef. You get used to it. So who are you dating?"

Dating. That word seemed weird to describe what she and Chance were doing. Mainly because she didn't know what she and Chance were doing. Besides taking every opportunity they could find to screw like bunnies. Chance had made it clear early that morning, sometime between her second and third orgasm, that tearing up the sheets with her was high on his list of priorities. She hadn't been in a position to argue.

Her face got hot just thinking about the position she'd been in.

"Whoo hoo." Her mother pushed her glass of water Jane's way. "There she goes again. Come Fourth of July, we won't need firecrackers. We can just light you up."

Allison bounced on her toes, her ample breasts jiggling. "*Who* is lighting Jane up? You guys are killing me."

"Only Pineville's newest fireman, Chance McGovern." Edith took a bite of pastry and moaned. "This is fabulous, Allison."

"I know." She gave Jane a wicked smile. "You work fast, girl. Didn't he just move to town?"

"Four weeks ago," one of the women at the next table said helpfully. Jane glared at her, and the woman went back to pretending not to listen. The total lack of conversation at her table indicated otherwise.

"Well, that's pretty quick, but not slutty fast." Allison poured herself a cup of coffee. Waggling her eyebrows, she asked, "So?"

"So what?" Jane had a pretty good idea what Allison wanted, but no way was she going to talk about how Chance was in bed. She didn't want to make the other woman jealous. "Besides, it wasn't fast at all. I've known Chance since we were kids."

"They were high school sweethearts," Edith said. "Kind of a boring couple. Her father and I never got a call from the cops telling us to pick up our daughter, never caught them dancing naked in a mud pit like my father caught me and hers. Frankly, it was a little disappointing."

"So sorry I wasn't the outlaw you wanted."

"Still," her mother continued, "Chance was a sweet boy who always treated our Janey right. Well, almost always." She patted Jane's hand. "But because of one mistake, Jane isn't willing to envision a future with him."

"Ooh, drama." Allison placed her hands on the counter and leaned forward. "What—"

"No," Jane said firmly. "No drama. We were both stupid kids and that's all I'm going to say about it." She paused. She really didn't want to talk about it, and not just because it was private. It no longer mattered.

She took a deep breath, her chest feeling light as a helium balloon. She was finally past it. Chance had been an ambitious eighteen-year-old, and Jane had been putting way too much pressure on their young relationship. It was over and done. Anything that happened between her and Chance now was on them, what they did in the present, and not what they'd done as teenagers.

Turning to her mom, Jane said in a low voice, "I'm leaving it in the past. I'm not saying anything will come of me and Chance, but . . . I'm willing to try."

A whiff of patchouli and a billow of chiffon swept around Jane as her mother hugged her. "Good for you, baby. It takes a strong woman to forgive."

"Thanks, Mom."

Edith pushed back and grabbed another pastry. "Besides, it's time I had grandchildren."

Jane's jaw dropped.

"Whoa," Allison said. "I hear that enough from my mom, I don't need to hear other mothers saying it to their kids. I'm going to head back to the kitchen. Any changes you want to make to the catering menu?"

"No, it was all delicious," Edith said. "Thanks, Allison. The dinner will be fantastic. And we'll sample your desserts tomorrow, right?"

Allison agreed and walked along the counter, picking up empty plates as she went.

As soon as the door to the kitchen swung shut, Jane turned to her mom. "We've been on one date." She tilted her head. "Maybe two. I'm not sure if the other one counted as a date. But still way too early to talk about grandkids."

"You've been on a lot more than two dates with Chance. You've known him almost your whole life." Edith took a sip of water. "Besides, none of us are getting any younger."

"When did my untraditional mother start sounding so conventional?"

Edith ignored her. "Just think. If you and Chance got married, I'd have a grandson ready-made. And I adore Josh. I'm happy to babysit anytime."

"You're not just putting the cart before the horse, you're putting a whole wagon train in front." Jane tapped her fork against her plate. Her hormones had been so eager to fall into bed with Chance that Jane hadn't thought through the implications of dating a single dad. Or soon-to-be single dad. She pursed her lips. Yeah, she still wasn't happy with that not-quite-divorced status.

If she and Chance got serious, she would be a big part of Josh's life. She tapped the fork a little faster. She cared about Josh. He was a sweet kid and a lot of fun to be around. But she'd be lying if she said the idea of being a substitute mother didn't freak her out a bit. She didn't know what she was doing. She could totally mess up a kid.

Her mother covered her hand with her own. "Breathe, Jane. You're going an odd shade of purple."

Jane let out the breath she'd been holding, sucked in another. And another.

"Whatever you're worried about," her mother said, "don't. Just let things happen naturally and you'll be okay. No one knows what they're doing. We're all just winging it. You'll be fine. I've seen it."

"Seen it?"

"You know I inherited my great-grandmother Nonni's third eye. I've seen you in the future, happy and well."

Yes, Jane's dad and Jane had seen "evidence" of Edith's third eye all throughout Jane's childhood. Every time Edith had pointed to a prediction no one could remember her making, her father had smiled indulgently and told his wife that she was amazing. Of the predictions that they did remember hearing, none had come true. Edith would shrug, say the future was never over and they'd just have to wait.

Not inspiring proof that Jane's future was a bouquet of roses.

"Come on." Edith stood. "We both have to get back to work. Walk with me back to my shop so you can pick up the other auction items."

Jane waved goodbye to Allison through the open kitchen window and followed her mother onto the sidewalk. Flipping her sunglasses down from their perch on her head, she breathed in the fresh air.

Pete, their local tow truck driver and owner of their sole taxi service, was parked in one of the new electric car plug-in spots, looking at the meter and scratching his head. Jane eyed his diesel truck, bit back a smile, and called out a greeting. Pete pointed at the new meter and shrugged before clambering back into his truck, and moving to a new spot.

Turning, Jane trailed after her mother, the sun warm on her face. From the moment she'd set foot in Pineville, she'd felt more grounded. Centered. The people might be a little nosy, but Jane knew they truly cared. The same women who almost fell out of their seats eavesdropping would be the first ones to drop a box of chocolates at her door if they found out a man had hurt her. And they'd make sure that man was the pariah of Pineville.

Her mom crossed the street, and Jane trotted to catch up. The geraniums were in full bloom in their baskets hanging from each light pole, and Jane brushed the fuchsia flowers from her face as she passed underneath.

"It's really nice of you to donate more stuff for the auction, Mom."

Edith pulled out a set of keys. "When I heard we were short, what else could I do? Also, I managed to get that cheapskate next door to donate a gift certificate."

Jane glanced at the line coming out of Soup's On. Even though she'd just eaten, the smell of pumpkin soup wafting out the front door beckoned to her.

"How did you get him to donate?" She followed her mom into her store. Several new bouquets of dried lavender hung from the ceiling, and Jane breathed in the floral scent.

Edith turned her back on Jane and went behind the counter. "Well, I, uh, appealed to his better nature." Lifting a large bag, she placed it on the counter. "I'm sure he has one somewhere," she muttered.

"Mom, what did you do? Did you threaten him?" Jane could just see the headlines now: Pineville FD Fundraiser Strong-Arms Citizens into Giving. "You didn't, did you?"

"No." Edith sounded genuinely shocked. "I just, might have, helped him out a little bit."

"You bought the gift certificate?" The income her mother earned from the Apothic Garden wasn't huge, and with her store shut down for almost a week, Jane knew things would be tight this month. "You didn't need to do that, Mom. We'd have made do."

"I didn't buy the whole thing. Mr. Kane did pony up some of the money."

"Uh-huh." *Five bucks tops*, Jane thought. She brushed a kiss on her mother's cheek. Jane had thought about bidding on the spa day as a treat for herself. Now she knew who deserved the little luxury more. "Thanks, Mom."

Turning to the bag, Jane pulled out a square frame, about two feet across, wrapped in a white T-shirt. "What's this?"

"That's a painting by someone in my class down at the community college." Edith carefully uncovered it, trailed her fingers over the wood frame. "He doesn't want to be identified, but I think he's really good. I bet it will sell for quite a lot at the auction."

Jane stared at the landscape. It was at a lake, Lake Travis if Jane had to guess, and the play of sunlight over the waves and through the trees on the shore was extraordinary. The painter had included some bathers in the distance, but their forms were indistinct. "It is good." She peered at the signature in the bottom corner, but the initials were an illegible scrawl. "Is he sure he doesn't want his name listed as a donor to the fundraiser?"

Edith pinched her mouth tight. "He's not sure of anything. But I think it will be best if it's anonymous. Hopefully, when he sees how many people like it, he'll come forward."

Jane looked at her mother curiously. "He's going to be at the ball? Are you and he . . . going together?"

"No." She wrapped the painting back up, placed it in the bag. "He and I are currently *not* doing anything together."

"Are you dating?" Jane couldn't smother the twinge of disappointment that shaded her words. She'd hoped her mom and the chief would come to something, but her mom had gone for an artist-type instead. It shouldn't surprise her. Her mother was artistic. Jane's father had been, too. Of course Edith would seek out someone similar.

Not wanting her mom to think she was disappointed in her, Jane quickly added, "Just so you know, I'd be okay with you dating."

"Oh, honey." Edith cupped her cheek. "That's nice to hear. But if I wanted to date, your disapproval wouldn't stand in my way."

Jane rolled her eyes and huffed out a laugh. Just when she thought she and her mom were having a nice moment.

"I'm my own woman, and I'm going to do what's best for me regardless of anyone else's opinion," Edith said.

"Okay, I get it." Jane picked up the bag.

"I mean, I'm always happier when you're happy," Edith continued, "but if I only lived my life the way you approved of, I wouldn't get much done. Nothing fun, that's for sure."

Jeesh. Really pound that nail in. "Really. I get it. You don't have to say anything else."

"Just like you need to live your life regardless of how I feel about it." Edith followed her to the door. "Just because I see you with my grandbabies and a certain hunky fireman doesn't mean you should do anything differently. Although, maybe you could wear sexier clothes. Men do appreciate it when you try a little for them."

"Oh good God." She pressed a hasty kiss to her mother's forehead, right where Edith claimed her third eye was, and escaped out the door. Lugging the bag of auction items across the street to her car, Jane thought about her mother's alleged sixth sense.

She knew it was all a part of her hippy-dippy persona, and there was nothing to the idea of a second sight.

But her mother's vision of Jane's future sounded wonderful. Chance and a houseful of babies.

Maybe just this once Edith's prediction would come true.

Chapter Seventeen

Chance threaded the strap through the buckle at Jane's waist and pulled it tight. Running his fingers along the harness that circled her thighs, he tested to make sure it was neither too snug nor too loose.

"I think it's good," Jane said, her voice low, breathy. "Please stop doing that in public when I can't do anything about it."

Satisfaction flooded Chance. He liked knowing he got to Jane as much as she got to him. "It's only fair." From his position on his knees in front of her, Chance's eyes were level with the quick rise and fall of her chest. He looked a little lower. This was a great position to be in.

"How's that?" she asked.

"That I drive you as crazy as you drive me." Keeping his hands on her outer thighs, he stood, dragging his palms up and over her hips and resting them at her waist.

She fiddled with the strap at her hip. "Maybe we should just forget this whole rappelling thing and go find an empty closet."

And that's when Chance realized that her rapid breathing and flushed skin weren't solely due to his touch. Jane was scared.

He moved his hands to her shoulders, massaged away the knots. "There's nothing to be nervous about. There's no way for you to fall, even if you tried. I've double-checked all the equipment, and Martinez is going to monitor the belay from up here while I rappel down beside you. You're completely safe."

Jane snorted. "I think your idea of safe and my idea of safe are two different things." She shuffled to the window of the cement training building, poked her head out and looked down. "Oh, holy crap. You really go down this thing?"

"*We're* really going to go down this thing." Grabbing her biceps, he tugged her away from the opening. "Do you think I'm a good fireman?" he asked, stepping into his own harness.

"I don't know," she said, brows drawn low. "I've never seen you in action."

He blew out an exasperated sigh. "Do you think I'm the kind of man who'd take chances with your safety? With my son's? Because I promised him I'd let him do this next week."

"No." She stared up at him, the gold flecks in her caramel eyes shimmering. "I trust you."

God, he was an idiot. Because those three little words slayed him. Rubbing his chest, Chance tried to think of something witty to say, something to lighten the mood, make her smile. He wanted a lifetime of making her smile. And for the first time, he thought that maybe they had a shot.

She trusted him. She'd forgiven him. He could see it in her eyes.

He pulled her close. The buckle in her harness dug into just the wrong spot, but he didn't care. "Thank you."

"Chance," she said, her voice muffled by his shoulder.

"Mm-hmm?"

"I still don't want to do this."

He chuckled. "But you're going to." Peeling her body off of his, he looked down into her worried eyes. This was familiar territory. Convincing her to go along with his harebrained schemes. "You can tell me what I can do to improve the experience before Josh gets in that harness. You do want him to have the best and safest experience, don't you?" He ignored her narrowed eyes. "Plus, do you want to hear from a five-year-old that he was brave enough to rappel down a little wall and you weren't? Because my son will mock you. He excels at that."

"I wonder where he learned it," she muttered.

A dark head followed by a navy uniform rose up from the stairs behind them. "We ready to get this show on the road?" Martinez asked. "A crowd's gathering down below. The guys don't want to miss this."

"A crowd?" Jane poked her head out the window, peered down. "What are they all doing here?"

Martinez grinned. "No one wanted to miss Dispatch Jane on her first rappel. Some of the guys are running numbers on it. Five has you wussing out, ten has you crying, and my personal favorite, twenty has you flipping ass over teakettle and going down Australian-style."

She lifted her chin. "I don't even know what that means, but I can assure you, none of those things will happen." Slapping Chance's chest, she nodded to the window. "Come on. Let's get going."

Like he was the one who'd been stalling. Chance smiled. Leading her to the opening, he instructed her on what to do. "Martinez will be watching your rope up top, as an extra safety measure, to make sure you don't descend too fast. Any questions?"

Taking a deep breath, Jane swung one leg over the sill. "Just one." She darted a glance at Martinez, leaned in close. "What's Australian-style?"

"It's when you rappel headfirst." Straddling the windowsill facing Jane, he patted her leg. "Don't worry. That usually doesn't happen."

A string of filthy curse words slipped past her pretty lips.

"Come on." He leaned into his rope, pulling it taut. "I put money on you rappelling like a champ. I'll buy you lunch with my winnings."

"You bet on me?" She looked at the ground far below, at Chance, and back again.

Putting a finger under her chin, he brought her around to face him. "I bet that you would succeed, and that's a bet I'll always make."

"Oh my God," Martinez muttered. "It's like I'm watching a chick-flick."

Jane squared her jaw. "Okay. Let's do this."

Chance couldn't resist. He knew the guys down below had a good view of them up in the window, would razz him later, but he leaned down and took her mouth. She was just so damn cute when she was being all kick-ass. He swallowed her little hum of pleasure, delved in for more.

Okay, new plan. When he'd accepted the job in Pineville, his idea for the future had been to work hard, take care of his son, and maybe in a couple of years, when Josh was old enough to understand, start dating again.

Threading his hands in her silky hair, he gently tugged her head back to a better angle.

But then he'd stumbled across Jane. His first love. A woman with heart, determination, and who was so damn sweet he'd have to start checking his blood-sugar levels like his sister. A woman he could build a lasting future with.

So, new plan. Date Jane for a year. There would have to be a lot of sneaking around so they didn't confuse Josh with another woman in Daddy's bed. But no way was he giving up Jane in his bed. Or in her bed. Or her kitchen table. He could even make the wall work.

She gripped his waist and scooted closer. Yeah, he wasn't giving this up. So a year of sneaking her into his bedroom. Then ask her to move in with them. Josh should be comfortable enough with her by then. His divorce would be final. And by the second year, marriage. His first marriage had been so awful, Chance couldn't believe he was already contemplating his second.

But with Jane, it didn't seem like a gamble. Marriage to her felt like a sure thing.

A solid plan. A sensible plan. One that would bring him and his son happiness and stability. He pulled his mouth from hers, lungs working like a bellows. So why did he feel like tossing her over his shoulder and driving to Atlantic City? Like if he didn't pin her down, she'd slip away?

"Wow," she whispered. She smiled up at him, all traces of fear evaporated. "That was quite a send-off." Lifting a hand, she rubbed her thumb over his lips, presumably to wipe off her lipstick since she no longer wore any. "I can't believe I'm going to say this, but let's go fall out of this building."

And just as he'd taught her, she leaned back, let the rope support her, and pushed out of the window.

Side by side, step for step, they dropped down the side of the building together.

"Say it again," Chance demanded.

Jane rolled her eyes. Jeesh. She never should have said it the first time. Once a man heard those words, it was all downhill from there. They got cocky. Smug.

Grabbing her around the waist, Chance tickled her side, holding her writhing body firmly in place until she gave up.

"Fine!" Jane wiped at her streaming eyes. "You were right. I was wrong. Rappelling was a lot of fun."

The tickling stopped, but he didn't release his hold. "I'm glad you're big enough to admit that, Janey-girl. Now if you'd just remember it for all future reference—"

Digging a knuckle into his kidney, Jane slipped from his grasp. She ran a hand through her hair and looked around Pineville's central square, hoping nobody had seen their undignified clinch. She and Chance had been wandering around the weekly farmers' market. He'd managed to lead her behind a clump of maple trees, giving them some semblance of privacy.

"For future reference," she said, "*I'm* rarely wrong. Like only point-zero-zero-one percent of the time. You'd do well to remember that."

"Using that math, you won't be wrong again until we're ninety years old."

"Uh-huh." She circled around the maple and headed back toward the impromptu stalls that covered the square's wide lawn. She'd seen jars of lavender-infused honey, and she wasn't going to let Chance distract her from her purpose again.

Falling into step beside her, he heaved a sigh. "You know—"

Jane walked a few more steps before realizing he was no longer keeping pace. Turning, she cocked her head. "What's wrong?"

The tendons running the length of his neck bulged. Jane followed his narrowed gaze. Blowing out a breath of relief, Jane shook her head, walked to Chance and patted his chest. "Jeez, I thought you'd seen a serial killer or something. Not Katie with the man I presume is Carter."

Whipping his head around, he nailed her with a glare. "You know who she's dating?"

"She told me a bit about him." Jane started walking to the market. "If you didn't get so bat-shit crazy about her dating life, she'd probably tell you about him, too."

"I don't like the look of him." His legs ate up the ground to catch up to Jane. "He put his arm around her!" A low growl mushroomed up from his chest.

Jane eyed the pair. "In a very sweet, non-creepy way. You need to calm down. Katie's a beautiful young woman and she's going to date." Waving at Allison and Judge Nichols across the way, she tugged Chance to the honey booth. "I only have two bucks in my purse. Buy me a jar."

He reached into his back pocket, removing his wallet without taking his eyes off Katie and Carter. "Does he look older than her to you?"

Jane peeled a ten out and handed it to the girl behind the booth. She gave Carter another look. "Maybe. But not by much." She cocked her head. "He's cute."

Chance scowled at her, but facts were facts. The man was tall and toned with caramel-colored skin and a thick crop of dark chocolate curls that just brushed his ears. Jane didn't recognize him, and with a face like his, she would have. He probably lived in one of the surrounding towns.

Carter stopped and bought a bouquet of daisies and handed them to Katie. Cradling them to her chest, she looked up into his face, her own smiling with delight.

"Isn't that sweet?" Jane asked. "He just bought her flowers."

Chance shoved his wallet in his pocket and grabbed the white paper bag from the girl behind the booth. "I bought you honey," he grumbled.

"And I really appreciate it." Rising up on her tiptoes, she kissed his cheek. "Thank you."

Looking slightly mollified, Chance wrapped an arm around her waist, resting his hand on her hip. Jane glanced around, caught a few knowing glances. Not that she thought she'd been fooling many people before by saying she and Chance were just old friends, but that pretext was now definitely finished. She and Chance were officially a couple.

She sneaked a glance at him. To the public anyway. To Chance . . . no. She forced the doubts away. He was serious about their relationship. He wasn't playing her. But he wasn't even divorced yet. Was she his rebound woman? Would he regret jumping into another relationship so soon after his marriage imploded?

Jane rubbed her temple. Her mother was right. She was wound too tight. Time to relax. Have fun. With Chance by her side, it wouldn't be hard.

"Look." Jane pointed. "They're holding hands now."

"Why would you point that out to me?" Leading Jane after the couple, Chance squeezed her to his side. "Are you punishing me for something?"

Jane steered him in another direction. "No. It's just fun to mess with you. And you're not going to introduce yourself when you look ready to rip the poor man's head off. Maybe we should get a beer or two into you before you meet Carter."

"If he gets scared away by a couple dark looks from me, he's not good enough for Katie," Chance argued. But he let her pull him to a booth selling sourdough bread.

Jane agreed, but it was up to Katie to determine whether Carter was good enough. It would only cause a rift between the siblings if Chance got involved.

Picking up a paper-wrapped loaf, she inhaled the ripe yeast aroma. "It's a good thing you have a son. I don't think you'd survive a daughter. Not once she turned into a teenager anyway."

Chance took the loaf from her, handed it to the baker along with some cash. "I hope to have a daughter someday." He looked down at Jane, eyes serious. "I'd like to have a couple more kids, if I'm lucky enough."

Jane sucked in a quick breath. Yep, he was serious about their relationship. Was *she* ready for such a life-changing relationship?

Their gazes held. Flecks of gold in his dark eyes caught the sun. Warmth started low in her belly, spread outward. She tucked her hand in his, tilted the corners of her mouth up. Chance wedged the loaf of bread under his other arm, nodded his thanks to the baker.

Being with Chance would be life changing, Jane had no doubt. But with his warm hand gripping hers, giving her strength, she knew he'd have her back when she got scared.

Chance looked over his shoulder, finding Katie in the crowd. "I want a daughter. But she's never dating."

Resting her head on his shoulder, Jane laughed.

Chapter Eighteen

"Jesus, you're racking up those frequent flyer miles, aren't you?" Chance pressed his hand against the doorjamb, blocking Annette's way into his house. The move was instinctual. She'd brought so much chaos with her, his body wanted to bar her physical entry into his life, as though that could keep the turmoil at bay.

She clasped a patent-leather clutch to her stomach. "I should charge you for the tickets. You're the one who moved our son across the country."

A fire blazed to life in his gut. "To keep him safe from your bookies. Don't forget that part."

Rolling her eyes, she tried to brush past him into the house. He didn't let her.

"Max wouldn't have hurt him," she said. "He was just trying to scare me." She pointed to his arm. "You going to let me in?"

Chance looked at that arm, at the fingers wrapped around the wood of the jamb. Did it make him a bad person that he wanted to wrap those same fingers around her throat? Maybe not squeeze the life out of her, but shake her back and forth for speaking so casually of their son's safety. Yeah, that would be satisfying.

And wrong, that annoying, law-abiding voice of his said. "Josh isn't here. Katie took him to soccer practice."

"Oh." She lost some of her starch, deflating before his eyes.

"If you'd called ahead, we could've arranged a time for you to visit. Instead of just showing up," he said pointedly.

"He's my son, too." Chance started to thaw, until she continued with, "You should be nicer to me. When I have full custody, I'll get to control when, or if, you see Josh."

The lava in his gut spread to his chest. *Oh, hell no*. Over his dead body was she getting full custody, locking him out of his son's life. Annette couldn't get it through her pea-sized brain that when she messed up as big as she had, she didn't get the privilege of unrestricted parenthood. There were consequences to her actions.

But what if she wins? What if Katie's right, and some stupid-ass judge awards her custody when she marries? A sliver of wood dug under his nail, he was gripping the frame so tight. He had to be smart. For Josh, he couldn't give in to the temptation to throw her off his property, tell her to go to hell.

"I'm not trying to keep you from him," he said evenly. "But Josh has a schedule. If you want to come by for dinner tonight, you can. Josh would love to see you." That was the truth. Another reason to try to make nice with this woman. Josh shouldn't see how much his mother disgusted his father.

"Thank you. Dinner will be good." Annette flipped her long swath of dark hair over one shoulder. "But I want some alone time with my son."

Chance opened his mouth.

"Before you say no, think about if the roles were reversed," she said. "Wouldn't you want to be able to take our son out to the park, or for some pizza, just the two of you? Do you always want me to be supervising your visits?"

She assumed she would be given custody. Just took it for granted. Just like she thought she'd always win the next horse race. But she wasn't wrong. He'd hate it if he couldn't take Josh out alone for some guy time.

Gritting his teeth, he gave her the nicest smile he was able to. "Tomorrow Josh has a playdate and I'm busy with our fundraiser. The ball is tomorrow night. Saturday is his soccer game. He usually goes out with the team afterwards. But Sunday, you can take him out that afternoon for a couple of hours. If you'll still be here?" *Please let her flight be tomorrow.*

"I'll be here." Spinning on her stiletto heel, she sashayed toward her rental car. "I'll see you tonight for dinner. And remember, make something vegetarian."

Chance was proud of himself for not slamming the door. But the tension coiled tighter and tighter through his body. That woman was a disease. And she was the most important woman in his son's life.

Chance punched the wall. Nope. Still pissed. That wasn't going to cut it. Jogging up the stairs, he pulled out his phone and started texting his sister. *Annette just here. I need to blow off some steam, maybe go pound the bag at the gym. You okay with Josh for a couple hours?*

While he waited for her response, he changed into a pair of running shorts and an old tee.

No prob. Team going to lunch after practice. Pizza Pit, again ☹. We'll be there for hours.

At some point Chance was going to have to explain to his son that pizza was not one of the four food groups. It wasn't intended for daily consumption. But not today. Right now he needed to pound out his anger.

He hit the sidewalk at a run and alternated between flat-out racing and sprinting as if a wolverine was chasing him. Sweat dripped into his eyes, burning, and his leg muscles screamed in protest. Yet the anger remained.

He pounded past the street that led to the gym, his body knowing that wasn't what he needed. Twenty-two minutes later, and his legs were almost too exhausted to climb the steps to her apartment. On a good day, he could jog for a solid hour and have plenty of energy left to strap on his gear and go to work. But the way his calves sent angry warning signals to his brain told Chance that balls-to-the-walls sprinting was something best left to the kids.

He knocked on her door, for the first time worrying that she might not be home. He should have called ahead. He should know her schedule better. Was she—

The door swung open, and she was there, delight in her eyes at seeing him. God, he missed seeing that from a woman. When had he resigned himself to the fact that his wife greeted him with indifference? When had it become normal to see the flicker of irritation cross Annette's face when he came home?

Jane stood in stretchy yoga pants and a baggy T-shirt, and no one had ever looked as lovely. Grabbing his hand, she pulled him into her apartment, her brows drawing together. "What's wrong?"

"Nothing. Annette. I just wanted to see you." The words were a jumble, his mind now as tired as his body.

She pushed him toward her bedroom. "Go to my bathroom and take your clothes off. And watch out for"—a hiss, a raging bundle of orange fur raced under his feet, making him stumble—"Cyclops."

Jane sighed. "He's got to get used to you eventually." She made little shooing motions before turning to her kitchen.

For once, Chance was happy to let someone else call the shots. He plodded into her small bathroom, leaned against the sink so he wouldn't fall over while taking off his clothes.

He was toeing off his sneakers when Jane came in, a large glass of water in her hand.

"Drink," she said. She finished pulling off his shoes and socks, slid his shorts and jockeys down his legs in one tug. Turning on the shower, she pulled off her own clothes. "Okay, into the shower." She prodded his shoulder until he stepped over the tub's edge.

"When did you get so pushy?" The spray of hot water hit his chest. Chance placed his hands on the cold tile below the nozzle and leaned into the stream. Damn, that felt good. Jane stepped behind him, her body brushing against his as she picked up one of those scrubby loofah things, and that felt even better.

She squeezed some soap into the loofah. "If I can push you around, you must not be feeling well. So just be quiet and let me take care of you."

Starting with his back, Jane wiped away his sweat right along with his tension. The soap was something fruity, girly, but Chance didn't care. If he spent the day smelling like Jane, it would be a good day. She moved down his back, rubbing his sore muscles as she went. Every part of him got her attention. He grunted in satisfaction when she massaged his glutes, and when she reached his abused calves, he almost wept in relief.

"Turn around," she said, her voice still bossy. Chance smiled, and obeyed. The sight of Jane on her knees in front of him perked his body up. Some parts more than others. Whereas her attentions to his back had been relaxing, the lathering up of his feet and shins made him impatient.

Those bits didn't matter. He'd give a month's salary if she'd only work a little higher, take care of him where he needed it.

She didn't disappoint. Pushing to her feet, she took Chance's offered hand to help stand. She wasted little time making a few swipes across his chest before hanging the loofah up on a suction-cup hook and filling her hands with a squirt of soap. She rubbed them together until a thick layer of foam coated them.

"Sweet Jesus." Chance leaned his head back on the tile. Her slippery hands stroked his length, cleaning each and every inch of him.

"Do you want to talk about it?" she asked.

"What? Annette? Now?" He barked out a harsh laugh. Opening his eyes, he looked down into her concerned gaze. "That's the last thing I want to talk about right now. In fact"—Chance removed her hands, though it just about killed him to do it, and moved her under the spray—"I don't want to talk at all." He filled his own hands with the liquid soap. "Now, you've been a dirty girl, dragging men into your apartment, stripping them naked, and it's time you got a good cleaning."

"You might have to scrub real good at some parts." She leaned back against the wall, lifted her arms and grabbed the shower head with both hands. "I can get awfully filthy."

Chance grinned. And he made sure to clean every bit of her. Her eyes were closed and the edges of her lips tilted up the slightest bit. She looked satisfied, taken care of, and Chance felt like he could take on a five-alarm fire single-handedly. He loved putting that look on her face.

Jane was always trying to take care of others. From conversations with Edith, Chance knew that Jane had followed her mother to Pineville to help her out. She had taken the lead with the fundraiser. And here she was, looking out for him, no questions asked when he'd appeared sweaty and tired on her doorstep.

But who had been taking care of Jane? Some small part inside Chance was happy that no one seemed to have taken that position in any significant way over the years. It was a vacancy he had every intention of filling.

Turning the water off, he grabbed a towel, swaddled it around Jane's shoulders, and climbed out of the tub with her. He dragged the terry cloth up and down her body until they were both breathing hard.

"The condoms still by your bed?" he asked.

"Just bought a new box." She nipped at his jaw. "But my legs don't want to move."

"Then it's a good thing there's a fireman in the house." Bending over, he threw her over his shoulder, not technically a fireman's carry, but good enough for his purposes. Jane squealed, and pushed her torso up off his back. "Watch your head," he told her as he stepped through the doorway.

"Put me down. We're too old for you to be picking me up like this."

"As you wish." Chance tossed her on her bed, enjoyed watching her bounce.

She gave him the evil eye. "That was uncalled for."

Smiling, he grabbed a condom from the box, sheathed himself. "But highly satisfying."

She harrumphed.

Chance settled on top of her, her skin still rosy and warm from the shower. Burying his nose in the crook of her neck, he inhaled, the scent of warm, sweet woman going straight to his head. He kissed the soft skin, licked across her collarbone. He couldn't get enough, would never get enough. She opened for him, and he nestled into the cradle of her thighs.

She sought out his mouth, and he gave it to her, their tongues tangling, sparring. Pressing closer to her, he felt her heart pound against his chest, its frantic beat a mirror to his own. Framing her face with his hands, he pressed a kiss to each eye, her nose, before lifting his head. "I love you, Jane."

Her eyes grew round, and her heartbeat kicked up a notch. She didn't say anything, and Chance's stomach churned. She had to have known where this was leading. With all their history, she couldn't have believed this was a casual fling, despite what she'd said at the beginning of the relationship. She needed to say something, anything, right damn now.

Jane bit her lip.

Biting back a curse, he sucked in a deep breath. Okay, he could work with this. So she wasn't there quite yet. Or she wasn't able to admit it. If he wanted to follow his plan, he still had a year to convince Jane to move in with him. He could do a lot in a year.

Jesus, why was she staring at him like that? Was she about to cry? Hearing he loved her made her cry? That wasn't a good sign. Sweat beaded at his hairline. His fingers pressed into her skull, and he had to force himself to relax his hands. He couldn't lose Jane now, not when he'd just found her. Life wouldn't screw with him like that. She just had—

"I love you, too." A tear escaped from the corner of her eye, and rolled down her cheek.

Chance's body sagged. Dropping his forehead to rest against hers, he muttered, "Thank God." A second later he pinned her with a glare. "Then why the hell are you crying?"

After the thirty seconds of hell she just put him through, Jane had the nerve to laugh. *Laugh!*

"God, you're dumb sometimes. But that's a common fault with your gender, so I forgive you."

He opened his mouth to protest, but she pressed her finger across his lips. "Chance, do you really want to argue right now?" She shimmied her body beneath his. "That would seem like a great waste of our time."

Chance groaned. "Do that again."

"What?" She smiled. "This?"

Her slow undulations rubbed her body over all the right places on his.

"Damn," he whispered. And because her smile held just a little too much of triumph over Chance for his liking, he did a little rubbing of his own.

A needy sigh escaped her lips, sending an arrow of heat through Chance.

He pressed against her. "Say it again," he growled.

"Which part?"

"You know damn well which part." Pressing in, he ran his hand down her thigh to hook behind her knee, brought her leg around his back.

"You want me to tell you you're dumb again now?" she teased. "I don't want to hurt your ego at this most critical time."

"Jane." His voice was a warning, a plea.

Her breath caught when he bottomed out. She wrapped her other leg around his waist. Fluttering her eyelids open, she pierced him with her gaze. "I love you. God help me, I love you so much."

A flare of primal satisfaction surged through him. She was his. His to love. His to care for. His Janey-girl.

Their future blossomed bright in front of him. Laughter, tears, brothers and sisters for Josh. With Jane by his side, Chance knew that even the bad moments would be good.

She rocked her hips, impatient, and Chance's thoughts narrowed from his wide-open future to the five-feet-something of Jane's body and nothing else.

He always wanted it to be good for his partner, but never had it felt as important as this. This wasn't just sex. It wasn't even making love. Chance had always felt like he'd been making love to Jane. There'd always been emotion behind it.

But this felt like a consummation. A turning point. And he was damn sure going to make it good for Jane.

So he went slow, and watched her body. He cataloged each reaction. Watched with pleasure as blood flushed her chest a pretty pink. Felt the burn of each of her ten fingernails as she raked them down his back. His thoughts tried to scatter, his body demanding its mindless pleasure, but he corralled them back to Jane.

A bead of sweat rolled down his spine. The slow pivot of his hips was killing him. He groaned. It felt so good, but he couldn't feel his toes, and it was killing him. When little whimpers escaped from her mouth, Chance told himself it was okay to thrust faster, it was what Jane needed, too.

Tugging at her lower lip, he sucked it into his mouth. She tasted of coffee and sugar. His favorite pick-me-up. He pounded harder.

He was pleading with her to *get there, get there, get there*, but it must have been only in his head because his lips were always full—of her mouth, her earlobe, her breast. If he wasn't past the point of reason, Chance might have worried about his raging desire to consume her. He wanted every part of her. To bite her, lick her . . . oh God, he wasn't going to last.

He needed to concentrate on something, anything other than Jane and the feel of her tight heat, her silky skin. He grunted with the effort. And then, thank the heavens, he didn't have to think, because she was there, her body writhing and clutching at his, her breath held tight in her lungs as her eyes went liquid, her gaze unfocused.

Chance stared into those whiskey eyes, got drunk on the ecstasy he saw there. Digging his fingers into her hair, he held her tight, wanting this moment to last forever but begging for it to end because he needed relief so badly it hurt.

She cupped his cheek with her hand. "Chance," she whispered, and he was gone.

His mind went white, his brain's only purpose to send bliss shooting through his body.

He threw his head back with a howl, and poured everything he had into her. He didn't worry if it was enough, what he had to give, if he and the woman beneath him could make it work. This was Jane. She was his.

It was more than enough. It was everything.

Chapter Nineteen

Jane accepted the drink with a smile. So far, the charity ball was a success. The finger foods Allison catered were delicious, there were plenty of names filling the silent auction forms, and the drinks were flowing. What they'd made on liquor sales alone would be a big contribution to the charity. Jane had told Chance his idea to set up a pay-bar for mixed drinks was silly; everyone would just drink the wine that was provided with the ticket purchase. She was too happy at the sight of the bulging credit card receipts to be put out that she was wrong and Chance was right.

She'd let him be right on some things. Occasionally.

In fact, the only fly in her ointment right now was the man standing next to her, tugging at his crooked bow tie. Leon had been a perfect gentleman, fetching her drinks, chatting about his new partner at game night, being no more boring than usual. Nothing was wrong with Leon except the fact that he wasn't Chance.

She stole a glance across the wine cave. Chance stood beside the entry doors, greeting any latecomers. The winery had placed two urns on either side of the entry, each containing a small faux tree, their branches lit with white lights and glowing pink blossoms. That, paired with the swathes of white lights draped over the wooden beams crisscrossing the ceiling, lent an ethereal feel to the ball.

Chance tossed his head back, laughed at something the mayor said. Jane's stomach did a backflip. He was breathtaking, so full of life. His energy had always drawn her, pulling her into his orbit.

And he said he loved her.

"Why are you smiling?" Leon asked. Poor guy must have known he hadn't said anything amusing.

Jane raised her wineglass to her lips. "Just enjoying the party."

Chance glanced over, found her immediately in the crowd. His gaze was searing, the emerald-green empire dress she wore feeling invisible. The mayor put a hand on his elbow, and Chance turned away to speak with the older man.

Releasing her breath, Jane tapped her fingers on her glass. She wanted to go over to him, spend the evening at his side. She looked over at the crowded dance floor that had been laid by the floor-to-ceiling windows. Maybe she could even convince him to dance, although that had never been easy.

But she'd promised herself she'd keep her obligation to Leon, and that included being a better date. She focused on him. "How's work going?"

"Uh?" He scratched his chin. "Fine? I mean, not much happens in Judge Nichols's courtroom. All I have to do is announce him. But I've started reading a new book. An Isaac Asimov. It's pretty good."

Jane didn't like science fiction and didn't want to start talking about it now. "The turnout's pretty good, don't you think?"

"Yeah, I guess." Leon checked his watch.

"And the auction setup is great." Jane looked at the far wall with satisfaction. The row of tables along the wall held twenty items that Pineville had donated, each with a placard describing the article. Framed photographs accompanied gift certificates, showing what the certificate could purchase. And next to the table, standing on easels, were two-foot-high poster-board photos of the bachelor firemen who were being auctioned off.

That seemed to be a favorite spot for the women to congregate.

"Uh-huh." Leon chewed on an ice cube.

Jane pursed her lips. This was going to be a long night.

Judge Nichols and Mr. Harraday were ambling around the room, and Jane flagged them down. "Mr. Harraday, I didn't think you'd be coming."

"Why?" He jabbed his cane into the floor, narrowly missing her foot. "You think I'm too old to come to a ball. That's discrimination."

"Saul." The judge shook his head. "You know she didn't mean it like that."

"I didn't think you'd want to come, what with there being a couple hundred people in one room and all." Stepping forward, Jane smoothed a crease in the lapel of his worn suit. A patch of bristly hairs had escaped his attempt to shave his neck. "You look very handsome, and our fire department appreciates your support."

He harrumphed, but his cheeks turned pink.

"How are the two of you enjoying the ball?" Judge Nichols asked. "Everything turned out great, Jane." With a curious glance at Leon, he said, "I'd thought you and Chance were going to come to this together. You two have another fight?"

Jane bit back a retort. They weren't *always* fighting. The man just excelled at frustrating her.

"No, Chance and I are fine." Jane patted Leon's arm. "Leon and I had agreed to come together a long time ago. And it's nice to go out with a friend sometimes."

"I wouldn't have minded if you wanted to go with Chance," Leon said.

Jane sighed. Of course he wouldn't. As long as there was food and drink, Leon would have been content to eat his way across the buffet, flying solo, playing sudoku on his phone. Well, she wasn't going to tell Chance that little tidbit.

"So, are the two of you having a good time?" she asked.

Harraday tugged at the knot in his tie. "'Course not. Why didn't you have any of them lady firemen up for sale? There's nothing here for a man to buy. It's discrimination."

Judge Nichols pursed his pink lips. "Pineville has only one female firefighter, and she's married."

"Besides," Jane added, "there's lots of items in the silent auction that you can bid on." Jane ran through the list in her mind. Nothing popped up as something the old man would like. "There's the, uh . . ."

"I've already made my bid," Harraday cut in. "I got the firefighter experience."

The firefighter experience? Jane shut her jaw with a snap. No way could Harraday do the rappelling. Even climbing into the fire engine would be a challenge for a man with a bum hip. Strapping into a harness and scaling the side of a building? She didn't even want to think about how badly Chance would mock her if old man Harraday made a successful rappel after all her whining.

"There's still an hour left in the silent auction," Leon pointed out. "Someone might outbid you."

Judge Nichols shook his head. "The top five donations win the day with a firefighter, and Saul made a very generous bid. He'll win it. He probably won't survive the experience, but he'll win it."

"I'll be fine," Harraday grumbled. "God wouldn't give me the easy way out before my move into Meredith's place."

"You're moving in with your daughter?" Jane asked. Harraday gave a brisk nod of his gray head. "That's wonderful news."

"Why?" he barked. "Just because I turned the sprinklers on you, you want me out of town?"

Judge Nichols widened his eyes. "You did what?"

Jane waved her hand. "There are no hard feelings over that." Just thinking about rolling around on the ground with a wet Chance did funny things to her stomach. No, she didn't want to make a habit out of a sprinkler attack, but she didn't begrudge the older man his fun. "I'm just happy you're going to be living with someone who cares for you. And you can help out watching your grandkids. It's a good solution for everyone."

Harraday narrowed his eyes, obviously searching for the flaw in her reasoning. Finding none, he cocked his head. "I don't want to be a full-time babysitter. Or a manny as you kids call it. I don't like my grandkids that much. But I could help out." He pursed his lips. "Yeah, Meredith might even be able to get some part-time work if I'm there to help out." His chest lifted.

Jane smiled at the man, understanding his position. It must be hard to go from a self-sufficient adult to being cared for. Everyone wanted to feel needed.

"But I'm not going till after I'm a fireman for a day." Pointing a bent finger in her face, he said, "Tell your boyfriend he'd better not go easy on me just 'cause he thinks I'm old. I can still do the job and I want the full experience."

The judge slapped his friend on the back. "I'm sure Mr. McGovern would be happy to throw you out of a window. Now let's leave the young people to enjoy themselves." Nudging Leon with his elbow, he nodded his head to the dance floor. "You should take your date for a spin." With a smile and a wink, he led Harraday away, slowing his pace to match.

Leon looked at her, eyes wide. "Uh . . . Did you want . . . ?"

Taking pity, she shook her head. "It's okay. We don't have to dance."

Ignoring his relieved sigh, she watched Harraday poke the back of Chief Finnegan's leg with his cane until the large man moved out of the way, a frown on his face.

Jane grinned. Chance had a whole day to spend with Harraday. With his insults, his complaints, and his physical assaults with his cane. No matter how well the physically challenged man did on the rappel, Chance would be too exhausted by the end of the day to bother saying "I told you so" over his idea being a success.

An arm circled around her waist, and Jane jumped before realizing it was Chance. "You scared me," she said.

Chance smiled. "Sorry," he said, not sounding sorry at all. Putting out his hand to the other man, he nodded. "Leon."

"Hi, Chance." Leon took his hand, his knuckles whitening as Chance squeezed. His eyebrows rose. "Uh"—he tugged his hand free, flexed it—"how've you been?"

"I've been doing real well." Chance looked down at Jane, pulled her tight against his hip. "Real well." Turning back to Leon, he said, "I want to thank you for entertaining my girl tonight. I'll be taking over after the ball." He bared his teeth. "Do you mind if I steal your date away for a dance, Leon?" He herded Jane toward the dance floor, not waiting for an answer. "I won't keep her long."

That surprised Jane enough to ignore the fact that she felt like a fire hydrant next to a dog. "You want to dance?" Her voice oozed disbelief.

"Yeah, I want to dance. With you." Finding a vacant spot on the floor, Chance pulled her into his arms.

"Since when?"

"What do you mean?" Placing his hand on her lower back, he tugged her closer. "It's a ball. You look amazing. I want to dance."

Jane snorted. "I had to beg you to take me to prom. And junior prom." Chance opened his mouth. "And spring fling," she continued. "You, Chance McGovern, don't like to dance."

His eyes crinkled. "When you're a kid, the only reason a boy dances with a girl is to get close to her, try to convince her to sleep with him. We were already sleeping together. Didn't need to dance you around."

Jane huffed in exasperation, but couldn't fault his logic. "What's changed? We're sleeping together now."

"Men aren't all raging hormones like boys are. I knew you wanted to dance, so I asked you to dance." Lowering his head, he whispered in her ear, "Besides, I don't think I could get away with taking you to the floor and screwing you senseless. Some of the cops in attendance might object. So holding you close is the next best thing."

Jane forced her voice steady. "So nothing's changed then. Still using dancing as a substitute for sex."

He swiped his hand lower, quickly returning it to her lower back, but not before sending a streak of heat straight to her core. "Now you've got us figured out. Every man in here is only dancing because we're not allowed to do what we want to be doing. Public indecency laws are the sole reason dancing exists."

Jane cocked her head back to look him in the eyes. "Are you sure it's just the men?"

He growled. "Baby, screw Leon—wait, poor choice of words. Forget about Leon. Spend the night with me. Right after the bachelor auction, let's get out of here. The guys and their wives at the fire-house will be expecting to watch Josh for several more hours yet."

She sighed. "It's just one night. I'm not going to ditch Leon now." Turning her head, she saw the bailiff playing something on his smartphone while wolfing down a mini–pot pie. "Although he'd probably be happy if we ended the evening early." She straightened her spine. "No. I'm not going to ditch him. But I will come over to your house later. It looks like Katie will be occupied, so it should be easy to sneak me in."

Chance craned his neck around. Seeing Katie wrapped in Carter's arms, Chance scowled. "I don't like him."

"Of course you don't."

"No, I mean it." A vein in his neck pulsed. "He's too old for her."

Jane rolled her eyes. "Katie told me he's twenty-six. Not exactly a May-December romance."

He set his jaw. "I don't like it."

Jane rubbed his shoulder. "But you're going to accept that your sister is an adult and can make her own choices on who she dates. Right?"

He stared over her head.

"Right?" She stepped on his foot and ground down. Just a little.

Chance jerked his foot out from under hers, stumbling into the guy next to them. "Christ! Yes. I'll be nice to my sister."

Resting her head against his chest, she wrapped her arms around his waist. "Good."

"As long as you make sure to come over tonight."

"Okay." The lapel of his tux tickled her nose and she wriggled it. "I'll distract you from locking your sister up by occupying you with sex."

"Going to need a lot of distraction." He rested his chin on her head. "And you're going to need to bid on me tonight for the bachelor auction."

She wrinkled her nose. "I organized the event. I don't think I should bid. Wouldn't that be some sort of insider trading?" Although she wanted to, the idea of raising her hand in the crowd, showing everyone how much she wanted him, made her stomach tense. If things didn't work out between them, she'd be the fool who couldn't even buy Chance's love.

"It's for charity," he said dryly. "Your money will be just as happily accepted as anyone else's."

"Still. It just feels wrong. And hokey." And daunting.

He shrugged, his chest heaving beneath her face. "Okay. If you're fine seeing me go out on a date with another woman, I don't have a problem with it, either."

Jane tightened her grip. Crap. He was right. She couldn't let that happen. Still, she didn't want to give up so easily. "Who said it'll be another woman who gets you? I've seen Paul eyeing your poster all night."

Chance pushed her away an inch so he could look down at her. "Paul? Who the hell is Paul?"

"Our florist."

Tipping his head to one side, he pursed his lips. "I inspected the florist shop on Third. Was that Paul?"

"Did you kick him out of his business, as well?" Jane couldn't keep the annoyance from her voice. Her mother was safely ensconced back in her own home now, but the memory of kale chips defiling her oven still brought a shudder to her bones. Some scars ran deep.

He tucked her close to his body, his heat soothing her irritation.

Snuggling in, she sighed. "Yes, that was Paul."

"Huh." Grabbing her hand, Chance spun her out, startling Jane, and pulled her back in. "He was built. But if you're fine, seeing me go out on a date with a hot guy . . ."

She laughed. That was what she'd missed most. Okay, the sex had become Oscar worthy and ran a close second. But she'd never laughed as much in her life as she did when she was with Chance. He could keep a smile on her face for hours. And that was something she didn't want to let go.

"We'll see." Jane looped her arms around his neck. "If it doesn't cut into my shoe budget, then maybe."

"I don't think I like how I rank."

"Then you're just going to have to work a little harder, aren't you?" She tried to smother her smile, but the edges of her lips tugged up.

Chance narrowed his eyes, bent his head down so his mouth brushed against the shell of her ear. "When I get you in bed tonight, you'll see just how hard I can work."

Holy Hades. Her temperature spiked. Being near Chance was like being pre-menopausal. Hot flashes popping up out of thin air. "I look forward to your efforts."

"Screw waiting. There's a gazebo outside. We're going—"

"Jane, there you are." Edith stepped next to them. She'd forgone her long, flowy dresses in favor of a fifties-style gown, its stiff skirt and sweetheart neckline giving her an hourglass figure.

"You look great, Mom."

Chance kissed Edith's cheek. "As beautiful as your daughter."

"I'm glad someone thinks so," Edith muttered.

Jane shared a look with Chance. He raised an eyebrow.

"Mom, what are you—"

"It doesn't matter. But Jane"—Edith tugged on Jane's arm—"Mrs. Bronkowski is saying that Mrs. Harper changed her one into a seven on the silent auction form to get the Lord of the Rings garden gnomes. She's threatening to call the *Pineville Gazette*. We don't want a scandal associated with our fundraiser."

"I hardly think that qualifies as a scandal," Jane said. Her mother gave her that look, the one that had sent her scurrying back to her room to do her homework. She sighed, stepping out of Chance's arms. "But I'll go see what I can do."

Chance took a step after her.

"And I should get back to Leon afterward," she added.

He put his hands on his hips, his mouth tight, but nodded. "I'll see you later." It was part demand, part plea, and the glower that accompanied it was all heat.

A delicious tingle kept her company as she walked away, adding a slight hip swing to her step, knowing Chance's eyes followed her. Tonight was going to be fun.

She approached the two bickering older women, one of them holding a stumpy Gandalf snug to her chest.

It would be fun *after* the ball, she promised herself, and dove into the melee. Twenty minutes later, she had both ladies moderately unhappy, a compromise they could each live with. Turning to look for Chance—nope, she meant Leon, he was her date—she was stopped once again by the sight of an unhappy woman. This time her mother.

Jane joined her in front of the painting by the unknown artist, which Edith had donated. "Mrs. Bronkowski isn't going to alert the media. You don't have to worry about that."

Her mother's shoulders slumped. "That's good."

"Mom, what's wrong?"

"Nothing. I've just been foolish." Edith stared at the painting. It rested on a low stand on the table. "A lot of people are bidding on this. I thought if he saw that, he'd understand how good his work is. But it just made him mad when I showed him. He said some things . . ."

Jane wrapped an arm around her mother's waist, rested her head against her silvering hair. "Who? Who painted this?"

Edith didn't answer. "I don't think he'll ever forgive me. He was so mad," she whispered.

A deep brogue thundered behind them. "Don't be daft, woman. I'm right ticked off, but I don't think there's anything you could do I wouldn't forgive."

Jane spun. "Chief Finnegan. You painted that?"

"Aye," he said, his gaze never leaving her mother.

Jane stepped closer to her mom. She'd noticed that the chief's accent intensified when he was upset. He'd been barely understandable over the radio when Sam Hunt had crashed an engine into a fire hydrant. Water had shot thirty feet in the air and flooded the street. His anger had been justified.

"And I didn't paint it so you could sell it. I painted it for you." Taking a step forward, he lifted Edith's hand. "I wanted you to have something of me."

Awww. Jane looked at the two of them. Her mom glowed, and the chief looked at her mother like he couldn't believe his luck. Her mom and Chief Finnegan. He was the man Jane would have chosen for her mother, and the sneaky woman had been seeing him all along. How had Jane missed this?

Skirt flouncing, Edith spun around and wrote an exorbitant amount down on the bidding sheet.

"Mom!" Jane widened her eyes. "That's really generous. Can you aff—"

"After all the money these guys saved me with my electrical upgrade, it's the least I can do." She threaded an arm through Finnegan's. "But I might need to borrow some money when I bid on Sean during the bachelor auction. I'm not letting this one get away."

Sean Finnegan whispered something in Edith's ear, and she flushed bright red.

Looking satisfied at her response, the chief nodded his head at Jane and pulled her mother away, a proprietary hand on her hip.

"Huh." Leon walked up to her, crunching ice. "I didn't know your mom and the chief were a couple."

"Neither did I."

"Isn't she a little old for him?" Leon asked.

Jane shot him a scathing look. "*Maybe* she's five years older. You wouldn't think anything of that if the roles were reversed."

He shrugged.

"I think the bachelor auction is going to start soon and I want to get my bidding placard." Jane strode toward the table near the stage, Leon trailing at her heels. "I hope you don't mind that I'm going to bid on Chance tonight."

Leon held up his hands, spilling a bit of his drink with the motion. "I've got no problems with Chance. Be sure to tell him I said that."

Jane patted his arm. "I'm sorry about that earlier. I'm going to have a chat with Chance about him trying to mark his territory."

Leon didn't look convinced. "Just tell him that we're friends. Just friends. Right?"

"He knows, Leon." Picking up a red placard, Jane practiced flashing it with a little wrist flick. She'd never participated in an auction before. Would the slightest move put her on the hook for a bid?

"Speak of the devil." Leon paused on their way across the floor, took a subtle step behind Jane. Chance and Katie stood a couple of feet ahead, their gazes trained on the dance floor.

Jane took a step forward, wanting to say hello to Katie. Hearing her name, she paused.

"So things sound like they're getting serious," Katie said, her shoulders moving to the beat of the music. "I'm glad you took my advice."

"What advice was that?" Chance asked.

Jane stepped back. She gave Leon an uncomfortable smile. She didn't want to eavesdrop, but if she approached them now, they might think that's what she'd been doing. She'd walk away with Leon and say hello to Katie another time.

But Katie's next words stopped her cold.

"That you get Jane to marry you to keep custody of Josh." Katie wound her arm around Chance's. "There's no way Annette will get her slimy hands on him once the judge sees sweet and sensible Jane as his new mother."

Jane fell back, stumbling on her heels. Only Leon's hand at her elbow kept her from taking a seat on the floor. Her head felt light, as if all the blood had drained from it, only to come thundering back, pounding in her temples. What the hell? Was Chance going to propose? And had he only gotten close to her in order to keep custody?

She sucked in a breath. Rubbing at the ache under her breastbone, she examined the facts. Chance loved Josh and would do anything to keep him. Jane had no illusions about how she ranked in Chance's life, and was fine with the pecking order. Josh should come first. But she wasn't willing to be an ignorant pawn in Chance's scheme.

Fact two, Chance had a history of screwing her over to achieve his goals. He hadn't cared about her feelings when she hadn't fit into his plans for college, just cut her out of his life.

She took another step back, saw Chance smile at his sister. She could no longer hear their conversation over the pounding in her ears.

She didn't need to hear. His smile said it all. He agreed with his sister. He'd made Jane a part of his plan and it was all falling into place.

"I have to leave," she whispered. People jostled into her from both sides, and the faintest hint of panic threaded through her body. Maybe she was claustrophobic. What else could explain why it felt like the walls were closing in on her? It didn't help that she was technically in a cave.

Leon's brows drew together. "Are you getting married, Jane?"

She huffed out a harsh laugh. "No."

"Then . . ." He looked stumped. "I don't get it."

Jane fled. Leon stopped her as she hit the dirt parking lot. "Hold up, Jane. Let me drive you home."

Leon was sweet. And she was an idiot for not falling for a man like him. Leon would never try to trick a woman into marrying him. But they'd driven to the ball separately, and she'd never been so happy to have her own wheels. She just wanted to get in her car and get the hell away from there. Alone.

"I'll be fine. But thanks." She'd be fine after a bottle or two of wine. Damn, she should have snagged a couple of bottles before leaving the cave. Chance's SUV sat in the pool of light cast from an overhead lamp, drawing her attention. Maybe she'd feel better if she ran her key along the door, she thought, knowing that was pointless and she'd never do it. But it was easier to feel betrayed and angry. If she didn't have those feelings, all she'd be left with was devastation.

"I don't think you should drive when you're this upset," Leon said. "I'll drive you home and have one of my buddies take your car to your house."

Lifting her chin, she wiped at her cheek. "Go back inside, Leon. Have a good time. If anyone asks, tell them I had a headache and went home."

That was pretty close to the truth. Only the organ that was aching was just below her head. As she stumbled to her car, her vision blurred. She got the door shut before she crumpled. A sob tore out of her throat, past the burn in her chest.

Twice. She'd fallen for his crap twice. But unlike in high school, this time Jane's feelings had matured. She loved him, the kind of love that would have fed her soul for the rest of her life.

And he'd broken her heart. Again.

Chapter Twenty

Jane rolled over in bed, peeled another tissue off her face. Her life seemed to have gone full circle, in more ways than one. If she cared about things like self-esteem and pride, she would have been disgusted by her behavior. Moping in bed. Over Chance. Again.

Picking up the damp tissue from her pillow, she blew her nose. She tossed it in the direction of her wastepaper basket. From the look of disgust in Cy's eye, she guessed she'd missed.

After sending a text to her mother, telling her she was okay but wanted to be alone, Jane had turned off her phone, unplugged her seldom-used landline, and ignored all knocks at her door. And there had been several. Some pounding and bellowing, too, but it was amazing how well a down comforter and pillow excelled at cancelling out the noise.

And so went Saturday. By Sunday, Jane knew she had to get her act together. She had a shift that afternoon, and no way would she let Chance reduce her to some nonfunctioning idiot who couldn't work because of man problems. That, and she was out of ice cream and Pop-Tarts. She needed to go out anyway.

She dragged through her shower, only put on the bare minimum of makeup. Girl sense, the fun neighbor of common sense, told her she should dress to impress, put on something tight and clingy in case she ran into Chance. But she couldn't muster the energy, and pulled on the first pair of baggy jeans she came across.

Crunching on a bowl of cereal, she stared at the desk where she'd laid *the card*. Would Chance have found something equally trite for his proposal? Had Hallmark come up with a little rhyme for that? *I don't love you, but want to make you my wife, to help keep my son in my life*?

Cy jumped onto her lap and kneaded his claws into her thigh. She grimaced before distracting him with a chin scratch. "I know I'm pathetic. You don't have to rub my nose in it." He circled three times before flopping down on his back, batting at her hand until she rubbed his stomach.

"I am not rolling over and playing dead. I'm just regrouping," she told Cy. He opened his good eye, looked at her with disbelief. His claw caught on the skin between her thumb and forefinger.

Shaking loose, Jane sucked at the tiny wound. "I never should have fed you and given you a home after I found you in that alley. You're supposed to take my side." He puffed out a breath, rolled onto his side, and curled into a ball. His purrs ripped through the living room. He knew she was a sucker and would never throw him out. He didn't have to play nice with her.

Her heart burned. She was a doormat. Apparently everyone had her figured out, and she was the last to know. She glared at the card through narrowed eyes. It was past time to change that. Cy could stay and keep walking all over her, literally and figuratively, but he was the only one. She needed to demand respect. No more pathetic dates with nice guys who didn't want anything more from her than a second player for their games. And no more falling for men who put their plans ahead of her needs. Time to take control of her life.

And that started with letting go of her past. Scooping up Cy, she deposited him on the cushion, ignoring his angry hiss. She strode to the desk, plucked up the card. She didn't look at it as she walked to the kitchen, pulled out a barbecue lighter from a drawer, and put a flame to it. The shiny cardstock burned an odd green, and the paper curled before turning black and flaking. Jane dropped it into the sink and watched it burn.

She didn't feel like a weight had lifted or that she'd overcome some great burden, but she wasn't sad to let that memory go. Even though the same man had screwed her over twice, she wasn't going to cling to the hurt. She was going to move forward with an open mind and heart. Her mother would be proud.

And she would start by stopping at Starbucks for a vanilla chai latte instead of her usual black coffee. Time to let loose.

She snorted. And if that wasn't absolutely pathetic, she didn't know what was.

Grabbing her keys, she swung open the door and ran into a hard wall of muscle. "What the hell?" She sputtered. "Were you squatting below the peephole?"

"Leaning on the wall next to the door. Waiting"—Chance checked his watch—"for hours."

Jane pulled the door shut. "Well, you can keep waiting. We're not talking."

Brushing past him, she trotted to the stairs.

His long-legged stride matched her pace. "Like hell we're not talking. I've been pounding on your door for a day and a half." He pushed open the door to the apartment building and held it. "I know what you think you heard. But if you'd just let me explain—"

"What I heard was self-explanatory. I don't need the footnotes." She hurried through the parking lot, head down. Pointing her key fob at her car, she unlocked the doors.

Chance ripped the car door from her grip, slammed it closed. "We're going to talk whether you want to or not," he growled. Placing his palm on her driver's-side window, he leaned against it, barring her entry. "When Katie said I should marry you—"

Jane snapped. She was supposed to be starting her new carefree lifestyle, not wallowing in the past and pathetic excuses. For the first time, Chance was ruining *her* plans. And it was pissing her off. She didn't want to listen to him, didn't want to hear his reasons. She grabbed a finger and yanked.

He yelped. "Christ!" Shaking his hand, he glared at her. "Stop acting like a child. Let's sit down somewhere and talk."

"Can't." She slid behind the wheel. "I'm getting a coffee then going to work."

"I'll buy you the damn coffee."

"No thanks." The slamming of her door cut off his reply. He reached for the door handle and Jane hit the locks.

Chance's eyes darkened to obsidian. Whoa, he was pissed. Well, he could stew in it for a while. She put the car in gear but waited for him to step back so she didn't run over his feet. She wasn't that pissed off. Probably.

He moved to the front of the car, put his hands on the hood, and glared at her through the windshield. Damn her conscience. She should have taken out a toe. And damn her penchant for backing into parking spaces. He had her boxed in. Unless she ran him down.

She shook her head. No. No running down her ex-boyfriend. No matter how manipulative he was. Besides, his arms were bulging under his T-shirt, his chest heaving with irritation. He looked kind of Hulk-like, and she didn't know if her small car would win in a battle between the two.

Putting the car into park, she rolled down her window. "You're going to want to move it."

"I thought you trusted me." She read his lips more than heard him. And she was glad of it. She didn't want to hear the hurt she saw written over his face. Didn't want to hear his side of the story. Her chest was tight, her eyes burned. She guessed she wasn't ready to let go of her hurts quite yet. She'd have to work on that. Tomorrow.

"And I thought you'd changed," she said. "That you weren't still a slave to your precious plans. I know you're desperate to keep Josh, but this plan really sucked. Now get out of my way."

Turning his head to the side, he took a deep breath. His shoulders slumped, and Jane knew he'd given up. A pin stabbed her heart. That was a good thing, him giving up. She wouldn't have to listen to his BS. Then why did she want to throw her arms around him and beg him not to leave?

He pushed off the car, gave her one last look, and walked away.

Jane let out a ragged sob. She should be as dehydrated as a raisin, but her eyes filled with more tears. How come he was the one who screwed her over and she was the one who felt like the bad guy? Gripping the steering wheel, she sucked in a shaky breath. Her lungs burned with the effort. Or was that her heart? It felt like it'd died. Only fitting it be cremated, too.

Pulling out of her parking space, she had to wipe her eyes twice in order to look both ways. No way was she stopping for coffee looking and acting like this. She went straight to work and settled in a half hour before her shift began.

A piece of chewing gum snapped. "Jane? What are you doing here so early?"

"Hi, Sharon." Jane turned on her computer. "Just thought I'd get some things organized."

A wall of dark hair crested the cubicle divider. "Uh-huh." Sharon rested her arms on the low wall. "So you coming in here early looking like you just saw *Sophie's Choice* has nothing to do with a certain fireman who you've been sleeping with for a month and who ran out of the ball before the bachelor auction looking for you?"

Jane scowled. "What have you heard about it?"

"There are a couple rumors." Sharon blew a bubble, sucked it back in. "One is that you're the secret mama to Chance's son, but because of your drug addiction, you gave Josh up to Chance and never looked back. You heartless bitch," she teased.

Jane dropped her face into her hands. "And the other?"

"That Chance asked you to marry him and because you don't want to be a mother, you dropped him." Sharon shook her head. "That's the one Leon's spreading, but it sounded fishy to me."

Jane sputtered. "How did Leon get that—" She rubbed her temples. "It doesn't matter. I'm not going to get mad at Leon, too, even if he is a moron."

"So what did happen?"

Picking up her headset, Jane twisted the cord around her finger. "I overheard Chance and his sister talking about him marrying me in order to keep custody of Josh. Apparently having a two-parent household sways judges in their consideration."

"And he never discussed this with you?" Sharon asked. She whistled at Jane's head shake. "So he led you on, acting like it was all a whirlwind romance when he really just wanted a baby mama?"

Christ, put like that, it sounded horrible. "Well . . ."

"That's fraud. Fraud and a con job." Sharon's red lips thinned. "I say tonight after work, we go out drinking. Then we find your con man, lure him out of his house, and—" Sharon ground her fist into her open palm.

"Give him an Indian burn?"

"No! We kick his ass. His hard, chiseled ass." Sharon's eyes went soft. "Since you're not seeing him anymore, you can tell me. Under that uniform, is he as hot as he looks?"

Jane's stomach plummeted. "Hotter." And she was never going to see it again.

"Nothing to ruin my fantasies? No third nipple or double toe?"

"I don't even know what that is, but no, he's pretty perfect." Damn him. "But what are you doing fantasizing about my . . ." Ex-boyfriend, ex-lover, ex-friend. She hated all those exes. "My almost fiancé?" Yeah, like that didn't sound pathetic at all.

Sharon raised a waxed eyebrow. "You're sounding awfully touchy for a woman who just dumped the man. What's the matter? You're not still attached to the slime, are you?"

"He's not slime." Jane felt her temper rise with her body temperature. "He's just worried about losing his son."

"Wait." Her friend's brow drew down. "I thought we were at the point where we bash the ex. Why are you defending him?"

"I'm not defending him."

"You sure about that? Because it kinda sounds like you are." She rested her head on her forearms. "You got in deep, didn't you?"

Shoulders slumped, Jane rubbed her forehead. "Sometimes it feels like with Chance, I never got out of it. I think I've loved him since high school. I don't want to believe he used me, but I know what I heard."

"Well, how does Chance explain it?" Sharon asked.

Jane sucked her bottom lip into her mouth.

Sharon cocked her head. "You did let Chance defend himself, right?"

Crickets chirped.

"Sweet Jesus. You don't think you owed him that much?" The condemnation in her friend's eyes shamed Jane.

Jane poked at a notepad, pushing it across her desk. "I didn't want to hear his excuses. All they'd do is insult me more."

Walking around the cubicle, Sharon came to stand in front of Jane. She looked down on her with sympathy. "Or maybe you don't want to hear that he didn't con you. You're using this as an excuse to cut and run."

"Why the hell would I do that?" Jane got to her feet, not liking her friend's height advantage. She also didn't like how reasonable she sounded. "I wanted nothing more than for Chance to be the guy I thought he was, to have a future with him."

"Honey, ever since I've known you, you've always sabotaged your romances." She raised a hand at Jane's protest. "First there was that Neanderthal from Clarion Township. You knew there was no future in that, but you wasted four months with him. And he didn't even show you a good time while you were dating."

"Marco wasn't that bad." He'd been worse. He'd grunt at her to pass the ketchup, and kissed like a fish.

"Please. He was barely literate. And you kept saying you thought he had a good soul underneath his rough exterior." Sharon snorted. "But he was crap all the way through."

"Okay, that's one. But—"

"And then there's Leon," Sharon continued.

"Leon's not a Neanderthal. He actually is a nice guy."

Shaking her head, Sharon sighed. "A nice guy who for the past eight months you've been going out with twice a week, knowing there was no way in hell you wanted a future with him. He was the safe date who kept you from having to think about going out with other men. You put yourself on the shelf."

"Hey." Jane's jaw dropped open. "I had fun with Leon."

"Playing board games." Tilting her head, Sharon gave her the stink eye.

"It was still fun." Most of the time. Depending on the game. And when Leon didn't get too serious about it. Which he usually did.

"No kissing. For *eight months*." Sharon crossed her arms as if the argument was won. And it was. Jane didn't have a counter to that annoying fact. Christ, had she been subconsciously sabotaging her love life? Was she one of those people who kept throwing up roadblocks in front of their own happiness? She hated those people.

Groaning, Jane fell back into her chair. Crap. She was one of those people. "Maybe I like being single and that's why I don't really want a relationship." She tried to salvage a victory. "There's nothing wrong with not getting married."

"Nothing at all," Sharon agreed. "Except you're not that person who doesn't want to get married. Don't pretend that you are."

"I hate you," Jane said, no heat in her voice.

Sharon grinned, her white teeth a beautiful contrast with her dark skin. "You love me. And if you love Chance, you need to give him, well, uh, a chance to explain." She wrinkled her nose. "His name's kinda annoying, though."

The phone rang and Sharon darted back into her cube to answer. Jane spun in her chair until the headset cord twisted around her body, then turned back the other way. What Sharon said was reasonable. She should have let Chance explain. So why hadn't she? Because she didn't want to hear his excuses, or because she was scared of reaching for the brass ring?

And there was no doubt in her mind that for her, Chance was the brass ring. If he hadn't tried to trick her into a marriage. And that was a very big if.

The phone rang, and Jane settled the headset on her hair. "This is 9-1-1. What's your emergency?"

"Jane? Is that you?" a small voice asked.

"Josh?" Bolting up straight, she scanned her computer screen, impatient for the data to pop up. "Are you okay? Is it your aunt?"

"Nooo." There was a scraping sound, then the rustle of fabric against fabric.

"Then what's wrong, buddy?" A phone number appeared on her screen, but no address information. He was calling from a cell. It would take longer to fix his location.

"Me and Mommy are out. Some men are yelling at her." He lowered his voice to a whisper. "I think they're bad men."

"Where are you, sweetie? Are you at a restaurant?" Drumming her fingers on the desk, Jane tried to make the address appear through force of will. Why was it taking so long?

"I'm in the car. Mommy and the men are outside."

"Look around you. Do you see anything you recognize?" Jane asked.

"Nuh-uh. We left Pineville."

Jane's pulse raced. Where the hell was Annette taking Josh? Was she driving away with him?

"He's grabbing her arm," Josh yelled, outrage in his high voice. "I'm going out."

"No!" She took a deep breath, ignoring Sharon, who'd popped her head over the wall in question. In a more controlled tone, she said, "Stay where you are, buddy. Stay out of sight." The address finally, finally, appeared on the screen. "Help is coming your way."

"I want my dad." The fear in Josh's voice broke her heart.

"And you're going to see him real soon." Jane pounded on her keyboard, alerting the police, and scribbled a note to Sharon. "I'm going to put you on the phone with my friend Sharon, and she's going to stay on the line until help arrives. I want you to stay on the phone with her. Can you do that for me?"

Sharon hustled around the cubicle and sat in Jane's seat when she got up. She motioned for the headset. Jane waited for Josh to agree before tossing the headset at her friend. Grabbing her keys, she ran from the courthouse.

Josh needed help, and sitting in dispatch just didn't cut it.

Chapter Twenty-one

Chance pounded his fists into the heavy bag hanging in the corner of the fire station's garage. The tape on his right hand had been scraped away, and he was leaving little red marks on the bag every time he hit it. The guys would love that. Hitting around his blood-stains.

Wrapping his left arm around the bag, he threw uppercuts into its midsection, like he was eviscerating some poor dude's gut. A hand clapped onto the back of his neck, pulling him away.

Chance whirled, a curse at the tip of his tongue. The chief stood before him, the look on his face telling Chance he wouldn't put up with any crap. Chance sucked a deep breath down into his stomach, tried to calm the roiling mess of vipers that had taken up residence there.

"Busting your hand isn't going to help with your situation," Finnegan said. "It's only going to put you out of commission. And since we save lives around here, that's going to piss me off." He shoved a bottle of water at Chance. "Want to talk about it?"

Shaking his head, Chance opened the bottle, swallowed deeply.

"Too damn bad. Follow me." The chief spun on his heel and stalked out of the garage into the driveway. Chance followed, feeling as sulky as Josh when told to go to bed.

Finnegan faced him. "I think we're far enough away from eaves-droppers."

Peering back into the dim garage, Chance didn't see anyone, but knew the chief was right. The guys were in the living room, and as soon as the chief left to talk to Chance, they would have been pressed against the door, eager to hear any dirt. Especially Martinez.

"Now"—Finnegan crossed his arms—"I understand you have a problem with your lady."

Chance kept his face impassive. "No problems. And no lady."

The chief snorted. "From the beggar to the king, we've all got problems. Now stop bullshitting me and tell me if there's anything I can do to help."

"No." Chance ran a hand through his sweaty hair. "There's nothing. Jane misheard something and won't let me explain her mistake. She ended it. Stubborn, bullheaded woman," he bit out.

"That's a quality that any woman who sticks with you is going to need," Finnegan said. When Chance glared at the chief, he shrugged, unapologetic. "Jane's what, five two?"

Chance wrinkled his forehead. "Five six. Why?"

"Still small," Finnegan said. "Hold her down. Make her listen."

A laugh escaped Chance. He tried to picture that scenario. It didn't end well for some of his most sensitive, and prized, parts. And he'd never thought of Jane as small. With her quiet strength, her innate kindness, she'd always seemed larger than life. And by her side, Chance had always felt like he could take on the world.

Until this morning. When she'd cut him into little bits and casually tossed him aside.

He needed to pound the bag some more. "Are we done here?"

"Not by a long shot, boyo." The Irish was coming up. Finnegan narrowed his eyes. "You'll bloody listen to what I say and then go fix it."

Chance gripped his hips. "I can't just fix it. Jane needs—"

"The girl needs to hear you love her. Edith says she's been in love with you for a decade." Placing a hand on Chance's shoulder, the chief squeezed. "You went out, got married, had a whole other life without her. It sounds like she's always been waiting for you. Of course she's going to be insecure, be looking for reasons why you don't care for her. She needs to hear how you feel."

"She hasn't been in love with me all this time," Chance said, his voice hoarse. He cleared his throat. "She couldn't have been." Could she? Those moments, when his marriage was going to hell and his thoughts had drifted back to the woman who'd always made him happy, his Janey-girl, had she been thinking of him, too? Had they always been connected?

"Edith says she hasn't had one serious relationship since you left." Finnegan blew out a breath. "She's going to kick my arse for telling you all this." His eyes lit up. "But I have ways to make her forgive me."

Yeah, Chance didn't need to know that. Edith had always acted like a second mom to him. He hoped the chief made her happy, but didn't want to think about how he was making her happy.

Finnegan clapped him on the back. "If your girl is anything like her mother, she's worth fighting for. Even if she is a pain in the butt every once in a while."

Chance's shoulders unbunched. Yeah, she was worth it. He didn't care about his plan for the future staying on schedule. He'd marry Jane tomorrow or in ten years, whenever she'd let him, but he knew she was a part of his future. She had to be. He and Josh wouldn't be happy without her.

So, like the chief said, he'd make her listen. Although the idea of sitting on her so she couldn't ignore him was appealing, he knew he wouldn't have to. He'd wear her down eventually. Get her to listen. It had only been two days since the fundraiser. She still hadn't had time to cool off properly.

Once she did, she'd give him a chance to explain.

If she didn't, then he'd sit on her. Or tie her to his bed. Heat flooded his body, and Chance smiled. He could get behind that idea.

"I don't even want to know what you're thinking," Finnegan said. He took a step back, crossed his arms. "She is the daughter of the woman I love, so behave, or I'll be forced to kick your arse." Raising his eyebrow, he shrugged. "But do what you need to, to get her back."

Chance intended to. He was on shift for another two days, but that didn't mean he couldn't start now. Flowers, balloons, that chocolate she liked. He'd avoid greeting cards. That was only sensible. But everything else was fair game. For the next two days, he'd launch a campaign that would not only show Janey-girl that he was sincere but that he wasn't giving up.

It wasn't the same as bringing her flowers in person, but it would have to be enough for now. But damn, he wanted to see her. Two days without seeing her smile, touching her soft skin. It was going to be hell. The one photo he had of her in his phone was going to get a lot of views.

That was the first thing he'd do when he got her back, take more pictures. Well, maybe the second or third thing. Definitely top ten.

Her smile came unbidden to his mind. The one she gave him right before . . . He ran a hand through his hair. Two more damn days. He'd never make it. He needed to see her, live, in person, right—

Her small blue car bounced over the curb, screeched to a stop at his feet. He and the chief jumped back, then Chance rushed forward as she lowered her window.

"Get in the car," she said, her face tight.

"What's wrong?" He scanned what he could see of her, didn't see any wounds. But she looked like she was in pain. "Are you—"

"It's Josh. He called me. He needs you." Her knuckles were white around the steering wheel. "Now get in the damn car."

Chance's feet were moving before his brain could catch up. Jane had been heading to work when he'd last seen her. So if Josh was calling her, he'd called her at work, dialed 9-1-1. He threw himself into the passenger seat. "Is it Katie? Did she pass out again?"

The chief jogged back into the station as they pulled away. They hadn't gotten a call yet, but Chance knew Finnegan would be making calls of his own to find out what was going on.

"It's not Katie." Picking her cell phone out of her cup holder, Jane pressed it between her ear and her shoulder. "Anything new?" she asked the person on the other end of the line. "Well, what do they say their ETA is?" Her jaw clenched, and Chance's pulse skyrocketed.

"Who are you talking to? What's going on?" he demanded.

Jane ignored him. "I know. Sharon, I know," she said, her voice getting heated. She pulled onto the highway onramp, cutting off a truck. "Look, I'm driving like crap. I'm going to put you down again. Hold on."

Dropping the phone back in the cup holder, Jane kept her eyes on the road, swerved around a slow-moving RV. "Josh called 9-1-1 about ten minutes ago. He said he was with his mom, and that some men were yelling at her." She darted a look at him. "One of them grabbed her. Josh is in the car."

"Where?" His voice came out harsher than he'd intended. It wasn't Jane's fault. God help him, he'd forgotten Josh was spending the afternoon with Annette. He'd been too wrapped up in thoughts of Jane. If one hair on his son's head was injured because of Annette, he'd strangle her this time.

"They're over in Clarion Township. At a gas station. Police are on their way."

He picked up the phone. "Sharon, this is Chance. Tell me what's going on."

"Hold on," she said. Chance heard her talking soothingly to someone else. He heard his son's name. She was talking to Josh. The pressure in his head popped, and he became dizzy. Josh was okay. As of now.

Sharon came back on his line. "Chance, Josh is still in the car. He's fine. But he's very upset. I'm going to patch you through so you can talk to him." Two clicks, and then he heard his son crying. *Crying*. His chest felt like it was caught in a vise.

"Hey, buddy. It's Dad. Everything's going to be fine." A road sign came up, whipped past. Clarion Township. Two miles. Jane needed to drive faster. "Can you talk to me?"

"Daddy?"

Christ. When was the last time Josh had called him daddy? His five-year-old had given up what he called "baby talk" at least a year ago.

"He . . ." A soft sob met Chance's ear, tore through his heart. "One of the bad men hit Mommy."

"Are the doors locked in the car?" Chance asked. It was only a small layer of protection. If Annette was outside, her keys probably were, too.

"Daddy, where are you?"

"I'm almost there." He looked at Jane, who nodded grimly. "We're almost there. Just stay in the car until I get you." Then the most beautiful sound came through the phone. The wail of a siren.

"P'weece are here," Josh yelled. "The men are running."

"And where's your mom?" Chance asked. "Do you still see her?"

"Yeah. She's sitting down."

Because she was injured, or upset? At that point, Chance didn't care. She'd frightened their son for the last time.

"An ociffer is knocking on the window," Josh said. A hint of excitement battled with the fear in his voice. Thank God kids were resilient. "I gotta go."

Chance stared at the phone. "He hung up on me."

Clutching his arm with one hand, Jane almost lost control of the car. "Oh my God. Did the men—"

"He's fine." Chance grabbed the steering wheel with his right hand, rubbed small circles into her shoulder with the other. "The police are there. Everything's going to be fine."

"Good." A tear rolled down her cheek. "That's good."

"Hey. Josh is safe. We're fine." Chance was tempted to tell her to pull over just so he could hold her. But there was too much unsaid between them. Jane was worried about his son. But she'd tensed under his touch.

"I know." She sniffed. "So why am I crying?"

Chance leaned back in his seat. "It's the adrenalin. You were pumped up for action, and now that it's over, your body doesn't know what to do with it."

"If anything had happened to him . . ."

"I know." Chance didn't want to think about it.

"I don't like your wife." Jane ran the back of her hand under her eyes.

"Ex-wife." He caught Jane's gaze. "It's official. I got the papers yesterday."

"Congratulations." She turned back to face out the windshield. "With this latest incident, I don't think you need to worry about custody. Any judge would grant custody to a single dad over that miserable excuse of an ex-wife."

"What if I don't *want* to stay single?"

"What?" Jane frowned.

"You're right. I don't need a wife to secure my son." Tucking a piece of hair behind her ear, Chance let his fingers trail down her neck. "So when I come for you, you'll know I'm doing it because I want to. Because I want you. You should have known that already."

Maybe berating her wasn't the smartest move to win her back, but dammit, he was pissed, too. Between his hurt and the influx of fear for his son, Chance wasn't in the mood to hold anything back. He couldn't. His control was on the edge of snapping.

She scraped her teeth over her bottom lip, darted a glance at him. "Why did Katie say that if it wasn't true?"

"Katie's got a big mouth and says whatever pops into her head." Speaking of, he should call his sister, tell her what had happened. Once he had Josh in his arms, he would. "She'd joked about that weeks ago. Thought she was being smart. It wasn't a plan I'd agreed to."

Jane turned onto a main street, and flashing red and blue lights came into sight. Josh sat on the hood of a patrol car, swinging his legs, chatting with a uniformed officer. Chance's whole body sagged. His son was okay. He didn't look around for Annette. Before Jane had put the car in park, Chance was out the door.

"Dad!" Josh yelled, just before Chance swept him into his arms. The cop gave them some space, and Chance leaned back against the hood and just enjoyed the feel of his son's small body, whole and safe, next to his.

Josh, however, wasn't as eager for a quiet bonding moment. "Did you see there are six p'weece here? Six." It was said as though that were a mystical number. "One gave me a badge"—he pointed to a sticker on his shirt—"but he wouldn't show me his gun. But cops get to carry guns and you don't." Josh wrinkled his nose. "I'm going to be a p'weece man when I grow up."

"Hey." Chance pulled back, looked his son up and down. Completely unharmed. The last of his tension rolled away. "I get to carry an axe sometimes. That's pretty cool."

Josh considered that. His face lit up. "Jane!" he screamed. Right in Chance's ear. But he couldn't blame the kid. He got that excited when he saw Jane, too. His son twisted away from his grip, threw himself at her.

Jane grabbed him before he fell. "Hey, buddy. Quite an adventure, huh?" Gathering him close, she put her nose on top of Josh's head, placed a kiss on his hair.

"I'm going to be a cop when I grow up."

Chance frowned. Josh obviously hadn't considered it as well as he'd hoped.

Jane laughed. "Whatever you do, I'm sure your dad will be very proud." She hefted Josh up, settled him more comfortably on her hip. "And I'm proud of you calling 9-1-1. Again. You're a really smart kid for knowing when to call for help."

"I know." He wiggled down Jane's body and grabbed Chance's hand.

Chance rolled his eyes. He would have to work with his son on his modesty. But today he'd let him enjoy his due props.

"Dad, Mom's over there. Come say hi." Josh started pulling, and reluctantly, Chance let himself be propelled over to her. He didn't even want to look at the woman much less talk to her. And nothing he wanted to tell her could be said in front of Josh.

Annette held an ice pack to one cheek and stood talking with a cop. She was pale, but her eyes warmed when they caught sight of Josh. And that right there was her sole redeeming quality.

"I'm sorry our afternoon got messed up," she said to Josh. "I promise next time we'll have fun."

Chance turned to the cop. "Can I speak with my ex-wife? Are you done taking her statement?"

The woman nodded. "She'll need to come down to the station to file a report." Flipping her notebook closed, she pushed it into her breast pocket. "When you get down to the station, ma'am, ask for me." She nodded at them both, smiled at Josh, and walked away.

Annette put down the ice pack, smiled as brightly as she could around her swollen cheek. "Well, who's for pizza? My treat."

Chance clenched his jaw so tight he could have ground diamonds into dust. He bared his teeth. "Buddy, go hang out with Jane for a bit. I need to talk to your mom."

Annette watched Josh run to Jane, a brittle smile on her face. "I know what you're going to say."

"I don't think you do." Chance forced his voice low. Josh couldn't hear all he had to say. "If you did, you'd be jumping in the back of that patrol car, begging the officer to get you away from me."

Annette rolled her eyes, and Chance felt the heat and anger that had settled in his gut rise through his body like it was on an express elevator. It was such an odd feeling that Chance stepped back, took a deep breath.

"It wasn't that big a deal," she said. "Josh shouldn't have called 9-1-1. There was just a misunderstanding."

He jerked his head at her face. "The bookie slipped and he accidentally hit you? You walked into his fist? How is that bruise a misunderstanding?"

Annette nudged a leaf with the toe of her brown suede pump. "That . . ." She cleared her throat. "He got more upset than he should have. I told him I'd pay! But when he found out I was from California, he thought I'd skip."

Which raised a gut-churning thought. "Why are you here?"

"To see my son. We've been over this."

Chance crossed his arms over his chest. Kept them from wrapping around Annette like a python, squeezing the life out of her. "Doesn't explain why you're in Clarion Township. A city twenty miles from

Pineville. Is it just because this is where your bookie works? And how you found a bookie in the few times you've been here I don't want to know. Or is it because Clarion Township is right next to the interstate? Just how far were you planning on going with Josh today?"

She shifted her eyes sideways.

"Son of a bitch!" Chance clenched his hands into fists. "I'm calling the cops back over here. You were going to kidnap Josh?"

Annette snapped her head up, poked a manicured nail into his chest. "He's my son, too. It wasn't kidnapping. You've had him long enough."

"Not according to the California court system. And I can guarangoddamn-tee that you will not be getting custody of Josh. Ever."

"You're going to have me arrested for kidnapping my own son?" A tinge of hysteria wound through her words. "You can't do that."

Chance looked over to where Josh and Jane sat on a bench. His son was head down over Jane's smartphone, but Jane watched them, concern and worry written all over her face. What would it do to his son if Annette was arrested? Would he have to testify against her?

Josh wiggled on his seat, pointed at something on the screen to Jane. Giving him a big smile, Jane put out her fist for Josh to bump.

No. Chance forced his swollen throat to swallow. He couldn't do that to his son. He faced Annette. "Here's what I'm going to do. I'm going to call my divorce attorney and tell him that you left rehab, continued to gamble, and put our son in danger. Again."

Annette started to protest, and Chance raised his hand. "Shut up," he said. "That's all public record now and I want the police report here to show up in the custody record. But the attempted kidnapping"—Chance swallowed again, barely able to breathe around those words—"I'll keep quiet about."

The strain in Annette's face dissolved. He didn't let her enjoy the moment long. "Provided you tell your attorney to write up the documents that give me full custody of Josh permanently."

"But—"

He stepped close. "You've lost custody of Josh either way. This way keeps you out of jail. For once in your life, do the right thing. You're no good for him."

The look she sent their son almost had Chance softening his words. Almost. He let a part of himself feel bad for his ex-wife. And he hoped that she'd work on her problems and end up having a role in Josh's life. But that role wasn't going to be full-time mother. Josh deserved better.

"I'll call my lawyer," she whispered. "You'll have the papers by the end of the month."

"Good."

"Can I say goodbye to him?" Annette asked.

"Yes." Chance waved at Jane, indicating they should come over. She leaned down, said something to Josh, and pointed his way. His son dropped the phone on the bench and tore over to them. Jane followed more sedately and stopped about twenty feet away, obviously not comfortable joining in.

Annette bent down. "I have to leave again. Go back home to California." She gave Josh a peck on the cheek, a small squeeze around his shoulders. "Be a good boy for your father and remember I love you."

"Why don't you just live here now?" Josh asked. "It's pretty nice."

Annette ran her hand over a cowlick on Josh's head. It popped back up. "It's not that simple, baby. But I'll talk with your dad, try to work out a time when I can come see you again."

Chance ground his teeth. He knew it was good for his son to know his mom cared, but he hoped she didn't call for a while.

"Okay. Bye." Josh stepped to his father's side, hooked a finger in Chance's pocket.

Annette looked between the two of them, nodded, and walked away. Only one patrol car remained, almost as if the incident had never occurred. Chance thought about how everything could have gone differently, and he scooped Josh into his arms, held tight.

Instead of trying to wiggle away, Josh wrapped his chubby arms around Chance's neck, laid his head on his shoulder. The feeling was just about perfect.

He locked eyes with Jane, took a step toward her. She gave him a small smile and started walking to meet him halfway.

"You smell funny, Dad."

Jane heard that from ten feet away, widened her smile.

"I was working out before I came to get you, buddy. I'll take a shower soon." For his son to comment, a boy who'd once made a fort out of garbage, Chance must smell pretty ripe. Normally he wouldn't inflict his sweaty body on a woman. Right now, he didn't care.

Holding out his arm, the one not wrapped around Josh, he paused, waiting for Jane to take the final steps. She moved into his body, wrapping her arm around his waist and resting her head on his chest. Obviously, she didn't care either.

Chance looked down at his two armfuls. His son and the woman he loved. Their bodies nestled against his, warming him from the outside in.

This feeling was absolutely perfect.

Chapter Twenty-two

Jane stood in the shadows off to the side of a small platform in city hall. The mayor and Judge Nichols were speaking to the assembled audience, giving a rundown on the fundraiser, how much money it'd raised for their charity. Soon the judge would introduce her and Chance as the cochairs, and they, along with Chief Finnegan, would present the absurdly oversize check to the representative of the charity.

Jane had argued over the added expense of the supersized cardboard check, saying it was a silly tradition. The judge had been adamant. Some traditions weren't altered. So the thirty-dollar tradition rested behind the podium, awaiting its presentation.

The fine hairs on the back of Jane's neck raised a second before a warm body pressed into her from behind.

"Those guys really like to talk," Chance said in her ear. "And the mayor wasn't even involved with the fundraiser. How can he find so much to say about it?"

Jane smiled. "He's a politician. Even for the local ones, it's a required skill, the ability to jabber on and say nothing for half an hour."

"Are they ever going to introduce us?" Chance sighed. "I'd much rather spend my time with you doing something else."

A finger trailed from her ear, over her neck, and down her spine. She shivered at his touch. "It doesn't even sound like they're close to wrapping this up. If this is boring for us, Josh must be about to explode."

"Your mom's keeping him entertained," Chance said.

Jane sought her mother in the crowd. Sure enough, she and Josh sat, heads together, eyes on identical game consoles, their fingers flying over the small buttons. "Before she met Josh, I don't think my mom ever played a video game. Now she has her own Nintendo 3DS."

Chance brushed his lips over her neck before heading back to her ear. "She said it's better for Josh if someone plays the games with him so it's not isolating. With all the babysitting she's been doing for us, getting her the game system seemed the least I could do."

Jane wondered if this was something she should be concerned about. She didn't want Josh, or her mother, getting addicted to playing video games. But Chance played outside with Josh every opportunity he got, and Edith had other things to distract her.

Her primary distraction sat on a folding chair near the other end of the platform, looking uncomfortable in his dress blues. Chief Finnegan twisted his neck to look back at Edith with a mournful expression. It was clear he'd rather be playing video games with the two of them than taking part in the ceremony.

Since the two of them had gone public with their relationship, the chief had spent most of his free time at Edith's apartment, and helping her around her shop. Watching the huge Irishman try to explain the benefits of lavender oil to a customer had been the highlight of Jane's week. She and Chance had laughed so hard they'd cried.

"I don't like waiting," Chance growled. His deep tone tickled her eardrum and did funny things to her stomach.

She huffed out a small laugh. "You're the king of waiting. If something's on your master plan ten years from now, you'll wait patiently for it to play out."

"I don't know how true that is anymore, but speaking of plans"—Chance pressed closer into her—"I have a question for you."

Jane leaned back, let her body relax into his. When would the mayor ever shut up? With Chance so close, she grew impatient, too. Their time could be much better spent doing other things. Naughty things. "If this is about that thing you asked me to do last night, the answer is still no."

His chest vibrated with quiet laughter. "Not about that," he whispered in her ear, "but I bet I can still convince you to do it."

"Only in your dreams." Maybe. Chance was awfully talented at convincing her to push past her limits.

"This is about the future," he said. "I want to know how long it will be before I can propose without having you think I'm asking because of Josh."

Jane's heart leaped around in her chest like a rabbit caught in a trap. Chance must have been able to feel it. He placed one hand on her hip, holding her to him like he thought she was about to run away.

Fat chance of that. If they hadn't been in a room full of people, Jane would have thrown her arms and legs around Chance and squeezed the breath out of him. He wanted to marry her. Her Chance. The man she'd thought she'd lost forever.

Sucking down deep breaths, she tried to calm her rioting emotions. She'd thought they might be heading in this direction. But thinking and knowing were two different things.

The mayor wrapped up his speech, and the judge stepped forward to introduce Jane and Chance. He raised an arm in their direction.

Not wanting to leave his embrace, but knowing she had to; Jane took a small step forward. She glanced back over her shoulder and caught his eye. A sliver of vulnerability crossed his face, but his eyes were full of determination. Once Chance set his sights on a plan, he'd do just about anything to make it happen.

She thought about teasing him. Making him work for it. But she was tired of games. She just wanted Chance. He was offering her a family, and she didn't want to live without it for one moment longer.

Grabbing his hand, she pulled him after her toward the stage. She leaned into him and whispered, "No time at all."

Don't miss Allyson Charles's next novel, available this November. Please read on for an excerpt.

Sadie Wilson doesn't think Christmas can get any worse. Her real estate staging business is going under, the house she inherited is a wreck, and she was just arrested for driving while texting. Then she learns that she's sentenced to one week of community service decorating the town's Christmas tree for the annual lighting ceremony—with the man whose truck she destroyed.

Colt McCoy has a contractor's business to run. He doesn't have time for forty hours of stringing tinsel, especially not with the uptight princess who totaled the truck his brother left to him. Between a Grinch stealing Christmas decorations, a father he just can't please, and unwanted lessons on the art of tree decorating from the fastidious yet sexy Sadie, Colt is ready for this holiday to be over.

As Sadie and Colt work together, tempers flare . . . and sparks fly. This Christmas just might remind these two that the best gifts are found under *The Christmas Tree*.

Chapter One

Sadie Wilson knew she shouldn't do it.

It was against the rules, and the key to her ordered life had always been to follow the rules. But the ping of her phone rang in her ears, a siren's call. It could be what she'd been waiting for.

She peered out her windshield up the street. Maple trees, bare of any leaves and wound with hundreds of white lights, lined the avenue, giving the dark night a cheery glow. Green wreaths with red bows hung from each light pole. And the dark streets were empty of traffic.

She glanced down at her phone. Shoulders slumping, she blew out a deep breath. The text wasn't the one she'd been praying to see.

And because that was just the way her life had been going lately, of course her lapse in judgment would come back to bite her in the end.

The raccoon didn't even try to avoid her car. It was a stationary shimmer of silver fur, black mask, and a raised paw, and she swore it was giving her the middle finger. She gasped, swerved. She pumped her brakes, knuckles whitening. The Nissan Maxima skidded sideways, executed a perfect pirouette, and slid inexorably toward the sidewalk.

The light pole on the sidewalk didn't stand a chance. The front end of her car struck the pole, her hood buckling with the crunch of metal. Her body trapped by the seat belt, Sadie's head and limbs snapped forward into the exploding air bag before she collapsed back into her seat.

Groaning, she rolled her head, trying to work through the ache in her neck. She pushed the deflated air bag out of the way and looked up. The raccoon waddled down the street to her left, unrepentant. But it was the movement she caught from the corner of her eye that stopped her heart. Peering through the windshield, she saw it again. A flutter of red.

Swaying in its moorings, the light pole wobbled like a metronome, the ribbon in its Christmas wreath trailing through the air.

"Please, please don't fall," Sadie whispered. The twinge in her neck from the collision forgotten, she prayed for further disaster to be averted.

Luck was not on her side. The thirty-foot aluminum pole tore from its bolts with a shriek and toppled away from the crumpled hood of her car, the ribbon flapping cheerfully. The cab of an F-150 Ford truck broke its fall.

"Oh God." She tore from her car and raced to the truck. The pole had fallen lengthwise down the center of the bed, creating a dent in the roof of the cab that nearly split the truck in two. The truck was parked on the side of the street so Sadie didn't *think* anyone was in it, but she wasn't positive.

Glass crunched under her three-inch Betsey Johnsons, and she steeled herself to peer in the driver's-side window. Her heart pounded, her palms growing clammy. If someone had been sitting in the cab, she didn't see how they could still be alive. Stepping to the window, she peered under the twisted metal and blew out the breath she didn't realize she'd been holding. Empty.

No one was hurt. That knowledge didn't stop the tremors that enveloped her body. Sadie wrapped her wool coat tighter around her, but her body didn't stop shaking.

She peered up and down the street. This late at night in downtown Pineville, no one was out and about. The sidewalks rolled up in this small Michigan town when the sun set. She had to call someone, but 9-1-1 didn't seem appropriate. The damage had been done. It was no longer an emergency.

A choking sound across the street made Sadie spin. A man stood in front of the large window of a darkened hair salon, mouth gaping, brown paper bag dangling from the tips of his fingers. He swiveled his head from the truck to Sadie and back again. The shock evaporated from his face, his lips pressing into a hard line, his chest expanding with a heated breath.

Roaring, he chucked his bag on the ground and ran across the street. A bear of a man, he was tall and well built, making her own five-foot-nine-inch frame feel insignificant. Or maybe it was his righteous fury that made her feel small. A black knit cap covered his head, but Sadie assumed his hair was the same color as his short beard, dark brown. A blue-checked shirt peeked out from under his worn pea coat, and jeans stretched tight across muscled thighs.

"What the hell happened to my truck?" His eyes traced the path of the fallen light pole from his truck to its base at the hood of Sadie's car. "You hit the light pole?"

She didn't answer such an obvious question. "I'm sorry. I have insurance. I'll pay for any damage."

"Any damage?" he shouted. "Are you an idiot?" His arm swept out to encompass the warped truck. "Of course there's damage!"

She stammered. "I meant I would cover anything insurance might not."

He stepped toward Sadie. His eyes, a deep, feral green and hard as agate, narrowed to slits. He surveyed her, taking in her Burberry coat and pearls, and snarled. "People like you think money solves everything. How did you even hit the pole? Were you drinking?" He leaned close and sniffed. She couldn't help but smell him back. If he wasn't such a jerk, she would have found his woodsy scent appealing.

"No, I wasn't drinking." She lifted her chin and an arc of pain shot through her neck. Rubbing it, she trotted after the bear.

He strode to her car and leaned in the open door.

"Hey, what are you doing?" she asked.

"What's your cell phone doing by the accelerator? Were you talking on the phone?" His nostrils flared, and he puffed clouds of condensation with each jerky breath, an angry dragon, ready to blow. He bent over, giving her a glimpse of his firm, denim-clad butt, then thrust her smartphone in her face. He growled. "You were texting."

She took a quick step back. The skin beneath his scruffy beard mottling, he appeared ready to strangle her. "I . . . I was expecting an important text. I didn't mean—"

"Of course you didn't mean anything by it. Your kind never does." He shoved her cell into her chest, reached into his front pocket and pulled his own phone free.

"Who are you calling?"

"The police," he said, his voice dripping with disdain. "Who do you think?"

Sadie clenched her fists. Of course the police needed to be called.

There was damage to city property, and who knew how much the truck would cost to repair. Her fingers kneaded the ache in her neck. This trip to Pineville had been a disaster from start to finish. Not that her life in Ann Arbor was going much better.

She released a deep breath. Her bangs blew up and drifted down, covering one eye. Brushing them aside, she glanced at the man. He gesticulated wildly at his truck, shouting at whoever was at the other end of the line. A person who couldn't see his gestures.

She snorted. He gazed at his truck like it was a dying family member. Why did men get so attached to their vehicles? He hadn't once even asked if she was all right. Sadie understood his being upset, but this rage seemed excessive.

He ended his call without a glance at her and walked to his truck. Resting his hands on an undamaged portion of the hood, he hung his head.

She shifted on her heels, uncertain. In a town this size, the police should be here soon. Sliding behind her wheel, she reached into her glove box. She approached the man still slumped against his truck.

"Perhaps we should exchange insurance information before the police arrive." She waved her insurance card under his nose.

"Son of a bitch!"

Sadie squeaked and ran around to the other side of the truck, ducking under the light pole on her way. Once the hood was between them, she stared at the man, breathing heavily.

"Oh, for Pete's sake, I'm not going to hurt you." He slammed his fist down on the hood of the truck. "My insurance ran out. The bill got lost in the mail, and I forgot to pay. I called, and it should be resolved in a couple of days, but that doesn't help me tonight, does it?"

"Tonight wasn't your fault. I think my insurance will pay for it." And would give her a hefty premium raise because of it, no doubt. One she wouldn't be able to afford.

The big man leveled her with a stare. "Oh, not just your insurance will pay, princess. You're going to pay, too. Personally. I *will* be pressing charges against you."

Sadie swallowed hard. "That isn't necessary." Could he even do that? "It was an accident."

"Accidents don't just happen. People make them happen through their carelessness"—his lip curled—"or their stupidity."

"I made a mistake, and I'm willing to make up for it." Sadie clenched her fists, the nails biting into her palms. "What more do you want?"

A cruiser rolled silently beside them, its red and blue lights flashing through the night. It pulled over and a uniformed cop emerged.

The man glanced at the cop and back at her, smiling darkly.

Her stomach flipped.

His lips curled, lopsided, devilish. Combined with his scruffy face, he looked like a pirate. An obnoxious, sexy pirate. Like someone who wanted to do wicked things to her, things that his eyes promised she'd enjoy.

He opened his mouth, ruining the fantasy. "What do I want, princess? I want to see your skinny ass in jail."

Sadie perched on the edge of a hard wooden bench in the old courthouse, awaiting her arraignment. The police officer the night before had insisted on taking her to the station to be booked for texting while driving and destruction of property, but was nice enough to allow her to sit, uncuffed, in the front seat of the cruiser on the drive over. She had been released on her own recognizance, under orders to show up for court the next morning.

She shifted on her seat, wishing the benches had a little padding. Bad enough she, someone who'd never gotten so much as a speeding ticket before, was now waiting to be *arraigned*, but by the time she left here she'd be nursing a sore behind, as well. Was that part of the judicial system's push against recidivism? Make the whole process from top to her bottom as uncomfortable as possible? The only thing that made this ordeal bearable was she wasn't there alone. After the fuss the big fur ball named Colt McCoy had made about her driving, she pointed out to the officer that perhaps Mr. McCoy shouldn't be tossing his verbal stones around so casually. He was, after all, driving without insurance.

On the other side of the empty courtroom and one row ahead, her co-arrestee sat stone-faced, arms crossed over his broad chest. He hadn't dressed up for court as she had, opting instead for cargo work pants and boots. In the light of day she saw that his facial hair couldn't quite qualify as a beard. Halfway between stubble and scruff, the man couldn't seem to make up his mind whether to grow it out or not. No matter that his jaw looked entirely too . . . pettable. His wannabe lumberjack appearance in a court of law was just one more nail in his coffin of rudeness. Remorseless, she loosely clasped her hands together. There was only so much apologizing a person could do, and she had reached her limit.

"All rise, the Honorable Judge Nichols presiding," the bailiff bellowed. Sadie, Colt, and the local prosecutor stood. Both Colt and Sadie had declined counsel. The white-haired judge shuffled behind his podium and lowered to his chair, settling his robes about him. "You may be seated." The bailiff walked to a desk beside the court reporter and sat, picking up a paperback book to read.

"Good morning, everyone. The criminal docket is especially busy this morning, with two violators." The judge's blue eyes twinkled. "Mr. Johnson, what are the formal charges you are bringing against the defendants?"

The prosecutor rose to his feet. "Your Honor, both Mr. McCoy and Ms. Wilson have pled no contest to the charges brought against them. One count of driving while uninsured and one count of texting while driving and destruction of property, respectively. First-time offenses for both, and the prosecutor's office recommends community service."

The judge shuffled through some papers on his desk. "Ms. Wilson and Mr. McCoy, please step forward." Sadie and Colt rose and stood next to the prosecutor. "Do you both understand your pleadings? This will show up as a misdemeanor conviction on both of your records."

"I understand," they said at the same time, glaring at each other.

"Hmm." The judge rubbed his hand over his round stomach, shifting his ebony robes. "I accept your pleas, and they shall be entered into the record. Now, as to your sentences." He peered at his file. "Ms. Wilson, I see that you are a professional stager. That's when you decorate a house to help it sell better?"

"Yes, Your Honor."

"And Mr. McCoy, you're a general contractor?" Colt nodded.

Sadie glanced down at his work boots. So he came by those scuffs honestly, at least, not as the local bully, kicking apologetic women when they were down.

"Well then," the judge said, "I have the perfect solution to a town problem." He rubbed his hands together, grinning. "Ms. Wilson, you're not local, so you might not be aware of our town's tradition of lighting a Christmas tree in the town square on the fifteenth of December. Last year our decorating committee ran into some . . . issues and it was decided, in the interest of public safety, to not allow the members of that committee to continue to decorate the town tree. However, no other town citizens have volunteered their services this year." The judge pursed his lips and raised an eyebrow, an annoyed Buddha.

He looked at Sadie and Colt, and a knot of dread formed in her stomach. She knew where this was going. "I can think of no better team to decorate our town tree than a designer and a contractor. Therefore, I sentence both of you to forty hours of community service getting our town Christmas tree ready for action. We have about a week until the fifteenth, so when the mayor flips the switch on a successfully decorated tree, your sentences will be up."

Allyson Charles lives in Northern California. She's the author of the contemporary romances *Putting Out Old Flames* and *The Christmas Tree* (Kensington Lyrical). A former attorney, she happily ditched those suits and now works in her pajamas writing about men's briefs instead of legal briefs. When she's not writing, she's probably engaged in one of her favorite hobbies: napping, eating, or martial arts (That last one almost makes up for the first two, right?). One of Allyson's greatest disappointments is living in a state that doesn't have any Cracker Barrels in it.

You can find her at www.allysoncharles.com or @1allyson charles.

CPSIA information can be obtained
at www.ICGtesting.com
Printed in the USA
LVHW02s1837290818
588518LV00002B/208/P

9 781601 836045